THERE WAS AN OLD WOMAN

THERE WAS AN OLD WOMAN

ELLERY QUEEN

HarperPerennial

A Division of HarperCollinsPublishers

Reprinted by arrangement with the Ellery Queen (Manfred B.
Lee and Frederic Dannay) Trusts and Scott Meredith Literary
Agency, Inc.

HarperCollins books may be purchased for educational, business, or sales promotional use. For information, please call or
write: Special Markets Department, HarperCollins Publishers,
Inc., 10 East 53rd Street, New York, NY 10022. Telephone: (212)
207-7528; Fax: (212) 207-7222.

First HarperPerennial edition published 1992.

Library of Congress Cataloging-in-Publication Data

Queen, Ellery
    There was an old woman / Ellery Queen.—1st HarperPerenni-
al ed.
        p. cm
    Originally published: New York : Little, Brown, c1943.
    ISBN 0-06-097440-0 (pbk.)
    I. Title
PS3533.U4T5   1992
813'.52—dc20   91-50534

92 93 94 95 96 RRD 10 9 8 7 6 5 4 3 2 1

Contents

Cast of Characters

Part One

1

Who Lived in a Shoe

The pearl-gray planet of the supreme court building, which lies in Foley Square, is round in shape; whereby you may know that in New York County Justice is one with universal laws, following the conscience of Man like the earth the sun. Or so Ellery Queen reflected as he sat on the southern extremity of his spine in Trial Term Part VI, Mr. Justice Greevey not yet presiding, between Sergeant Thomas Velie of Homicide and Inspector Queen, waiting to testify in a case which is another story.

"How long, O Lord?" yawned Ellery.

"If you're referring to that Gilbert and Sullivan pipsqueak, Greevey," snapped his father, "Greevey's probably just scratching his navel and crawling out of his ermine bed. Velie, go see what's holding up the works."

Sergeant Velie opened one aggrieved eye, nodded ponderously, and lumbered off in quest of enlightenment. When he lumbered back, the Sergeant looked black. "The Clerk says," growled Sergeant Velie, "that Mr. Justice Greevey he called up and says he's got an earache, so he'll be delayed two hours gettin' down here while he gets—the Clerk says 'irritated,' which I *am*, but it don't make sense to me."

3

"Irritation," frowned Mr. Queen, "or to call it by its purer name 'irrigation'—irrigation, Sergeant, is the process by which one reclaims a dry, dusty, and dead terrain...a description, I understand, which fits Mr. Justice Greevey like a decalcomania."

The Sergeant looked puzzled, but Inspector Queen muttered through his ragged mustache: "Two hours! *I'd* like to irrigate him. Let's go out in the hall for a smoke." And the old gentleman marched out of Room 331, followed by Sergeant Velie and—meekly—Ellery Queen; and so barged into the fantastic hull of the Potts case.

For a little way down the corridor, before the door of Room 335, Trial Term Part VII, they came upon Charley Paxton, pacing. Mr. Queen, like the governor of Messina's niece, had a good eye and could see a church by daylight; so he noted this and that about the tall young man, mechanically, and concluded [a] he was an attorney (brief case); [b] his name was Charles Hunter Paxton (stern gilt lettering on same); [c] Counselor Paxton was waiting for a client and the client was late (frequent glances at wrist watch); [d] he was unhappy (general droop). And the great man, having run over Charles Hunter Paxton with the vacuum cleaner of his glance, made to pass on, satisfied.

But his father halted, twinkling.

INSPECTOR: Again, Charley? What is it this time?

MR. PAXTON: *Lèse-majesté*, Inspector.

INSPECTOR: Where'd it happen?

MR. PAXTON: Club Bongo.

SERGEANT VELIE (*shaking the marble halls with his laughter*): Imagine Thurlow in that clip joint!

MR. PAXTON: And he got clipped—make no mistake about that, my friends. Clipped on the buttonola.

INSPECTOR: Assault and battery, huh?

MR. PAXTON (*bitterly*): Not at all, Inspector. We mustn't break our record! No, the same old suit for slander. Young Conklin Cliffstatter—of the East Shore Cliffstatters. Jute and shoddy.

4

SERGEANT: Stinking, I bet.

MR. PAXTON: Well, Sergeant, just potted enough to tell Thurlow a few homely truths about the name of Potts. (*Hollow laugh.*) There I go myself—"potted," "Potts." I swear that's all Conk Cliffstatter did—make a pun on the name of Potts. Called 'em "crack-Potts."

ELLERY QUEEN (*his silver eyes gleaming with hunger*): Dad?

So Inspector Queen said Charley-Paxton-my-son-Ellery-Queen, and the two young men shook hands, and that was how Ellery became embroiled—it was more than an involvement—in the wonderful case of the Old Woman Who Lived in a Shoe.

A court officer plunged his bald head into the cool of the corridor from the swelter of Room 335, Trial Term Part VII.

"Hey, Counselor, Mr. Justice Cornfield says Potts or no Potts he ain't waitin' much longer for your cra—your client. What gives, in God's good name?"

"Can't he wait another five minutes, for goodness' sake?" Charley Paxton cried, exasperated. "They must have been held up—Here they are! Officer, tell Cornfield we'll be right in!" And Counselor Paxton raced toward the elevators, which had just discharged an astonishing cargo.

"There she is," said the Inspector to his son, as one who points out a clash of planets. "Take a good look, Ellery. The Old Woman doesn't make many public appearances."

"With the getup," chortled Sergeant Velie, "she could snag a job in the movies like that."

Some women grow old with grace, others with bitterness, and still others simply grow old; but neither the concept of growth nor the devolution of old age seemed relevant to Cornelia Potts. She was a small creature with a plump stomach and tiny fine-boned feet which whisked her about. Her face, like a tangerine, was almost entirely lacking in detail; one was surprised to find embedded in it two eyes, which were as black and hard as coal

5

chips. Those eyes, by some perverse chemistry of her ego, were unwinkingly malevolent. If they were capable of changing expression at all, it was into malicious rage.

If not for the eyes, seeing Cornelia Potts in the black taffeta skirts she affected, the boned black lace choker, the prim black bonnet, one would have thought of her as a "Sweet old character," a sort of sexless little kobold who vaguely resembled the Jubilee pictures of Queen Victoria. But the eyes quite forbade such sentimentalization; they were dangerous and evil eyes, and they made imaginative people—like Ellery—think of poltergeists, and elementals, and suchlike creatures of the unmentionable worlds.

Mrs. Cornelia Potts did not step sedately, as befitted a dame of seventy years, from the elevator—she darted from it, like a midge from a hot stream, followed by a widening wake of assorted characters, most of whom were delighted ladies and gentlemen of the press, and at least one of whom—palpably *not* a journalist—was almost as extraordinary as she.

"And who," demanded the astonished Mr. Queen, "is that?"

"Thurlow," grinned Inspector Queen. "The little guy Charley Paxton was talking about. Cornelia's eldest son."

"Cornelia's eldest *wack*," Sergeant Velie, the purist, said.

"He resents," winked the Inspector.

"Everything," said the Sergeant, waving a flipper.

"Always taking—what do you educated birds call it?— umbrage," said the Inspector.

"Resents? Umbrage?" Ellery frowned.

"Aw, read the right papers," guffawed the Sergeant. "Ain't he *cute?*"

With a thrill of surprise Ellery saw that, if you were so ill-advised as to strip the black taffeta from old Mrs. Potts and reclothe her in weary gray tweeds, you would have Thurlow, her son.... No, there was a difference. Thurlow radiated an inferior grade of energy. In a race with his mother, he would always lose. And, in fact, he was losing the present race; for he toddled hurriedly along in the Old Woman's wake, clutching his derby to his little belly, and trying without success to overtake her. He was panting, perspiring, and in a pet.

A lean glum man in a morning coat, carrying a medical satchel, stumbled after mother and son with a sick smile which seemed to say: "I am not trotting, I am walking. This is not reality, it is a bad dream. Gentlemen of the press, be merciful. One has to make a living."

"I know *him*," growled Ellery. "Dr. Waggoner Innis, the Pasteur of Park Avenue."

"She treats Innis like some people treat dogs," said Sergeant Velie, smacking his lips.

"The way he's trotting after her, he looks like one," said the Inspector.

"But why a doctor?" protested Ellery. "She looks as healthy as a troll."

"I always understood it was her heart."

"What heart?" sneered the Sergeant. "She ain't got no heart."

The cortege swept by and through the door of Room 335. Young Paxton, who had tried to intercept Mrs. Potts and received a blasting "Traffic!" for his pains, lingered only long enough to mutter: "If you want to see the show, gentlemen, you're welcome"; then he dashed after his clients.

So the Queens and Sergeant Velie, blessing Mr. Justice Greevey's earache, went in to see the show.

Mr. Justice Cornfield, a large jurist with the eyes of an apprehensive doe, took one look from the eminence of his bench at the tardy Old Woman, damp Thurlow Potts, blushing Dr. Waggoner Innis, and their exulting press and immediately exhibited a ferocious vindictiveness. He screamed at the Clerk, and there were whisperings and scurryings, and lo! the calendar was readjusted, and the case of *Potts v. Cliffstatter* found itself removed one degree in Time, so that *Giacomo v. Jive Jottings, Inc.*, which had been scheduled to follow it, now found itself with priority.

Ellery beckoned Charley Paxton, who was hovering about Mrs. Cornelia Potts; and the lawyer scooted over thankfully.

"Come on outside. This'll take hours."

They shouldered their way out into the corridor again.

"Your client," began Mr. Queen, "fascinates me."

"The Old Woman?" Charley made a face. "Have a cigaret? It's Thurlow, not Mrs. Potts, who's the plaintiff in this action."

"Oh. From the way he was tumbling after his mother, I gathered—"

"Thurlow's been tumbling after Mama for forty-seven years."

"Why the elegant Dr. Waggoner Innis?"

"Cornelia has a bad heart condition."

"Nonsense. From the way she skitters about—"

"That's just it. Nobody can tell the old hellion *anything*. It keeps Dr. Innis in a constant state of jitters. So he always accompanies the Old Woman when she leaves the Shoe."

"Beg pardon?"

Charley regarded him with suspicion. "Do you mean to say, Queen, you don't know about the *Shoe*?"

"I'm a very ignorant man," said Ellery abjectly. "Should I?"

"But I thought everybody in America knew! Cornelia Potts' fortune was made in the shoe business. *The Potts Shoe.*"

Ellery started. "*Potts Shoes Are America's Shoes—$3.99 Everywhere?*"

"*That's* the Potts."

"No!" Ellery turned to stare at the closed door of Room 335. The Potts Shoe was not an enterprise, or even an institution; it was a whole civilization. There were Potts Shoe Stores in every cranny of the land. Little children wore Potts Shoes; and their mothers, and their fathers, and their sisters and their brothers and their uncles and their aunts; and what was more depressing, their grandparents had worn Potts Shoes before them. To don a Potts Shoe was to display the honor badge of lower-income

America; and since this class was the largest class, the Potts fortune was not merely terrestrial—it was galactic.

"But your curious reference," said the great man eagerly, turning back to the lawyer, "to 'when she leaves the Shoe.' Has a cult grown up about the Pottses, with its own esoteric terminology?"

Charley grinned. "It all started when some cartoonist on a pro-Labor paper was told by his editor to squirt some India ink in the general direction of Cornelia. Don't you remember that strike in the Potts' plant?" Ellery nodded; it was beginning to come back to him. "Well, this genius of the drawing board drew a big mansion—supposed to represent the Potts Palace on Riverside Drive—only he shaped it like an old-fashioned high-top shoe; and he drew Cornelia Potts like the old harridan in the *Mother Goose* illustration, with her six children tumbling out of the 'shoe', and he captioned it: 'There Was an Old Woman Who Lived in a Shoe, She Had So Many Children She Couldn't Pay Her Workers a Living Wage,' or something like that. Anyway, the name's stuck; she's been 'the Old Woman' ever since."

"And you're this female foot potentate's attorney?"

"Yes, but most of my activity is devoted to Thurlow, bless his sensitive little heart. You saw Thurlow? That tubby little troglodyte with the narrow shoulders?"

Ellery nodded. "Built incredibly like a baby kangaroo."

"Well, Thurlow Potts is the world's most insultable man."

"And the money to do something about it," mourned Mr. Queen. "Very sad. Does he ever win one of these suits?"

"Win!" Paxton swabbed his face angrily. "It's driven me to sobriety. This is *the thirty-seventh suit for libel or slander* he's made me bring into court! And every darned one of the first thirty-six has been thrown out."

"How about this one—the Club Bongo imbroglio?"

"Cornfield'll throw it out without a hearing. Mark my words."

"Why does Mrs. Potts put up with this childishness?"

"Because in her own way the Old Woman's got an even crazier pride in the family name than Thurlow."

"But if the suits are all silly, why do you permit them to come to court, Charley?"

Charley flushed. "Thurlow insists, and the Old Woman backs him up.... I know I've been accused of milking them, Queen." His jaw shot forward. "I've earned every damn cent I've ever collected being their attorney, and don't you think I haven't!"

"I'm sure you have—"

"I've had nightmares about them! In my dreams they have long noses and fat little bottoms and they spit at me all night! But if *I* didn't do it, they'd find a thousand lawyers who'd break their necks to get the business. And wouldn't be so blamed scrupulous, either! Beg your pardon. My nerves—"

Sergeant Velie stuck his head out of Room 335. "Charley! The judge settled that hot-trumpet case, and the Old Woman's bellowin' for you."

"May she crack a cylinder," muttered Counselor Paxton; and he marched back into Trial Term Part VII with the posture of one who looks forward only to the kiss of Madame Guillotine.

"Tell me, Dad," said Ellery when he had fought his way back with Sergeant Velie to the Inspector's side. "How did Charley Paxton, who seems otherwise normal, get mixed up with the Pottses?"

"Charley sort of inherited 'em," chuckled Inspector Queen. "His pappy was Sidney Paxton, the tax and estate lawyer—fine fella, Sid—many a bottle of beer we cracked together." Sergeant Velie nodded nostalgically. "Sid sent Charley to law school, and Charley got out of Harvard Law with honors. Began to practice criminal law—everybody said he had a flair for it—but his old man died, and Charley had to chuck a brilliant career and step in and take over Sid's civil practice. By that time the Potts account was so big Sid had had to drop all his other clients. Now Charley spends his life trying to keep out of the nut house."

Thurlow Potts could scarcely contain himself at the front of the room. He squirmed in his seat like a fat boy at the circus, the two gray tufts behind his ears standing up nervously. He exuded a moist and giggly fierceness, as if he were enjoying to the full his indignation.

"That little man," thought Ellery, "is fitten fodder for a psychiatrist." And he watched even more intently.

Ensued a brilliant but confusing battle of bitternesses. It was evident from the opening sortie that Mr. Justice Cornfield meant to see justice done—to Mr. Conklin Cliffstatter, who sat bored among his attorneys and seemed not to care a tittle whether justice were done or not. In fact, Ellery suspected Mr. Cliffstatter suckled only one ambition—to go home and sleep it off.

"But Your Honor—" protested Charley Paxton.

"Don't Your Honor me, Counselor!" thundered Mr. Justice Cornfield. "I'm not saying it's your fault—heaven knows lawyers have to live—but you ought to know better than to pull this stunt in my court for—how many times does this make?"

"Your Honor, my client has been grossly slandered—"

"My Honor my eye! Your client is a public nuisance who clutters up the calendars of our courts! I don't mind his wasting *his* money—or rather his mother's—but I do mind his wasting the taxpayers'!"

"Your Honor has heard the testimony of the witness—" said Counselor Paxton desperately.

"And I'm satisfied there was no slander. Case dismissed!" snapped Mr. Justice Cornfield. He grinned evilly at the Old Woman.

To Charley Paxton's visible horror, Thurlow Potts bounced to his feet. "Your Honor!" Thurlow squeaked imperiously.

"Sit down, Thurlow," gasped Charley. "Or rather let's get out of here—"

"Just—one—moment, Counselor," said Mr. Justice Cornfield softly. "Mr. Potts, you wish to address the Court?"

"I certainly do!"

"Then by all means address it."

"I came to this court for justice!" cried Thurlow, brandishing his arms as if they were broadswords. "And what do I get? *Insults*. Where are the rights of Man? What's happened to our Constitution? Don't we live in the last refuge of personal liberty? Surely a responsible citizen has the right of protection by law against the slanders of *drunken, irresponsible persons?*"

"Yes?" said Mr. Justice Cornfield. "You were saying—"

"But what do I find in this court?" screeched Thurlow. "Protection? No! Are my rights defended by this court? No! Is my name cleared of the crude insinuations of this defendant? No! It is a valuable name, Your Honor, an honorable name, and this person's slander has reduced its value by considerable sums—!"

"I'll reduce it still more, Mr. Potts," said the judge with enjoyment, "if you don't stop this outrageous exhibition."

"Your Honor," Charley Paxton jumped forward. "May I apologize for the hasty and ill-considered remarks of my client—"

"*Stop!*" And the Old Woman arose, terrible in wrath.

Even the judge quailed momentarily.

"Your *Dis*honor," said Cornelia Potts, "—I can't address you as Your Honor, because you haven't any—Your Dishonor, I've sat in many courtrooms and I've listened to many judges, but never in my long life have I had the misfortune to witness such *monkey's* antics, in such a court of Baal, presided over by such a wicked old *goat*. My son came here to seek the protection of the court in defense of *our good name*—instead he is insulted and ridiculed and our good name further held up to *public scorn....*"

"Are you quite finished, Madam?" choked Mr. Justice Cornfield.

"No! How much do I owe you for contempt?"

"Case dismissed! Case dismissed!" bellowed the judge; and he leaped from his leather chair, girding his robe about him like a young girl discovered *en déshabille*, and fled to chambers.

* * *

"This is surely a bad dream," said Ellery Queen exultantly. "What happens next?"

The Queens and Sergeant Velie joined the departing Potts parade. Bravely it swept into the corridor, Queen Victoria in the van flourishing her bulky bumbershoot like a cudgel at the assorted bondsmen, newspaper folks, divorce litigants, attorneys, attendants, rubbernecks, and tagtails who had joined the courtroom exodus. The Old Woman, and then steaming little Thurlow, and red-faced Dr. Innis, and Charles Hunter Paxton, and Sergeant Velie, and the Queens *père et fils*. Bravely it swept onto the balcony under the rotunda, and into the elevators, and downstairs to the lobby.

"Uh, uh. Trouble," said Sergeant Velie alertly.

"How she hates cameramen," remarked Inspector Queen.

"Wait—no!" shouted Ellery. "Charley! Somebody! Stop her. For goodness' sake!"

The photographers had lain in ambush. And she was upon them.

The guns of Cornelia Potts's black eyes sent out streams of tracer bullets. She snarled, grasped her umbrella handle convulsively, and rushed to the attack. The umbrella rose and fell. One camera flew through the air to be caught willy-nilly by a surprised man in a derby. Another fell and tumbled down the steps leaving a trail of lens fragments.

"Break it up, break it up," said Sergeant Velie.

"That's just what she's doing," panted a cameraman. "Joe, did you get anything?"

"A bust in the nose," groaned Joe, regarding his encarmined handkerchief with horror. He roared at the old lady: "You old crackpottia, you smashed my camera!"

"Here's the money to pay for it," panted Cornelia Potts, hurling two hundred-dollar bills at him; and she darted into her limousine and slammed the door shut behind her, almost decapitating her pride and heir, Thurlow, who was—as ever—just a step too late.

"I *won't* have public spectacles!" she cried through her tonneau window. The limousine jerked away, slamming the old lady against her physician, who had craftily sought the protection of the car before her, and leaving Thurlow, puffing and blowing, on the field of glory where, after a momentary panic at thus being left exposed alone to the weapons of the enemy, he drew himself up to his full five foot and grimly girded his not inconsiderable loins.

"Happens this way every time," said Inspector Queen from the top of the courthouse steps.

"If she's smashed one camera, she's smashed a hundred," said Sergeant Velie, shaking his head.

"But why," wondered Ellery, "do the cameramen keep trying? Or do they make a profit on each transaction? I noticed two rather impressive-looking greenbacks being flung at the victim down there."

"Profit is right," grinned his father. "Take a look. That fella who had his camera broken. Does he look in the dumps?"

Ellery frowned.

"Now," instructed his father, "look up there."

Ellery sighted along the Inspector's arm to a window high in the face of the courthouse. There, various powerful camera eyes glittered in the sun, behind them human eyes intent on Thurlow Potts and Charley Paxton on the sidewalk before the courthouse.

"Yes, sir," said Sergeant Velie with respect, "when you're dealing with the Old Woman you just naturally got to be on your toes."

"They caught it all from that window," exclaimed Ellery softly. "I'll bet that smashed camera was a dummy and Joe a rascally, conniving stooge!"

"My son," said the Inspector dryly, "you've got the makings of a detective. Come on, let's go back upstairs and see if Mr. Justice Greevey's over his irrigation."

* * *

"Now listen, boys," Charley Paxton was shouting on the sidewalk. "It's been a tough morning. What d'ye say? Mr. Potts hasn't one word for publication—You better not have," Charley said through his teeth three feet from Thurlow's pink ear, "or I walk out, Thurlow—I swear I walk out!"

Someone applauded.

"You let me alone," cried Thurlow. "I've got *plenty* to say for publication, Charles Paxton! I'm through with you, anyway. I'm through with *all* lawyers. Yes, and judges and courts, too!"

"Thurlow, I warn you—" Charley began.

"Oh, go fish! There's no justice left in this world—not a crumb. Not a particle!"

"Yes, little man?" came a voice.

"No Justice, Says Indignant Citizen."

"Through with all lawyers, judges, and courts, he vows."

"What a break for all lawyers, judges, and courts."

"What you gonna do, Pottso—protect your honor with *stiletti?*"

"You gonna start packing six-shooters, Thurlow-boy?"

"Thurlow Potts, Terror of the Plains, Goes on Warpath, Armed to the Upper Plates."

"Stop!" screamed Thurlow Potts in an awful voice; and, curiously, they did. He was shaking in a paroxysm of rage, his small feet dancing on the sidewalk, his pudgy face convulsed. Then he choked: "From now on I take justice in my own hands."

"Huh?"

"Say, the little guy actually means it."

"Go on, he's hopped to the eyeballs."

"Wait a minute. Nuts or no nuts, he can't be left running around loose. Not with *those* intentions, brother."

One of the reporters said, soberly: "Just what do you mean—you'll take justice in your own hands, Mr. Potts?"

"Thurlow," muttered Charley Paxton, "haven't you raved your quota? Let me get you out of here—"

15

"Charles, take your hand off my arm. What do I mean, gentlemen?" said Thurlow quietly. "I'll tell you what I mean. I mean that I'm going to buy myself a gun, and the next person who insults me or the honorable name I bear won't live long enough to hide behind the skirts of your corrupt courts!"

"Hey," said a reporter. "Somebody better tip off Conk Cliffstatter."

"This puffball's just airy enough to do it."

"Ah, he's blowing."

"Oh, yeah? Well, maybe he'll blow bullets."

Thurlow launched himself at the crowd like a little ram, butting with his arms. It parted, almost respectfully; and he shot through in triumph. "He'll get a bullet in his guts, that's what he'll get!" howled the Terror of the Plains. And he was gone in a flurry of agitated little arms and legs.

Charley Paxton groaned and hurried back up the steps of the courthouse.

He found Ellery Queen, Inspector Queen, and Sergeant Velie emerging from Room 331. The Inspector was holding forth with considerable bitterness on the subject of Mr. Justice Greevey's semicircular canals, for it appeared that the justice had decided to remain at home sulking in an atmosphere of oil of wintergreen rather than venture out into the earacheless world; consequently the case which had fetched the Queens to court was put off for another day.

"Well, Charley? What's happening down there?"

"Thurlow threatened to buy a gun!" panted the lawyer. "He says he's through with courts—the next man who insults him gets paid back in lead!"

"That nut-ball?" scoffed the Sergeant.

Inspector Queen laughed. "Forget it, Charley. Thurlow Potts hasn't the sand of a charlotte russe."

"I don't know, Dad," murmured Ellery. "The man's not balanced properly. One of his gimbals out of socket, or something. He might mean it, at that."

"Oh, he means it," said Charley Paxton sourly. "He means it *now*, at any rate. Ordinarily I wouldn't pay any attention to his ravings, but he's been getting worse lately and I'm afraid one of these days he'll cross the line. This might be the day."

"Cross what line?" asked Sergeant Velie, puzzled.

"The Mason-Dixon line, featherweight," sighed the Inspector. "What line do you think? Now listen, Charley, you're taking Thurlow too seriously—"

"Just the same, don't you think we ought to take precautions?"

"Sure. Watch him. If he starts chewing his blanket, call Bellevue."

"To buy a gun," Ellery pointed out, "he'll have to get a license from the police department."

"Yes," said Charley eagerly. "How about that, Inspector Queen?"

"How about what?" growled the old gentleman in a disgusted tone. "Suppose we refuse him a license—then what? Then he goes out and buys himself a rod without a license. Then you've got not only a nut on your hands, but a nut who's nursing a grudge against the police department, too. Might kill a cop. ...And don't tell me he can't *buy* a gun without a license, because he can, and I'm the baby who knows it."

"Dad's right," said Ellery. "The practical course is not to try to prevent Thurlow from laying hands on a weapon, but to prevent him from using it. And in his case I rather think guile, not force, is what's required."

"In other words," said the Sergeant succinctly, "yoomer the slug."

"I don't know," said the lawyer with despair. "I'm going bats myself just trying to keep up with these cormorants. Inspector, can't you do *anything*?"

"But Charley, what d'ye expect me to do? We can't follow him around day and night. In fact, until he pulls something our hands are tied—"

17

"Could we put him away?" asked Velie.

"You mean on grounds of insanity?"

"Whoa," said Charley Paxton. "There's plenty wrong with the Pottses, but not to that extent. The old girl has drag, anyway, and she'd fight to her last penny, and win, too."

"Then why don't you get somebody to wet-nurse the old nicky-poo?" demanded Inspector Queen.

"Just what I was thinking," said the young man cunningly. "Uh—Mr. Queen...would *you*—?"

"But definitely," replied Mr. Queen with such promptness that his father stared at him. "Dad, you're going back to Headquarters?"

The Inspector nodded.

"In that case, Charley, you come on up to my apartment," said Ellery with a grin, "and answer some questions."

2

She Had So Many Children

Ellery mixed Counselor Paxton a scotch and soda.

"Spare me nothing, Charley. I want to know the Pottses as I have never known anybody or anything before. Don't proceed to the middle until you've arrived at the end of the beginning, and then repeat the process until you reach the beginning of the end. I'll try to have something constructive to say about it from that point on."

"Yes, *sir*," said Charley, setting down his glass. And, as one who is saturated with his subject, the young lawyer began to pour forth facts about the Pottses, old and young, male and female—squirting them in all directions like an overloaded garden hose relieving itself of intolerable pressure.

Cornelia Potts had not always been the Old Woman. Once she had actually been a child in a small town in Massachusetts. She was a ragged Ann, driven from childhood by a powerful purpose. It was to be rich and to live upon the Hill. It was to be rich and to live upon this Hill and any hill that was higher than its neighbor. It was to be rich and to multiply.

19

Cornelia became rich and she multiplied. She became rich almost wholly through her own efforts; to multiply, unhappily, it was necessary to enlist the aid of a husband, God having so ordered the creation. But the least Cornelia could do was improve upon the holy ordinance. This she did by taking, not one, but two husbands; and thus she multiplied mightily, achieving six children—three by her first husband, and three by her second—before that other thing happened which God has also ordained.

("The second husband," said Charley Paxton, "is still around, poor sap. I'll get to *him* in due course.")

Husband the First was trapped by Cornelia in 1892, when she was twenty and possessed the dubious allure of a wild-flower growing dusty by the roadside. His name was Bacchus, Bacchus Potts. Bacchus Potts was that classic paradox, a Prometheus bound—in this case, to a cobbler's bench, for he was the town shoemaker, a man of whom all the girls in the village were gigglingly afraid, for by night he wandered in the woods and sang rowdy songs under the moon while his feet danced a dance of impotent wanderlust.

It has been said of the Old Woman (said Charley) that if she had married the village veterinary, she would have turned him into a Pasteur; if she had married the illegitimate son of an illegitimate son of an obscure sprig of the royal tree, she would have lived to be queen. As it was, she married a cobbler; and so, in time, she made him the leading shoe manufacturer of the world.

If Bacchus Potts dreamed defeated dreams over his bench, it was surely not of larger benches; but larger benches he found himself possessor of, covering acres and employing thousands. And it happened so quickly that he, the dreamer, could not grasp its dreamlike magic; or perhaps he wished not to. For as Cornelia invested his life's savings in a small factory; as it fed, and bulged, and by process of fission became two, and the two became four...Bacchus could only sit helplessly by, resenting the miracle and its maker.

Every so often he would vanish. When he returned, without money, dirty, and purged, he crept meekly back to Cornelia with the guilty look of a repentant tomcat.

After some years, no one paid any attention to Bacchus' goings or comings—not his employees, not his children, certainly not his wife, who was too busy with building a dynasty.

In 1902, ten years after their marriage, when Cornelia was a plump and settling thirty, and the Pottses owned not only factories but retail stores over all the land, Bacchus Potts one day dreamed his greatest dream. He disappeared for good. When months passed and he did not return, and the authorities failed to turn up any trace of him, Cornelia shrugged him off and became truly Queen of Egypt land. After all, there was a great deal of work involved in building a pyramid, and she had three growing children to care for between crackings of the overseer's whip. If she missed Bacchus, it was not for any reason discernible in daylight.

Then came the seven fat years, at the expiration of which the queen exhorted the lawmakers; and the law, that stern Pharaoh, being satisfied, Bacchus Potts was pronounced no longer a living man but a dead one, and his wife no longer a wife but a widow, able to take to herself without contumely another husband.

That she was ready and willing as well became evident at once.

In 1909, at the age of thirty-seven, Mrs. Potts married another shy man, Stephen Brent, to whom even at the altar she flatly refused to give up her name. Why she should have felt a loyalty to that first fey spouse upon whom she had founded her fortune remained as much a mystery as everything else about her relationship with him; or perhaps there was no loyalty to Bacchus Potts, or sentiment either, but only to his name, which was a different thing altogether, since the name meant the Potts Shoe, $3.99 Everywhere.

Cornelia Potts not only refused to give up her name, she also insisted as a condition of their marriage that Stephen Brent give up his. Brent being the kind of man to whom argument is an evil thing, to be shunned like pestilence, feebly agreed; and so Stephen Brent became Stephen Potts, according to legal process, and the Potts dynasty rolled on.

It should be remembered (Charley Paxton reminded Ellery) that in December of 1902 Cornelia had moved her three father-less children to New York City and built a house for them—the Potts "Palace," that fabulous square block of granite and sward on Riverside Drive, facing the gentle Hudson and the smoky greenery of the Jersey shore. So Cornelia had met Steve Brent in New York.

"It's a wonder to me," growled the young attorney, "that Steve tore himself away from Major Gotch long enough to be alone with the old girl and ask her to marry him—if he did ask her."

Stephen Brent had come to New York from the southern seas, or the Malay Peninsula, or some such romantic place, and with him, barnacle-like, had come Gotch—two vagabonds, of the same cloth, united by the secret joy of idleness and tenacious in their union. They were not bad men; they were simply weak men; and men of weakness seemed to be Cornelia's weakness.

Perhaps this was why, of the two wanderers, she had chosen Steve Brent to be her prince consort, and not Major Gotch; for Major Gotch evinced a certain minor firmness of fiber, not exact-ly a strength but a lesser weakness, which happily his friend did not possess. It was this trait of his character which enabled him to stand up to Cornelia Potts and demand sanctuary with his Pythias. "Marry Steve—yes, ma'am. But Steve, he'll die without me, ma'am. He's just a damn' lonesome man, ma'am," Major Gotch had said to Cornelia. "Seeing that you're so well-fixed, seems to me it won't ruffle your feathers none if I sort of come along with Steve."

"Can you garden?" snapped Cornelia.

"Now don't get me wrong," said Major Gotch, smiling. "I ain't asking for a job, ma'am. Work and me don't mix. I'll just come and set. I got a bullet in my right leg makes standin' something fierce."

For the first time in her life Cornelia gave in to a man. Or perhaps she had a sense of humor. She accepted the condition, and Major Gotch moved right along in and settled down to share his friend's incredible fortune and make himself, as he liked to say, thoroughly useless.

"Was Cornelia in love with Stephen?" asked Ellery.

"In love?" Charley jeered. "Say, it was just animal magnetism on Cornelia's part—I'm told Steve had 'pretty eyes,' though they're washed-out now—and a nice business deal for old Steve. And it's worked out not too badly. Cornelia has a husband who's given her three additional children, and Steve's lolled about the rich pasture after a youth of scratching for fodder. Fact is, he and that old scoundrel Major Gotch spend all their time together on the estate, playing endless games of checkers. Nobody pays any attention to them."

"The three children of the Old Woman's first marriage—the offspring of Cornelia and the 'teched' and vanished Bacchus Potts—are crazy," Charley continued.

"Did you say 'crazy'?" Ellery looked startled.

"You heard me." Charley reached for the decanter.

"But Thurlow—"

"All right, take Thurlow," argued young Mr. Paxton. "Would you call him sane? A man who spends his life trying to hit back at people for imaginary insults to his name? What's the difference between that and a mania for swatting imaginary flies from your nose?"

"But his mother—"

"It's a question of degree, Ellery. Cornelia's passion for the honor of the Potts name is kept within bounds, and she doesn't hit out unless she has a vulnerable target. But Thurlow spends his life hitting out, and most of the time nothing's there but a puzzled look on somebody's face."

23

"Insanity is a word neurologists don't like, Charley," complained Ellery Queen. "At best, standards of normality are variable, depending on the age and mores. In the Age of Chivalry, for example, Thurlow's obsession with his family honor would have been considered a high and virtuous sign of his sanity."

"You're quibbling. But if you want proof, take Louella, the second child of the Cornelia-Bacchus union....I'll waive Thurlow's hypersensitivity about the name of Potts; I'll accept his impractical extravagant nature, his childish innocence on the subject of business values or the value of money—as the signs of merely an unhappy, maladjusted, but essentially sane man.

"But Louella! you can't argue about Louella. She's forty-four, never married, of course—"

"What's wrong with Louella?"

"Louella believes herself to be a great inventor."

Mr. Queen looked pained.

"Nobody pays much attention to Louella, either," growled Charley. "Nobody except the Old Woman. Louella's got her own 'laboratory' at the house and seems quite happy. There's an old closet in the Potts zoo where the Old Woman throws Louella's 'inventions.' One day I happened to catch the old lady sitting on the floor outside the closet, crying. I admit," said Charley, shaking his head, "for a few weak seconds I felt sorry for the old she-pirate."

"Don't stop now," said Ellery. "What about the third child of the first marriage?"

"Horatio?" The lawyer shivered. "Horatio's forty-one. In many ways Horatio's the queerest of the trio. I don't know why, because he's not at all the horrible object you might think. And yet...I never see him without getting duck bumps."

"What's the matter with Horatio?"

"Maybe nothing," said Charley darkly. "Maybe everything. I just don't know. You'll have to see and talk to him in his self-made setting to believe he really exists."

Ellery smiled broadly. "You're very clever. You've already learned that my type of mind simply can't resist a mystery."

Paxton looked sheepish. "Well...I want your help."

Ellery stared at him hard. "Charley, what *is* your interest in this extraordinary family?" The lawyer was silent. "It can't be merely professional integrity. There are some jobs that aren't worth any amount of compensation, and from what I've seen and heard already, being legal adviser to the Pottses is one of them. You've got an ax to grind, my friend, and since it doesn't seem to be made of gold...what *is* it made of?"

"Red hair and dimples," said Charley defiantly.

"Ah," said Mr. Queen.

"Sheila's the youngest of the three children who resulted from the marriage of Cornelia and Steve. *They're* rational human beings, thank God! Robert and Mac are twins—a sweet pair—they're thirty." Charley flushed. "I'm going to marry Sheila."

"Congratulations. How old is the young lady?"

"Twenty-four. Can't imagine how Sheila and the twins got born into that howling family! The Old Woman still runs the Potts Shoe business, but Bob and Mac really run it, with the help of an old-timer who's been with Cornelia for I don't know how many years. Nice old Yank named Underhill. Underhill superintends production at the plants; Robert's vice-president in charge of sales, Mac's vice-president in charge of advertising and promotion—"

"What about Thurlow?"

"Oh, Thurlow's vice-president, too. But I've never found out what he's vice-president of: I don't think he has, either. Sort of roving nuisance. And, speaking of nuisances, how are we going to prevent Thurlow from doing something silly?"

Ellery lit a cigaret and puffed thoughtfully. "Assuming that Thurlow meant what he said when he threatened to get a revolver, have you any idea where he'd go to buy one?" he asked.

"Cornwall & Ritchey, on Madison Avenue. He has a charge there—keeps lugging home sports equipment he never uses. It's the logical place."

Mr. Paxton was handed the telephone. "Call Cornwall & Ritchey and make discreet inquiries."

Mr. Paxton called that purple house of commerce and made discreet inquiries. When he set the telephone down, he was purple, too. "He meant it!" cried Charley. "Know what the wack's done? He must have hotfooted it down there right from the Supreme Court Building!"

"He's bought a gun?"

"*A* gun? He's bought *fourteen!*"

"What!"

"I spoke to the clerk who waited on him. Fourteen assorted pistols, revolvers, automatics," groaned Paxton. "Said he was starting a collection of 'modern hand weapons.' Of course, they know Thurlow well down there. But see how cunning he's becoming? Knew he had to give an extraordinary excuse for purchasing that number of guns. Collection! What are we going to do?"

"Then he must have had a license," reflected Ellery.

"Seems he came magnificently prepared. He's planned this for a month—that's obvious now. Must have got his wind up in that last libel suit he lost—the one before Cliffstatter. He *does* have a license, a special license he snagged by pull somewhere. We've got to have that license revoked!"

"Yes, we could do that," agreed Ellery, "but my father was right this morning—if Thurlow's denied the legal right to own a gun, he'll get one somewhere illegally."

"But fourteen! With fourteen guns to play with, he's a menace to the public safety. A few imaginary insults, and Thurlow's likely to start a one-man purge!"

Ellery frowned. "I can't believe yet that it's a serious threat, Charley. Although obviously he's got to be watched."

"Then you'll take over?"

"Oh, yes."

"White man!" Charley wrung Ellery's hand. "What can I do to help?"

"Can you insinuate me into the Potts Palace today without getting everybody's wind up?"

"Well, I'm expected tonight—I've got some legal matters to go over with the Old Woman. I could wangle you for dinner. Would tonight be too late, do you think?"

"Hardly. If Thurlow's the man you say he is, he'll be spending the afternoon fondling his fourteen instruments of death and weaving all sorts of darkly satisfactory dreams. Dinner would be splendid."

"Swell!" Charley jumped up. "I'll pick you up at six."

3

She Didn't Know What to Do

"We're going to call for somebody," announced counselor Paxton as he drove Ellery Queen downtown that evening. "I particularly wanted you to meet this person before—well, before."

"Aha," said Ellery, deducting like mad, but to himself.

Charley Paxton parked his roadster before an apartment building in the West Seventies. He spoke to the doorman, and the doorman rang someone on the house phone. Charley paced up and down the lobby, smoking a cigaret nervously.

Sheila Potts appeared in a swirl of summery clothes and laughter, a small slim miss with nice red hair. It seemed to Ellery that she was that peculiar product of American society, a girl of inoffensive insolence. She would insist on the rightness of things and cheerfully do wrong to make them right; she would be impatient with men who beat their breasts, and furious with the authors of their misery. (Ellery suspected that Mr. Paxton beat his breast upon occasion for the sheer glum pleasure of calling attention to himself.) And she was delicious and fresh as a mint bed by a woodsy brook. Then what, wondered Ellery as he took Sheila's gloved hand and heard her explanation of having been visiting—"Don't dare laugh, Mr. Queen!"—a sick friend, was wrong? Why that secret sadness in her eyes?

He learned the answer as they drove west to the Drive, the three of them crowded into the front seat of the roadster.

"My mother's against our marriage," said Sheila simply. "You'd have to know Mother to know just how horrible that can be, Mr. Queen."

"What's her reason?"

"She won't give one," complained Charley.

"I think I know her reason," said Sheila so quietly Ellery almost missed the bitterness. "It's my sister Louella."

"The inventor?"

"Yes. Mother makes no bones about her sympathies, Mr. Queen. She's always been kinder to the children of her first marriage than to Bob and Mac and me. Maybe it's because she never did love my father, and by being cold to us she's getting back at *him*, or something. Whatever it is, I do know that Mother loves poor Louella passionately and *loathes* me." Sheila sucked in her lower lip, as if to hide it.

"It's a fact, Ellery," growled Paxton. "You'd think it was Sheila's fault that Louella's a skinny old zombie, swooping around her smelly chem lab with an inhuman light in her eye."

"It's very simple, Mr. Queen. Rather than see me married while Louella stays an old maid, Mother's perfectly willing to sacrifice my happiness. She's quite a monster about it."

Ellery Queen, who knew odd things, thought he saw wherein the monster dwelt. The children of the Old Woman's union with Bacchus Potts were off normal. On these, the weaklings, the misfits, the helpless ones, Cornelia Potts expended the passion of her maternity. To the offspring of her marriage with Stephen Potts, *né* Brent, therefore, she could give only her acid anger. The twin boys and Sheila were what she had always wanted fussy little Thurlow, spinster-inventor Louella, and the still-unglimpsed Horatio to be. This much was clear. But there was that which was not.

"Why do you two stand for it?" Ellery asked.

Before Charley could answer, Sheila said quickly: "Mother threatens to disinherit me if I marry Charley."

"I see," said Ellery, not liking Sheila's reply at all.

She read the disapproval in his tone. "It's not of myself I'm thinking! It's Charley. You don't know what he's gone through. I don't care a double darn whether I get any of Mother's money or not."

"Well, I don't either," snapped Charley, flushing. "Don't give Ellery the impression—The hours I've spent arguing with you, sweetie-pie!"

"But darling—"

"Ellery, she's as stubborn as her mother. She gets an idea in her head, you can't dislodge it with an ax."

"Peace," smiled Ellery. "This is all new to me, remember. Is this it? If you two were to marry against your mother's wishes, Sheila, she'd not only cut you off but she'd fire Charley, too?" Sheila nodded grimly. "And then, Charley, you'd be out of a job. Didn't I understand that your whole practice consists in taking care of the Potts account?"

"Yes," said Charley unhappily. "Between Thurlow's endless lawsuits and the legitimate legal work of an umpteen-million-dollar shoe business, I keep a large staff busy. There's no doubt Sheila's mother would take all her legal work elsewhere if we defied her. I'd be left pretty much out on a limb. I'd have to start building a practice from scratch. But I'd do it in a shot to get Sheila. Only—she won't."

"No, I won't," said Sheila. "I won't ruin your life, Charley. Or mine for that matter." Her lips flattened, and Charley looked miserable. "You'll hate me for this, Mr. Queen. My mother's an old woman, a sick old woman. Dr. Innis can't help that awful heart of hers, and she won't obey him, or take care of herself, and we can't make her....Mother will die very soon, Mr. Queen. In weeks. Maybe days. Dr. Innis says so. How can I feel anything but relief at the prospect?" And Sheila's eyes, so blue and young, filled with tears.

Ellery saw again that life is not all caramel candy and rose petals, and that the great and hardy souls of this earth are women, not men.

"Sometimes," said Sheila, sniffing, "I think men don't know what love really is." She smiled at Charley and ruffled his hair. "You're a jerk," she said.

The roadster nosed along in traffic, and for some time none of them spoke.

"When Mother dies, Charley and I—and my dad, and the twins—we'll all be free. We've lived in a jail all our lives—a sort of bedlam. You'll see what I mean tonight....We'll be free, and we'll change our names back to Brent, and we'll become folks again, not animals in a zoo. Thurlow's furious about the name of Brent—he hates it."

"Does your mother know all this, Sheila?" frowned Ellery.

"I imagine she suspects." Sheila seized her young man's arm. "Charley, stop here and let me out."

"What for?" demanded Charley suspiciously.

"Let me out, you droogler! There's no point in making Mother madder than she is already. I'll cab home from here, while you drive Mr. Queen into the grounds—then Mother can only *suspect* I've been seeing you on the side!"

"What in the name of the seven thousand miracles," demanded Ellery as he got out of his host's roadster, "is *that*?"

The mansion lay far back from the tall Moorish gates and iron-spiked walls which embraced the precious Potts property. The building faced Riverside Drive and the Hudson River beyond; between gates and house lay an impressive circle of grass and trees, girded as by a stone belt with the driveway which arched from the gates to the mansion and back to the gates again. Ellery was pointing an accusing finger at the center

31

of this circle of greenery. For among the prim city trees stood a remarkable object—a piece of bronze statuary as tall as two acrobats and as wide as an elephant. It stood upon a pedestal and twinkled and leered in the setting sun. It was the statue of an Oxford shoe. A shoe with trailing laces in bronze.

Above it traced elegantly in neon tubing were the words:—

THE POTTS SHOE
$3.99 EVERYWHERE

4

She Gave Them Some Broth Without Any Bread

"It's a little early for dinner," said Charley, his robust voice echoing in the foyer. "Do you want to absorb the atmosphere first, or what? I'm your man."

Ellery blinked at the scene. This was surely the most wonderful house in New York. It had no style; or rather, it partook of many styles, borrowing rather heavily from the Moorish, with Gothic subdominant. It was large, large; and its furnishings were heavy, heavy. There was a wealth of alfresco work on the walls, and sullen, unbeautiful hangings. Knights of Byzantium stood beside doorways stiffly on guard against threats as empty as themselves. A gilded staircase spiraled from the foyer into the heaven of this ponderous dream.

"Let me take the atmosphere in bits, please," said Ellery. He half-expected Afghan hounds to come loping out of hidden lairs, bits of rush clinging to their hides, and Quasimodos in nut-brown sacking and tonsured pates to serve his shuddering pleasure. But the only servant he had seen, an oozy prig of a man in butler's livery, had been conventional enough. "In fact, Charley, if you could give me a glimpse of the various Pottses before dinner in their native habitat I should be ever so much obliged."

"I can't imagine anyone wanting to meet them except through necessity, but I suppose that's what distinguishes you from all other men. This way, Professor. Let's see which Potts we can scare up first."

At the top of the staircase stood a landing, most specious and hushed, and long halls leading away. Charley turned a corner, and there yawned the entrance to what looked like a narrow tower. "That's just what it is," nodded Charley. "Up wi' ye!"

They mounted a steep coil of steps. "I didn't notice this campanile from outside. Why, Charley?"

"It's a peculiarity of construction. The tower faces an inner court and can't be seen from the street."

"And it leads where?"

"To Louella's lair...Here."

Charley knocked on a door with a grille in it backed by thick glass. A female face goggled through the glass, eyed Mr. Paxton with suspicion, withdrew. Bolts clanked. Ellery felt a sensible prickling along his spine when the door screeched open.

Louella Potts was not merely thin—a more desiccated figure he had not seen outside the Morgue. And she was utterly uncared-for. Her gray-dappled coarse brown hair was knotted at her scrawny neck and was all wisps and ends over her eyes. The eyes, like the eyes of the mother, fascinated him. But these, while brilliant, were full of pain, and between them the flesh was set in a permanent puzzle of inquiry. Louella Potts wore a laboratory smock which fitted her like a shroud, and shapeless *huaraches*. No stockings, Ellery noted. He also noted varicose veins, and looked away.

The laboratory was circular—a clutter of tables, retorts, goose-necked flasks, Bunsen burners, messy bottle-filled shelves, taps, benches, electrical apparatus. What it was all for Ellery had no idea; but it looked impressive in a cinematic sort of way.

"Queen?" she shrilled in a voice as tall and thin as herself. "Queen." The frown deepened until it resembled an old knife wound. "You aren't connected with the Mulqueen General Laboratories, are you?"

"No, Miss Potts," said Ellery tensely.

"You see, they've been after my invention. Just thieves, of course. I have to be careful—I do hope you'll understand. Will you excuse me now? I have a tremendously important experiment to conclude before dinner."

"Reminds you of the Mad Scientist in *The Crimson Clue*, doesn't she?" Charley shuddered as they made their way down the tower stairs.

"What's she inventing?"

"A new plastic to be used in the manufacture of shoes," replied Charley Paxton dryly. "According to Louella, this material she's dreaming up will last forever. People will be able to buy one pair of shoes and use them for life."

"But that would ruin the Potts Shoe Company!"

"Of course. But what else would you expect a Potts to spend her time inventing? Come on—I'll introduce you to Horatio."

They were in the foyer again. Charley led the way towards a panel of tall French doors set in a rear wall.

"House is built in a U," he explained. "Within the U are a patio and an inner court, and more grounds, and Horatio's dream house and so on. I've had architects here who've gone screaming into the night...Ooops. There are Steve and the Major."

"Sheila's father and the companion of his Polynesian youth?"

They were two crimson-cheeked elderly men, seemingly quite sane. They were seated in a small library directly off the rear of the foyer, a checkerboard between them. The rear wall of the library was a continuation of the French doors, looking out upon a flagged, roofed terrace which apparently ran the width of the house.

35

As the two young men paused at the foyer doorway, one of the players—a slight, meek-eyed man with a straggly gray mustache—looked up and spied them. "Charley, my boy," he said with a smile. "Glad to s-see you. Come in, come in. Major, I've got you b-beaten anyway, so s-stop pretending you'll w-wiggle out."

His companion, a whale of a man with a whale's stare, snorted and turned his heavy, pocked face towards the doorway. "Go away," he said testily. "I'll whip this snapper if it takes all night."

"And it will," said Stephen Brent Potts in a rush. Then he looked frightened and said: "Of course we'll p-play it out, Major."

Paxton introduced Ellery, the four men chatted for a moment, and then he and Ellery left the two old fellows to resume their game.

"Goes on by day and by night," laughed Charley. "Friendly enemies. Gotch is a queer one—domineering, swears all over the place, and swipes liquor. Otherwise honest—it pays! Steve lets Gotch walk all over him. And everybody else, for that matter."

They left through the French doors in the foyer and crossed the wide terrace, stepping out upon a pleasant lawn, geometrically landscaped, with a path that serpentined to a small building lying within the arms of the surrounding garden walls like a candy box.

"Horatio's cottage," announced Charley.

"Cottage?" gulped Ellery. "You mean—someone actually lives in it? It's not a mirage?"

"Positively not a mirage."

"Then I know who designed it." Ellery's step quickened. "Walt Disney!"

It was a fairy-tale house. It had crooked little turrets and a front door like a golden harp and windows that possessed no symmetry at all. Most of it was painted pink, with peppermint-striped shutters. One turret looked like an inverted beet—a turquoise beet. The curl of smoke coming out of the little chimney was green. Without shame Ellery rubbed his eyes. But when he looked again the smoke was still green.

"You're not seeing things," sighed Charley. "Horatio puts a chemical from his chem set on the fire to color the smoke."

"But *why?*"

"He says green smoke is more fun."

"The Land of Oz," said Ellery in a delighted voice. "Let's go in, for pity's sake. I *must* meet that man!"

Charley played on the harp and it swung inward to reveal a very large, very fat man with exuberant red hair which stood up all over his head, as if excited, and enormous eyes behind narrow gold spectacles. He reminded Ellery of somebody; Ellery tried desperately to think of whom. Then he remembered. It was Santa Claus. Horatio Potts looked like Santa Claus without a beard.

"Charley!" roared Horatio. He wrung the lawyer's hand, almost swinging the young man off his feet. "And this gentleman?"

"Ellery Queen—Horatio Potts."

Ellery had his hand cracked in a fury of welcome. The man possessed a giant's strength, which he used without offense, innocently.

"Come in, come in!"

The interior was exuberant, too. Ellery wondered, as he glanced about, what was wrong with it. Then he saw that nothing was wrong with it. It was a perfect playroom for a child, a boy, of ten. It was crowded with large toys and small—with games, and boxes of candy, and construction sets, and unfinished kites, with puppies and kittens and at least one small, stupid-looking rabbit which was nibbling at the leg of a desk on which were piled children's books and scattered manuscript sheets covered in a large, hearty hand with inky words. A goosequill pen lay near by. It was the jolliest and most imaginatively equipped child's room Ellery had ever seen. But where was the child?

Charley whispered in Ellery's ear: "Ask him to explain his philosophy of life to you."

Ellery did so.

"Glad to," boomed Horatio. "Now you're a man, Mr. Queen. You have worries, responsibilities, you lead a heavy, grown-up sort of life. Don't you?"

"Well...yes," stammered Ellery.

"But it's so simple!" beamed Horatio. "Here, sit down—throw those marbles on the floor. The happiest part of a man's life is his boyhood, and I don't care if he was brought up in Gallipolis, Ohio, or Hester Street, New York." Ellery wiggled his brows. "All right, now take *me*. If I had to make shoes in a factory, or tell other men to make 'em, or write advertising, or dig ditches, or do any of the tiresome things men have to do to be men—why, I'd be like you, Mr. Queen, or like Charley Paxton here, who always goes around with a worried look." Charley grinned feebly. "But I don't have to. So I fly kites, I run miniature trains, I build twelve-foot bridges and airplane models, I read Superman and Hairbreadth Harry, detective stories, fairy tales, children's verses...I even write 'em." Horatio seized a couple of highly colored books from his desk. "*The Little Old Dog of Dogwood Street*, by Horatio Potts. *The Purple Threat*, by Horatio Potts. Here are a dozen more boys' stories, all by me."

"Horatio," said Charley reverently, "publishes 'em himself, too."

"Right now I'm writing my major opus, Mr. Queen," roared Horatio happily. "A new modern version of *Mother Goose*. It's going to be my monument, mark my words."

"Even has his meals served there," said Charley as they strolled back to the main house. "Well, Ellery, what do you think of Horatio Potts?"

"He's either the looniest loon of them all," growled Mr. Queen, "or he's the only sane man alive on the planet!"

*   *   *

Dinner was served in a Hollywood motion-picture set by extras—or so it seemed to Ellery, who sat down to the most remarkable meal of his life. The dining-room ceiling was a forest of rafters, and one had to crane to count them. Everything was on the same Brobdingnagian scale—a logical outgrowth, no doubt, of the giant that was Pottsism. Nothing less than a California redwood could have provided the one-piece immensity of the table. The linen and silver were heavier than Ellery had ever hefted, the crockery was grander, and the stemware more intricate. The *credenza* groaned. If the Old Woman was hen of a batty brood, at least she did not make them scratch for their grub. This was the board of plenty.

The twins, Robert and Maclyn, had not appeared for dinner. They had telephoned their mother that they were held up "at the office."

Cornelia Potts was a not ungracious hostess. The old lady wanted to know all about "Mr. Queen," and Mr. Queen found himself talking when he had come to listen. If he was to gauge the temper and the sanity of Thurlow Potts, he could not distract himself with himself. So he was annoyed, deliberately. The Old Woman stared at him with the imperial surprise of a woman who has lived seventy years on her own terms. Finally she rejected him, turning to her children. Ellery grinned with relief.

Sheila ate brightly, too brightly. Her eyes were crystal with humiliation. Ellery knew it was for him, for being witness to her shame. For Cornelia ignored her, as if Sheila were some despised poor relation instead of the daughter of her flesh. Cornelia devoted herself almost wholly to Louella, who bothered not at all to respond to her mother's blandishments. The skinny old maid looked sullen; she ate wolfishly, in silence.

Had it not been for Stephen Potts and his friend Major Gotch, the dinner would have been intolerable. But the two cronies chattered away, apparently pleased at having a new ear to pour their reminiscences into, and Ellery had some difficulty extricating himself from Papuan paradises, Javanese jungles, and "the good old days" in the South Seas.

Thurlow had come to the table bearing two books. He set them down beside his service plate, and once in a while glanced at them or touched them with a glowering pleasure. From where Charley Paxton sat he could read the titles on their spines; Ellery could not.

"What are those books, Charley?" he mumbled.

Charley squinted. *"The History of Dueling—"*

"History of dueling!"

"The other is *A Manual of Firearms.*"

Mr. Queen choked over his melon.

During the soup course—an excellent chicken consommé—Ellery looked about and looked about and finally said in an undertone to Charley: "I notice there's no bread on the table. Why is that?"

"The Old Woman," Charley whispered back. "She's on a strict diet—Innis has forbidden her to eat bread in any form—so she won't have it in the house. Why are you looking so funny?"

Thurlow was explaining to his mother with passion the code of duello, and Major Gotch interrupted to recall some esoteric Oriental facts on the broader subject; so Mr. Queen had an opportunity to lean over to his friend and chant, softly:—

> "There was an *old woman* who lived in a *shoe,*
> She had *so many children* she didn't know what to do,
> She gave them some *broth without any bread ...*"

Charley gaped. "What are you talking about?"

"I was struck by certain resemblances," muttered Ellery. "The Horatio influence, no doubt." And he finished his broth in a thoughtful way.

Suddenly Louella's cricket-voice cut across the flow of table talk. "Mother!"

"Yes, Louella?" It was embarrassing to see the eagerness in

40

the old lady's face as her elder daughter addressed her.

"I need some more money for my plastic experiments."

"Spend your allowance already?" The corners of the Old Woman's mouth sank, settled.

Louella looked sullen again. "I can't help it. It's not going just right. I'll get it this time sure. I need a couple of thousand more, Mother."

"No, Louella. I told you last time—"

To Ellery's horror the forty-four-year-old spinster began to weep into the puddle in her consommé cup, weep and snuffle and breathe without restraint. "You're mean! I hate you! Some day I'll have millions—why can't you give me some of my own money now? But no—you're making me wait till you die. And meanwhile I can't finish my greatest invention!"

"Louella!"

"I don't care! I'm sick of asking you, asking you—"

"Louella dear," said Sheila in a strained voice. "We have guests—"

"Be quiet, Sheila," said the Old Woman softly. Ellery saw Sheila's fingers tighten about her spoon.

"Are you going to give me my own money or aren't you?" Louella shrieked at her mother.

"Louella, leave the table."

"I won't!"

"Louella, leave the table this instant and go to bed!"

"But I'm hungry, Mother," Louella whined.

"You've been acting like an infant. For that you can't have your supper. Go this instant, Louella."

"You're a horrible old woman!" screamed Louella, stamping her foot; and, bouncing up from the table, she stormed from the dining room, weeping again.

Mr. Queen, who had not known whether to rise for the woman or remain seated for the child, compromised by assuming a half-risen, half-seated posture; from which undignified position he murmured, but to himself:—

41

"And whipped them all soundly and put them to bed. ..."

After which, finding himself suspended he lowered himself into his chair. "I wonder," he wondered to himself, "how much of this a sane mind could take."

As if in answer, Sheila ran from the dining room, choking back sobs; and Charley Paxton, looking grim, excused himself after a moment and followed her. Steve Potts rose; his lips were burbling.

"Stephen, finish your dinner," said his wife quietly.

Sheila's father sank back in his chair.

Charley returned with a mumble of apology. The Old Woman threw him a sharp black look. He sat down beside Ellery and said in a strangled undertone: "Sheila sends her apologies. Ellery, I've got to get her out of this lunatic asylum!"

"Whispering, Charles?" Cornelia Potts eyed him. The young man flushed. "Where is Sheila?"

"She has a headache," muttered Charley.

"I see."

There was silence.

5

There Was a Little Man and He Had a Little Gun

From the moment Robert and Maclyn Potts entered the dining room to be introduced to the guest and seat themselves at table, a breath of sanity blew. They were remarkably identical twins, as alike in feature as two carbon copies. They dressed alike, they combed their curly blond hair alike, they were of a height and a thickness, and their voices had the same pleasant, boyish timbre.

Charley, who introduced them, was obviously at a loss; he made a mistake in their identities at once, which one of them corrected patiently. They tackled their broth and chicken with energy, talking at a great rate. It seemed that both were angry with their eldest brother, Thurlow, for having interfered in the conduct of the business for the hundredth time.

"We wouldn't mind so much, Mother—" began one, through a mouthful of fried chicken.

"Yes, Robert?" said the Old Woman grimly. She, at least, could distinguish between them.

"If Thurlow'd restrict his meddling to unimportant things," continued the other. *Ergo*, he was Mac.

"But he doesn't!" growled Robert, dropping his fork.

"Robert, eat your dinner."

"All *right*, Mother."

"But Mother, he's gone and—"

"One moment *please*," said Thurlow icily. "And what is it I'm supposed to have done this time, Maclyn?"

"Climb off it, Thurl," grumbled Mac. "All right, you're a vice-president of the Potts Shoe Company—"

"You pretend you're running a God-knows-how-many-million-dollar firm," exploded Robert, "and that's okay as long as you pretend—"

"But why in hell don't you stick to wasting the family's money on those silly lawsuits of yours—"

"Instead of canceling our newspaper-advertising plans for the Middle West, you feeble-minded nitwit?"

"Robert, don't speak to your eldest brother that way!" cried their mother.

"How you protect your white-haired boy, Mother," grinned Robert. "Although there isn't much of it left....You know Thurlow would ruin the business if—"

"Just—one—moment, *if* you please," said Thurlow. His fat nostrils were quivering. "I've got as much to say about running the company as you two have—Mother said so! Didn't you, Mother?"

"I won't have this disgraceful argument at the dinner table, boys."

"He said I'd ruin the business!" cried Thurlow.

"Well, wouldn't you?" asked Bob Potts with disgust.

"Bob, cut it out," said his twin in a low voice.

"Cut nothing out, Mac!" said Robert. "We always have to sit by and watch old fuddy-pants pull expensive boners, then we've got to clean up his mess. Well, I'm damned good and tired of it!"

"Robert, I warn you—!" shouted Thurlow.

"Warn my foot. You're a nice fat little bag of wind, Brother

Thurlow," said Bob Potts angrily, "a fake, a phony, and a blubbering jerk, and if you don't keep your idiotic nose out of the business—"

Thurlow grew very pale, but also a look came into his eyes of cunning. He snatched his napkin, jumped up, ran over to where Robert was watching him with a puzzled expression, and then whipped the napkin over his younger brother's face with an elegance—and a force—that caused Bob's mouth to open.

"What the devil—"

"You've insulted Thurlow Potts for the last time," choked the chubby little man. "Brother or no brother, I demand satisfaction. Wait here—I'll give you your choice of weapons!" And, triumphantly, Thurlow stalked out of the dining room.

Surely, thought Ellery Queen, this is where I wake up and stretch.

But there was the doorway through which Thurlow Potts had passed, here was the long board with its congress of amazed faces.

"Well, I'll be a monkey's uncle," said Mac, looking blank. "Thurlow's gone clean off his chump at last! Pop—did you hear that?"

Steve Potts rose indecisively. "Maybe if I g-go speak to Thurlow, Mac—"

Mac laughed. "He's stark, raving mad!"

Bob was feeling his cheek. "Why don't you face the facts, Mother? How can you sit by and let Thurlow have anything to do with the business? If Mac and I didn't countermand every stupid order he gives, he'd run us into bankruptcy in a year."

"You baited him, Robert. Deliberately!"

"Oh, come, Mother—"

Suddenly the air was windy with recriminations. The only member of the household who seemed to enjoy it was Major Gotch, who sat back puffing a pipe and following the play of words like a spectator at a tennis match.

"That book, Ellery," exclaimed Charley Paxton under cover of the argument. "Reads *The History of Dueling* and challenges Robert to a duel!"

"He can't be serious," muttered Ellery. "Can't be."

Thurlow popped in, his eyes shining. Ellery rose like a released balloon. Thurlow was brandishing two pistols.

"It's all right, Mr. Queen," said Thurlow gently. "Sit down, please."

Mr. Queen sat down. "What interesting-looking little guns," he said. "May I look at them, Mr. Potts?"

"Some other time," murmured Thurlow. "From now on, we must do everything according to the code."

"The code?" Ellery blinked. "Which code is that, Mr. Potts?"

"The code of duello, of course. Honor before everything, Mr. Queen!" And Thurlow advanced upon his brother, who sat transfixed. "Robert, take one of these. The choice is yours."

Bob's hand came up in a mechanical motion; it fell grasping a shiny nickel weapon which Ellery recognized as a Smith & Wesson, "S. & W. .38/32," a .38-caliber revolver. It was not a large weapon, being scarcely more than half a foot long, yet it hung like a submachine gun from Robert's paralyzed hand. Mac sat by his twin with an identical expression of stupefaction.

Thurlow glanced down at the weapon remaining—a Colt "Pocket Model" automatic pistol of .25 caliber, a flat and minia-ture gun which looked like a toy beside the small revolver in Robert's hand, for it was only 4½ inches long. Thurlow with a flourish put the little automatic into his pocket. "Mr. Queen, you're the only outsider here. I ask you to act as my second."

"Your—" began Ellery, finding the word stick to his gums.

But Charley Paxton whispered frantically to him: "Ellery, for Pete's sake! Humor him!"

Mr. Queen nodded wordlessly.

Thurlow bowed, a not inconsiderable feat; but the action had a certain dignity. "Robert, I'll meet you at dawn in front of the Shoe."

"The Shoe," said Bob stupidly.

Ellery caught a clairvoyant glimpse of the two brothers in the

46

coming dawn approaching from opposite directions that ugly bronze on the front lawn, and he almost laughed. But then he glanced at Thurlow again, and refrained.

"Thurlow, for the love of Mike—" began Mac.

"Keep out of this, Maclyn," said Thurlow sternly, and Mac glanced quickly at his mother. But the Old Woman simply sat, a porcelain. "Robert, each one of these weapons has one bullet in it. You understand?"

Bob could only nod.

"I warn you, I'll shoot to kill. But if you miss me, or just wound me, I'll consider my honor satisfied. It says so in the book."

It says so in the book, Ellery repeated to himself, dazed.

"Dawn at the Shoe, Robert." A huge contempt came into Thurlow's penny-whistle voice. "If you don't show up, I'll kill you on sight." And Thurlow left the dining room a second time, prancing, like a ballet dancer.

Sheila came running into a thickly inhabited silence. "I just saw Thurl go up to his bedroom with a little gun in his hand—" She stopped, spying the glittering nickel in Bob's hand.

The Old Woman simply sat.

Charley got up, sat down, got up again. "It's nothing, Sheila. A—joke of Thurlow's. About a duel at dawn at the Shoe on the front lawn, or some such nonsense—"

"A duel!" Sheila stared at her brother.

"I still think it's some weird gag of Thurl's," Bob said with a shaky smile, "although God knows he's never been famous for a sense of humor—"

"But why are you all *sitting* here?" cried Sheila. "Call a doctor, a psychiatrist! Call Bellevue!"

"*Not while I live,*" said the Old Woman.

Her husband's face waxed and waned, purple and white. "Not while you live!" he spat at her. Then he ran from the room, as if ashamed...as he had been running, Ellery suddenly knew, for over thirty years.

47

"You're grown men, aren't you?" The old lady's mouth was wry.

"Mother," said Mac. "You can stop this craziness. You know you can. All you have to do is say a word to Thurlow. He's scared to death of you ..." She was silent. "You *won't?*"

The Old Woman banged on the table. "You're old enough to fight your own battles."

"If precious li'l Thurl wants a duel, precious li'l Thurl gets it, hey?" Mac laughed angrily.

But his mother was on her way to the door.

Sheila stopped her with a choked cry. "You never interfere except when it suits you—and this time it doesn't suit you, Mother! You don't care anything about the twins and me—you never have. Your darling Thurlow—that poor, useless lunatic! You'd let him have his way if he wanted to kill the three of us...the three of us!"

The Old Woman did not even glance at her younger daughter. She eyed Ellery instead. "Good night, Mr. Queen. I don't know what Charles Paxton's purpose was in bringing you here tonight, but now that you've seen my family, I hope you'll be discreet enough to hold your tongue. I want no interference from strangers!"

"Of course, Mrs. Potts."

She nodded and swept out.

"What do you think, Ellery?" Charley's tone was brittle, ready to crack. "It's a bluff, isn't it?"

The twins stared at Ellery, and Paxton, and Sheila...but not Major Gotch, who, Ellery suddenly realized, was no longer among those present. The canny old goat had managed to slip out some time during the farce.

"No, Charley," said Mr. Queen soberly, "I don't think this is a bluff. I think Thurlow Potts is in earnest. Of course, he's touched; but that won't keep Bob Potts out of the way of a bullet tomorrow morning. Let's put our heads together, the five of us."

6

Ellery Betrays the Code of Duello

"The steps we can take," said Ellery without excitement, "are legion, but they have a common drawback—they involve the use of force. Thurlow can be arrested on some picturesque charge—there may be an old statute on the law books which forbids the practice of dueling, for example. Or he might be charged with threatening homicide. And so on. But he'd be out on bail—if I read your mother correctly—before he was fairly in the clink, and moreover he'd be smarting under a fresh 'injustice.' Or we could ship him off to Bellevue for observation. But I doubt if there are sufficient grounds either to keep him there or put him away in a mental hospital...No; can't be force."

"Bob could duck out of town," suggested Mac.

"Are you kidding?" growled his twin.

"Besides, Thurlow would only follow him," said Sheila.

"How about humoring him?" Charley scowled.

Ellery looked interested. "What do you mean exactly?"

"Why not go through with the duel, but pull its teeth?"

"Charley...that's it!" cried Sheila.

"Fake it?" frowned Bob.

"But how, Charley?" asked Mac.

"Thurlow said he'd be satisfied if each man fired a single shot, didn't he? In fact, he said each gun was loaded with just one bullet. All right. *Let* each man fire one cartridge apiece tomorrow morning, but see that those cartridges are *blank*."

"The legal mind," moaned Ellery. "These simple solutions! Charley, you're a genius. My hand, sir."

They shook hands solemnly.

"I knew I'd fallen in love with a Blue Plate special," laughed Sheila. She kissed Charley and then put her arms about her twin brothers.

"What d'ye think, Bob?" asked Mac anxiously.

The intended victim grinned. "To tell the truth, Mac, I was frightened blue. Yes, if we substitute blank cartridges for the real ones in the two guns, old Nutsy'll never know the difference."

Sheila was to decoy Thurlow into the library at the rear of the house, on the ground floor, and keep him there while the men did the dirty work.

"The real dirty work's *my* assignment," said Sheila darkly. And she sallied forth to find Thurlow.

Mac volunteered to stand guard at the outpost. Ellery and Charley, it was agreed, must do the actual deed. Bob was to stay out of everything.

Within ten minutes Mac was back with a report, his blue eyes glittering. He had seen Thurlow and Sheila come down from upstairs, chatting earnestly. They had gone into the library. Sheila had shut the door, winking at the hidden twin that all, so far at any rate, went well.

Ellery stood musing. "Bob—can you shoot a revolver?"

"If you show me the place where the blame thing goes off."

"Ouch," said Mr. Queen. "Can Thurlow?"

"He can shoot," said Mac shortly.

"Oh, my. In that case, this mustn't fail. Charley, where's The Purple Avenger's lair?"

The twins sped upstairs to their room. Charley Paxton and Ellery followed, and Charley led the great man to one of the numerous doors studding the upper hall.

"Thurlow's?"

Charley nodded, looking around uneasily.

Ellery listened for a moment. Then, boldly, he went in. He stood in a tall and pleasant sitting room, profuse with fresh flowers and easy-chairs and books, and furnished with surprising good taste. Aside from a rather sexless quality, the room was cloistered and fragrant peace for anyone.

"I see what you meant by Thurlow's potentialities, Charley," remarked Ellery. "Did he fix this up himself?"

"All by his little self, Ellery—"

"The man has dignity. I wonder what he reads." He ran his eye along the bookshelves. "Mm, yes. A little heavy on Paine, Butler, and Lincoln—ah, of course! Voltaire. No light reading at all, of course ..."

"Ellery, for heaven's sake." Charley glanced anxiously at the door.

"It gives the man a perspective," mused Ellery, and he moved on to Thurlow Potts's bedroom. This was a wee, chaste, almost monastic chamber. A high white bed, a highboy, a chair, a lamp. Ellery could see the little man clambering with agility into his bed, clad—no doubt this was an injustice—in a flannel nightshirt, and clutching a volume of *The Rights of Man* to his thick little bosom.

"There it is," said Charley, who had his mind on his work.

The Colt automatic lay on top of the highboy. Ellery picked it up negligently. "Doesn't look very formidable, does it?"

"Has it got one cartridge in it, as Thurlow said?"

Ellery investigated. "But of course it would. He's an honest man. Let us away, Charles." He slipped the Colt into his jacket

51

and they left Thurlow's apartment, Charley acting furtive and relieved at once.

"Where the devil do we get blank cartridges this time of night?" he asked in the hall. "All the stores are closed by now."

"Peace, peace," said Ellery. "Charley, go downstairs to the library and join Sheila in keeping Mr. Thurlow Potts occupied. I don't want him back in his bedroom till I'm ready for him."

"What are *you* going to do?"

"I," quoth Mr. Queen, "shall journey posthaste to my daddy's office at Police Headquarters. Don't stir from the library till I get back."

When Charley had left him, Ellery ambled to the door through which he had seen Bob and Mac Potts disappear, knocked gently, was admitted, gave his personal reassurances that everything was going off as planned—and requisitioned Robert's Smith & Wesson.

"But why?" Bob asked.

"Playing it safe," grinned Ellery, from the hall. "I'll put a blank in this one, too."

"But I don't like it, Ellery," grumbled Inspector Queen at Head-quarters, when his son had told him and Sergeant Velie the story of Thurlow Potts's great adventure.

"It ain't decent," said Sergeant Velie. "Fightin' a duel in the year of our Lord!"

Ellery agreed it was neither decent nor to be condoned; but what, he asked reasonably, was a sounder solution of the problem?

"I don't know. I just don't like it," said the Inspector irritably, jamming a blank cartridge into the magazine of the Colt. He tossed it aside and slipped a center-fire blank into the top chamber of the Smith & Wesson.

"That den of dopes've been in every screwball scrape you can imagine," complained the Sergeant, "but this one takes the hand-embroidered bearskin. Fightin' a duel in the year of our Lord!"

"With the sting removed from Thurlow's stingers," argued Ellery, "it makes a good story, Sergeant."

"Only story *I* want to hear," grunted his father, handing Ellery the two weapons, "is that this fool business is over and done with."

"But Dad, there's no danger of anything going wrong when both guns are loaded with blanks."

"Guns are guns," said Sergeant Velie, who was the Sage of Center Street.

"And blanks are blanks, Sergeant."

"Stop chattering! Velie, you and I are going to watch Thurlow Potts's duel at dawn tomorrow from behind that big Shoe on the front lawn," snapped Inspector Queen. "And may God have mercy on all our souls if anything goes haywire!"

Ellery slipped back into the Potts mansion under an impertinent moon; but he made sure only the moon's eye saw him. Mr. Queen had a way with front doors.

The foyer was empty. He stole towards the rear, listened for voices at the study door, nodded, and made his way in noiseless leaps up the staircase.

Several minutes later he knocked on the twins' door. It opened immediately.

"Well?" asked the Potts twins in one voice. They were nervous: cigaret butts littered the trays, and a bottle of Scotch had been, if not precisely killed, then at least criminally assaulted.

"The deed is done," announced Mr. Queen, "the Colt and its blank are back on Thurlow's highboy, and here's your Smith & Wesson, Bob."

"You're sure the damned thing won't kill anybody?"

"Quite sure, Bob."

Robert placed it gingerly on the night table between his bed and Mac's.

"Then nothing can go wrong tomorrow morning?" growled Mac.

"Oh, come. You're acting like a couple of children. Of course nothing can go wrong!"

Ellery left the twins and cheerily went downstairs to the library. To his surprise, he found Thurlow in a mood more mellow than melancholy.

"Hi," said Thurlow, describing a parabola with his left hand. His right was clasped about a frosty glass. "My second, ladies 'n' gentlemen. Can't have a duel without a second. Come in, Misser Queen. We were just discussing the possibility of continuing our conversation in more con-congenial surroundings. Know what I mean?" And Thurlow leered cherubically.

"I know exactly what you mean, Mr. Potts," smiled Ellery. Perhaps Thurlow in his cups might prove a saner man than Thurlow sober. He nodded slightly to Sheila and Paxton, who looked exhausted. "A hot spot, eh, kid?"

"Hot spot 'tis," beamed Thurlow. "Tha's my second, ladies 'n' gentlemen. Won'erful character." And Thurlow linked his arms in Ellery's, marching him out of the library to the tune of a rueful psalm which went: "Eat, drink, an' be merry, for tomorrow I'll be glad when you're dead, you rascal youuuuu ..."

Thurlow insisted on Club Bongo. All their arguments could not dissuade him. Ellery could only hope fervently that Mr. Conklin Cliffstatter, of the East Shore jute and shoddy Cliffstatters, was getting drunk elsewhere this night. In the cab on their way downtown, Thurlow fell innocently asleep on Ellery's shoulder.

"This seems kind of silly," giggled Charley Paxton.

"It is not, Charley!" whispered Sheila. "Maybe we can get him into such a good mood he'll call the duel off."

"Hush. Uneasy lies the head." And indeed at that moment Thurlow awoke with a whoop and took up his dolorous psalm.

Mr. Queen, Miss Potts, her eldest brother, and Mr. Paxton spent the night at Club Bongo, keeping its death watch with the curious characters who seemed to find its prancing maidens and tense comedians the most hilarious of companions.

Fortunately, Mr. Cliffstatter was not among them.

Mr. Queen was his suavest and most persuasive; he inserted little melodies of reasonableness into the chit-chat; he suggested frequent libations at the flowing bowl.

But all his efforts, and Sheila's, and Charley's, availed nothing. At a certain point, diabolically, Thurlow stopped imbibing; and to all suggestions that he call off the duel and make a peace with Bob, he would smile sadly, say, "Punctilio is involved my good frien's," and applaud the *première danseuse* enthusiastically.

7

Pistols at Dawn

They got back to the Potts grounds on the drive at a quarter of six. The dawn was dripping and jellyfish-gray, not cheerful. The thing was beyond reason, but there it was. A duel was to be fought in this clammy dawn, with pistols, on a sward, and with trees as sentinels.

The three were exhausted; but not baggy-pantsed, tweed-coated Thurlow. He egged them on in his high-pitched voice, made higher than ordinary by a sort of ecstasy. Sheila and Charley and Ellery could scarcely keep step with him.

They went directly from the sidewalk before the front gates across the grass to the obscene bronze bulk of the Shoe, above which the neon inscription, THE POTTS SHOE, $3.99 EVERYWHERE, still glowed faintly against the early morning sky.

Thurlow glanced up at the silent windows of his mother's mansion beyond the Shoe. "Mr. Queen," he said formally, "you will find my pistol on the highboy in my bedroom."

Ellery hesitated; then he bowed and hurried off to the house. In every story Ellery had ever read about a duel, the seconds bowed.

As he rounded the Shoe, the Inspector's voice came to him in a low and wondering snarl. "He's going through with it, Velie!"

"They'll never believe this downtown," whispered the Sergeant with hoarse awe. "Never, Inspector."

The two men nodded tensely to Ellery as he strode by, and he nodded back. It wasn't so bad, he thought, as he vaulted up the front steps. In fact, it was rather fun. He realized how gay life had been for those old boys of the romantic age, and felt almost thankful to Providence for having brought Thurlow Potts into the world a century or two late.

He realized, too, that part of his enjoyment derived from a certain giddiness of the brain, which in turn came from having tried to set Thurlow a Scotch example all night. Things were a little hazy as he tiptoed into the house, having used his magic on the lock of the front door.

Where was everybody? Wonderful household! Two brothers are to duel to the death, and of their blood none cares sufficiently to let off snoring and be miserable. Or perhaps the Old Woman was awake, peering through the curtains of her bedroom window at the scene in miniature to be enacted on the grass before her Moloch. What could she be thinking, that extraordinary mother? And where was Steve Brent Potts? Probably drunk in his bed.

Ellery stopped very suddenly halfway up the main staircase leading from the foyer to the bedroom floor. The house was silent, with that eeriest of silences which pervades a house at dawn, the silence of gray light.

Not a sound. Not even a shadow. But—something?

It seemed to be on the bedroom floor, and it seemed to pass the door of Thurlow Potts's apartment. Was it...*someone coming out of those two rooms?*

Ellery sped up the remaining steps and stopped catlike on the landing to survey the hall, both ways. No one. And the silence again.

Man? Woman? Imagination? He listened very hard.

But that deep, deep silence.

He went into Thurlow's apartment, shut the door behind him, and began to search for more palpable clues. He spared neither time, eyesight, nor his clothes. But crawl and peer and pry as he might, he could detect no least sign that anyone had been there since he himself had left the premises the night before on his last visit. The tiny Colt lay exactly where he had placed it with his own hand after his trip to Police Headquarters for the blank cartridges—on Thurlow's highboy.

Ellery seized Thurlow's automatic and left the apartment.

Robert and Maclyn Potts appeared promptly at six. They marched from the house shoulder to shoulder, appeared not to notice Inspector Queen and Sergeant Velie in the shadows at the base of the Shoe's pedestal, rounded the Shoe, and stopped.

The two parties stared solemnly at each other.

Then Thurlow bowed to his brothers.

Bob hesitated, glanced at Ellery, then bowed back. Behind Thurlow, Charley grinned and clasped his hands above his head. Bob's left eyelid drooped ever so little in reply.

But Mac's expression was serious. "Look here, Thurl," he said, "hasn't this fool farce gone far enough? Let's shake hands all around and—"

Thurlow glared disapprovingly at his adversary's twin. "You will please inform the gentleman's second," he said to Ellery, "that conversation with the principals is not considered good form, Mr. Queen."

"I so inform him," replied Mr. Queen frigidly. "Now what do I do, Mr. Potts?"

"I should be obliged if you would act as Master of Ceremonies as well as my second. It's a little irregular, but then I'm sure we can take a few liberties with the code."

"Oh, of course," said Ellery hastily. Improvise, Brother Queen, improvise. Must be some sense in the code of duello somewhere, or was. "Mr. Thurlow Potts, your weapon," said Ellery in a grave voice. He handed the Colt, walnut stock forward, to his man.

Mr. Thurlow Potts dropped the automatic into the right pocket of his coat. Then he turned and walked off a few paces, to stand there stiffly, a man alone with his Maker. Or so his back said.

"I believe," continued Ellery, turning to Maclyn Potts, "that as your principal's second you should be addressed. The Master of Ceremonies should ask somebody if the duelists won't call the whole thing off. What say?"

Before Mac could reply, Thurlow's voice came, annoyed. "No, no, Mr. Queen. As the offended party, the option is mine." It didn't sound right to Mr. Queen; more like a business conference. "And I insist: Honor satisfied."

"But isn't there something in the code," the Master of Ceremonies asked respectfully, "about the duel being called off if the offender apologizes, Mr. Potts?"

"I'll apologize. I'll do any blasted thing," snapped Bob, "to get off this damp grass."

"No, *no!*" screamed Thurlow. "I won't have it that way. Honor satisfied, Mr. Queen, honor satisfied!"

"Very well, honor satisfied," replied Mr. Queen hastily. "I think, then, that the principals should stand back to back. Right here, gentlemen. Mac, is your man ready?"

Mac nodded disgustedly, and Robert took from his pocket the Smith & Wesson Ellery had returned to him the night before. Robert and Thurlow now approached each other, Thurlow producing from his pocket the Colt Ellery had just handed him and gripping it nervously. Thurlow was pale.

"Back to back, gentlemen."

The brothers executed the *volte-face*.

"I shall count to ten. With each number of the count," continued Ellery with stern relish, "you gentlemen will walk one pace forward. At the end of the count you will be twenty paces from each other, facing in opposite directions. Is that clear?"

Thurlow Potts said in a strained voice: "Yes." Robert Potts yawned.

"At the end of the count, I shall say 'Turn!' You will then turn and face each other, raise your weapons, and take aim. I will thereupon count to three, and at three you each fire just one shot. Understand?"

Sheila giggled.

"Very well, then. Start pacing off. One. Two. Three…" Ellery counted solemnly. When he said "Ten," the two men obediently stopped pacing. "Turn!" They turned.

Thurlow's chubby face gleamed wet in the gray light. But his mouth was set in a stubborn line, and he scowled fiercely at his brother. He raised his Colt shoulder high, aiming it. Robert shrugged and aimed too.

"One," said Ellery. This is all wrong, he thought testily. I should have read up on it. Maybe when Thurlow finds out how I've messed up his duel, he'll insist on a retake.

"Two." And what were the Inspector and Velie thinking behind that horrible statue? He'd never hear the end of this. He spied the two men's heads peeping cautiously from behind the pedestal.

"Three!"

There was one cracking report. Smoke drifted from the muzzle of Thurlow's little weapon.

Ellery became aware of a leaden silence, and of a curious look on Thurlow Potts's face. He whirled. Behind him Sheila gurgled, and Charley Paxton said: "What the—" and Maclyn Potts stared at the grass. And Inspector Queen and Sergeant Velie were racing around the pedestal, waving their arms frantically.

For Robert Potts lay on the grass, on his face, the undischarged Smith & Wesson still in his hand.

"Bob, Bob, get off the grass." Mac kept saying. "Stop clowning. Get the hell up off the grass. You'll catch cold—"

Somebody—it was Charley—took Mac's arm and steered him, still prattling, off to one side.

"Well?" asked the Inspector in an unreal voice.

Ellery rose, mechanically brushing at grass stains on his trouser knees which would not come off. "The man's dead."

Sheila Potts ran blindly for the house. She made a wide, horrified detour around Thurlow, who was still standing there, gun in hand, looking at them all with a bewildered expression.

"Smack in the pump," breathed Sergeant Velie, pointing. Ellery had turned Bob Potts over: there was a dark spot on his clothing, from which an uneven bloodstain had spread, like the solar corona.

Thurlow threw down his automatic as if it burned his hand. He walked off unsteadily.

"Hey—!" began Sergeant Velie, taking a step toward him. But then the Sergeant stopped and scratched his head.

"But—how?" howled the Inspector, finding his normal voice. "Ellery, I thought you said—"

"You'll find the blank cartridge you yourself placed in Robert's Smith & Wesson still in the chamber," Ellery said in a stiff tone. "He never even fired. There *was* a corresponding blank in Thurlow's Colt too—when I deposited it on Thurlow's highboy last night after my trip to Headquarters. But someone—*someone in this house*, Dad—substituted a *real* bullet for the blank you'd put in Thurlow's gun last night!"

"Murder," said the Inspector. He was white.

"Yes," mumbled Ellery. "Murder to which we were all eyewitnesses—yet none of us lifted a finger to stop it...in fact, we aided and abetted it. *We saw the man who fired the shot, but we don't know who the murderer is!*"

Part Two

8

The Paramount Question of Opportunity

A premeditated murder is not unlike a child. First it must be conceived, second gestated; only then can it be born. These three steps in the fruition of the homicide are usually unwitnessed; when this occurs, there is a Mystery, and the function of the Detective is to go back along its blood line, for only in this way can be established the paternity of the crime—which is to say, solve the mystery.

Ellery Queen had never before been privileged to attend the delivery, as it were; and the fact that, having attended it, he knew as little about its parentage as if he had not neither irritated nor angered him, for if a murder had to be committed and could not be averted, then Ellery preferred it to be a mystery at the beginning, just so that he could dig into it and trace it backward and explain it to himself at the end.

He stood by himself, deep in thought, in the lightening morning under one of the Old Woman's pedigreed blue spruces, watching his father and Sergeant Velie go to work. He stood by, musing, as Hesse, and Flint, and Piggott, and Johnson, and others of the Inspector's staff arrived, as radio patrol cars gathered on the Drive outside the high wall, as the police photographer came, the fingerprint men, and Dr. Samuel Prouty, Assistant Medical Examiner of New York County—petulant at having had to leave spouse, progeny, and couch so early of a summer morning. As of old, Doc Prouty and Inspector Queen set about snarling at each other over Robert Potts's sprawled corpse, like two fierce old dogs over a bone. As always Sergeant Velie, the Great Dane, chuckled and growled between them. Eventually the body was lifted to an improvised stretcher, under the fussy superintendence of Doc Prouty; a moment later Dr. Waggoner Innis's big sedan roared up under police motorcycle escort, and the doctor's long legs carried him in almost eager strides after the cortege, to confer with the assistant Medical Examiner over the technical details of the homicide. The whole party disappeared into the house, leaving Inspector Queen and his son, alone, at the pedestal of the bronze Shoe.

The air was chill, and the Inspector shivered a little. "Well?" he said.

"Well," said Ellery.

"We'd better talk fast," said the Inspector after a pause. "The newspapers will be here soon, and we'd better figure out what to say to them. At the moment, my mind's a blank."

Ellery frowned over his cigaret.

"A duel," the Inspector continued with bitterness. "I let myself be talked into a duel! And this happens. What'll I say to the boss? What'll I say to anybody?"

Ellery sighed and flipped his butt into the damp grass. The sun was struggling to wipe the clouds from its eye; the feeble glance that escaped flung the ugly shadow of the Shoe toward the Hudson. "Why," complained Mr. Ellery Queen, "does the sun invariably stay hidden when you want it, and come out when it doesn't matter any more?"

"What are you talking about?"

"Well, I mean, " smiled Ellery, "that if the light had been better we might have been able to see something."

"Oh. But what, Ellery? The dirty work was done during the night."

"Yes. But—a glance, a change of expression. You never know. Little things are so important. And the light was dismal and gray, and details likewise." And the great man sank into silence again.

The Inspector shook his head impatiently. "Light or no light, the point is: Who could have substituted a live bullet for the blank I put in Thurlow's automatic at Headquarters last night?"

"Opportunity," murmured Ellery. "Dat ol' debil. Yes. In a moment, Dad. But tell me—you've examined the shell?"

"Of course."

"Anything unusual about it?"

"Nope. The cartridge used was ordinary Peters 'rustless.' M.C. type of bullet for a .25 automatic, 2-inch barrel. Ballistics penetration of three inches, figured on the usual seven-eighths pine board. Exactly the ammunition that was in the automatic when you handed it to me at Headquarters."

"Really?"

"Don't get excited," scowled the Inspector. "That ammunition can be bought any place."

"I know, but it's also the ammunition Thurlow used, Dad. Have you checked with Thurlow's supply? He must have got some at Cornwall & Ritchey's when he bought the guns yesterday."

"I told Velie to root around."

And indeed at this moment Sergeant Velie swung out of the house and came rocking across the lawn to the Shoe. "What kind of buggery is this, anyway?" he exploded. "Here's a guy dead, murdered, and most of his folks don't even seem to care. What am I saying? Care? They're not even payin' attention!"

"You'll find them a rather unorthodox family, Sergeant," said Ellery dryly. "Have you checked back on Thurlow's ammunition?"

"I ain't had a chance yet to look at it myself, but Little Napoleon says he bought a lot of ammunition yesterday, and the box of .25 automatic cartridges has got some missing out of it, he says. A handful. Says *he'd* only took out one last night—the one he put into the Colt automatic. Can't understand what all the fuss is about, he says. 'It was a duel, wasn't it?' he grouses to me. 'All right, so my brother got laid out,' he says. 'So what's the cops here for?' he says. 'It's all legal and aboveboard!'" And the Sergeant shook his head and stamped back to the mansion.

"The big point is, Thurlow's already checked back on his ammunition supply," murmured Ellery. "Then he doesn't know about the blanks, does he, Dad?"

"Not yet."

"Worried. All legal and aboveboard, but—worrisome, too, Dad. I think you'd better locate Mr. Thurlow's armory and appropriate it with dispatch. The stuff's a menace."

"It's a cinch he's cached it somewhere cute, like the squirrel he is," growled the Inspector, "and nobody but he knows where. The boys are keeping an eye on Mr. Thurlow, so it'll hold for a few minutes. What about this opportunity business, Ellery? Let's go over the ground to make sure. Just what did you do last night after you left Headquarters with the Colt and S. & W.?"

"I returned to the house here immediately, slipped back into Thurlow's bedroom, replaced the blank-loaded Colt automatic on the highboy exactly where I'd found it earlier in the evening, then I went to the twins' room and gave Bob Potts the blank-loaded Smith & Wesson."

"Anybody spot you entering or leaving Thurlow's room?"

"I can't swear, but I'm convinced no one did."

"The twins knew about it, though, didn't they?"

"Naturally."

"Who else?"

"Charley Paxton and Sheila Potts. All the others had left by the time we discussed the plan to substitute blanks for the live cartridges in the two guns."

"All right," grunted his father, "you left the Colt right where you found it, in Thurlow's bedroom, you gave Robert his doctored revolver, and then what?"

"I left the twins in their room and went downstairs to the library. Charley and Sheila still had Thurlow cornered down there, as I had instructed. Thurlow was in a gay mood—Sheila'd fed him some drinks in an effort to restore his sanity. He insisted on our all going out on a tear, which we did, just as we were— the four of us. We left the house in a group, from the library, cabbed downtown, and spent the entire night at Club Bongo, on East 55th Street. We didn't get back to the Palace—"

"The what?"

"Forgive me. I'm only using the family's own terminology. We got back here about a quarter of six this morning."

"Was Thurlow, Paxton, or Sheila in a position to get to that Colt automatic in Thurlow's room at any time during the night, after you left it there?"

"That's what makes this part of it so beautiful," declared Ellery. "No, those three were with me, within sight and touch, from the moment I stepped into the library until we got out of the cab at dawn this morning."

"How about when you got back? What happened?"

"I left Thurlow, Charley, and Sheila on the lawn, right over there, as you saw. Thurlow'd sent me into the house to fetch his gun. I went up and—" He stopped.

"What's the matter?" asked his father quickly.

"I just remembered," muttered Ellery. "It seemed to me as I went up that spiral staircase to the landing that I...not exactly *heard*, but *felt* someone or something moving in the hall outside the bedrooms."

"Yes?" said the Inspector sharply. "What? Who?"

"I don't know. I even had the feeling it came from around the area of Thurlow's door. But that may have been an excited imagination. I was *thinking* of Thurlow's apartment."

"Well, was it or wasn't it, son? For the love of Peter's pants!

Did somebody come out of Thurlow's rooms around six A.M.?"

"I can't say yes, and I can't say no."

"Very helpful," groaned the Inspector. "You got the gun and came right back down here to the lawn? No stops?"

"Exactly. And handed the gun to Thurlow. He dropped it in the right-hand outside pocket of his tweed jacket the moment I handed it to him." The Inspector nodded; he had observed the same action. "He didn't touch it again until he was ordered to during the duel. I had my eyes on him every second. Nor did anyone approach near enough to him to have done any funny work."

"Right. I was watching him, too. Then the only possible time the blank could have been removed and the live cartridge substituted in the Colt was during the night—between the time you left it on Thurlow's highboy last night and the time he sent you up there at six this morning to get it for the duel. But where does that take us? Nowhere!" The Inspector waved his spindly arms. "Anybody in this rummy's nightmare could have sneaked into Thurlow's room during those ten hours or so and made the switch of bullets!"

"Not anybody," said Ellery.

"What? What's that?"

"Not anybody. Anybody," said Ellery patiently, "minus three."

"Talk so that my simple mind can understand, Mr. Queen," said the Inspector testily.

"Well, Thurlow couldn't have sneaked into his bedroom during those hours," murmured Mr. Queen. "Nor Charley Paxton. Nor Sheila Potts. Couldn't possibly. Those three are eliminated beyond the least shadow of the least doubt."

"Well, of course. I meant one of the others."

"Yes," mused Ellery, "here's a case in which we can actually delimit and define the suspects. The rest of the Potts menagerie were in the house during the period of opportunity, and so any one of them could have made the switch from blank to lethal bullet. Aside from the servants, there are: the Old Woman herself, her husband Steve, that old parasite Major Gotch, Louella the 'scientist,' Mac the twin, and Horatio."

"That's the son you told me sleeps in some kind of—what did you call it, Ellery?"

"Fairy-tale cottage. Yes," replied the great man crossly. "Yes, the Philosopher of Escapism could have done it, too, even though he sleeps in his dream cottage. Horatio could have slipped into the main house through the inner court, patio, and French doors, and slipped out again via the same route, without necessarily being seen."

"Six likely suspects," mumbled the Inspector. "Not so bad. Let's see how they stand on motive. As far as the old hell-cat's concerned ..."

Ellery yawned. "Not now, Dad. I'm not Superman—I need sleep occasionally, and last night was heigh-de-ho. Ditto Sheila and Charley. Let us all sleep it off."

"Well, you ring me here from home when you wake up."

"When I wake up," announced his son, "I shall be practically at my father's elbow."

"Now what's *that* mean?"

"I'm requisitioning a bed in the Potts Palladium. And if you don't think," added the Inspector's pride and joy, "that I'll investigate it microscopically before I climb in to make sure it isn't the bed of Procrustes ..."

"Who's that?"

"A Greek robber who occasionally whittled his victims down to size," said Ellery with another yawn.

"You won't need his bed to do that," said the Inspector grimly. "I have a hunch this case'll do it for you, my son."

"Making any bets?" Ellery drifted off toward the house.

9

The Narrow Escape of Sergeant Velie

Ellery fell asleep like a cat and awoke like a man. As his senses unfolded he became conscious of unnatural quiet and unnatural noise. The house, which should have been filled with the sounds of people, was not; the front lawn, which had been empty, was filled with the sounds of people.

He leaped from his borrowed bed and ran to one of the windows overlooking the front lawn. The sun was high now, in a hot blue sky, and it glared down upon a swarm of men. They surrounded the Shoe, near the base of which the Inspector stood at bay. There was a great deal of shouting.

Ellery threw on his clothes and raced downstairs. "Dad! What's the trouble?" he cried, on the run.

But the Inspector was too busy to reply.

Then Ellery saw that this was not a mob, but a group of reporters and newspaper photographers engaged—if a trifle zealously—in the underpaid exercise of their duty.

"Ah, here's the Master Mind!"

"Maybe *he's* got a tongue."

72

"What's the lowdown, Hawkshaw?"

"Your old man's all of a sudden got a stiff upper lip."

"Say, there's nothing lenient about the lower one, either!"

"Loosen up, you guys. What are you holding so tight?"

"What gives here at six A.M.?"

Ellery shook his head good-humoredly, pushing his way through the crowd.

The Inspector seized him. "Ellery, tell these doubting Thomases the truth, will you? They won't believe *me*. Tell 'em the truth so I can be rid of 'em and get back to work—God help me!"

"Gentlemen, it's a fact," said Ellery Queen. The murmurs ceased.

"It's a fact," a reporter said at last, in a hushed voice.

"A real, live, fourteen-carat *duel*?"

"Right here, under the oxford?"

"Pistols at twenty paces and that kind of stuff?"

"Hey, if they wore velvet pants I'll go out of my mind!"

"Nah, Thurlow had on that lousy old tweed suit of his—"

"And poor Bob Potts wore a beige gabardine—wasn't that what Inspector Queen said?"

"Nuts. I'd rather it was velvet pants."

"But, my God—"

"Listen, Jack, not even the readers of *your* rag'll believe this popeyed peep show!"

"What do I give a damn whether they believe it or not? I'm paid to report what happened."

"Me, I'm talking this over with the boss."

"Hold it, men—here comes the Old Woman."

She appeared from the front door and marched towards the marble steps, flanked on one side by Dr. Innis and on the other by Sergeant Thomas Velie. Each escort, in his own fashion, was pleading with her.

The reporters and cameramen deserted the Queens shamelessly. In a twinkling they had raced across the lawn and set up shop at the foot of the steps.

"Bloomin' heroes," said Ellery. He was squinting at the Old Woman, disturbed.

There was no sign of grief on that face; only rage. The jet snake's eyes had not wept; they had kept the shape and color of their reptilian nature. "Get off my property!" she screamed.

Cameras were raised high; men fired questions at her.

If these intrepid explorers of the news had the wit, thought Ellery, they would shrink and flee before an old woman who accepted her young son's bloody murder without emotion and grew hysterical over a transitory trespass on the scene of his death. Such a woman was capable of anything.

"It's the first peep out of her today," remarked the Inspector. "We'd better get on over there. She may blow her top any minute."

The Queens hurried toward the house. But before they could reach the steps, Cornelia Potts blew, and blew in an unexpected manner.

One moment she was standing there like an angry pouter pigeon, glaring down at her tormentors; the next her claws had flashed into a recess in the overlapping folds of her taffeta skirt and emerged with a revolver. It was absurd, but there it was: an old lady, seventy years old, pointing a revolver at a group of men.

Somebody said: "Hey," indignantly; then they grew very quiet.

It was a long-barreled revolver alive with blue fires in the sun. All eyes were on it.

Dr. Innis took a quick backward step. On the Old Woman's other side, Sergeant Velie looked dazed. Ellery had seen the Sergeant disarm five thugs all by himself, without excitement laying them out in a neat and silent row; but the spectacle and the problem of a septuagenarian who resembled Queen Victoria brandishing a heavy revolver evidently frustrated him.

"One of Thurlow's mess of guns," the Inspector said bitterly, eyes intent on the talon that was crooked about the trigger. "So she knew where Thurlow'd hid 'em after all. I swear, anyone who mixes with these crazy drooglers gets addled—even me."

"Someone ought to stop her," said Ellery nervously.

"Care to volunteer your services?" And since there was no answer, his father lit a stogie and began to puff on it without relish. "Mrs. Potts," he called, "put that naughty thing down and—"

"Stand where you are!" said the Old Woman grimly to the Inspector; at which he looked surprised, for he had exhibited no least intention of moving from the spot. She turned back to the fascinated group below her. "I told you men to get off my property." She waved the revolver shakily.

One witless enthusiast raised his camera for a furtive shot of Cornelia Potts Draws Bead on Press. There was a shot, but it came towards the camera, not from it. It was a bad shot, merely nicking one edge of the lens and ricocheting off to bury itself in the grass; but it had the magical property of causing a group of grown men to disappear from the foot of the steps and reintegrate behind the solid bronze of the Shoe some yards away.

"She's loco," said the Sergeant hoarsely to Dr. Innis.

"Get out!" shrieked Cornelia Potts to the men cowering behind the Shoe. "This is my family's business and I won't have it all over the dirty newspapers. Out!"

"Piggott, Hesse," said the Inspector wearily. "Where in time are you men? Escort the boys from the grounds."

Several heads peered from behind several trees, and it was seen that they were the heads of several large persons—what was more shameful, of detectives attached to Inspector Queen's staff.

"Well, go on," said the Inspector. "All she can do is kill you. That's what you're paid for, isn't it? Get these brave men out of here!"

The detectives emerged, blushing. Whereupon Mr. Queen enjoyed the spectacle of numerous male figures scampering helter-skelter toward the front gates, their flank covered, as it were, by plain-clothes men who were running as energetically as they.

Within seconds only the three at the top of the steps and the two a short way off on the grass were left to watch the fires burn blue on the barrel of the faintly smoking revolver.

"That's the way it is," said the Old Woman with satisfaction. "Now what are *you* men waiting for?" The barrel waggled again.

"Madam," said the Inspector, taking a step.

"Stop, Inspector Queen."

Inspector Queen stopped.

"I'll say this now, and not again. I don't *want* you. I don't *want* an investigation. I don't *want* police. I don't want *any* outside interference. I'll handle my son's death in my own way, and if you don't think I mean it—"

Ellery said respectfully: "Mrs. Potts."

She gave him a sharp glance. "*You've* been hanging around to no good, young man. What d'ye want?"

"Do you quite realize your position?"

"My position is what I make it!"

"I'm afraid not," said Ellery sadly. "Your position is what your impulsive son Thurlow has made it. Or rather whoever was using Thurlow as a witless fool to commit a revolting crime. You can't get out of your position, Mrs. Potts, with revolvers, or threats, or loud tones of voice. Your position, Mrs. Potts, if you'll reflect for a moment, dictates that you hand that revolver to Sergeant Velie, go into your house, and leave the rest to those whose business it is to catch murderers."

Sergeant Velie, thus obliquely brought into the conversation, gave a nervous start and cleared his throat.

"Don't move," said Cornelia Potts sharply; and the Sergeant gave a feeble laugh and said: "Who, me, Mrs. Potts? I was just shiftin' to the other foot."

She backed up, grasping the revolver more firmly. "Did you hear what I said? Get out, Innis—you too!"

"Now, Mrs. Potts," began the physician, pallidly. "Mr. Queen is quite right, you know. Besides, all this excitement is bad for your heart, very bad. I shan't be responsible—"

"Oh, fiddlesticks," she snapped. "My heart's my own. I'm sick of you, Dr. Waggoner Innis, and what I've been thinking of to let you mess around me I can't imagine." Dr. Innis drew himself up. "For the last time, you men—are you going to leave, or do I have to shoot one of you to convince you I mean what I say?"

Inspector Queen said: "Velie, take that gun away from her."

"Dad—" began Ellery.

"Yes, sir," said Sergeant Velie.

Several things happened at once. Dr. Innis stepped aside with extraordinary agility to get out of the way of Sergeant Velie, who was advancing cautiously towards the old lady; and of the old lady, who had twisted about to train her revolver on the advancing Sergeant. At the same moment Ellery darted from his station on the grass and hurled himself at the steps. Simultaneously the front door opened and eyes clustered, staring, while on the grass Inspector Queen took two kangaroo steps to the left, pulling from his pocket as he did so his large and ponderous fountain pen, and let fly.

Ellery, pen, and Cornelia Potts met at the identical instant that the revolver cracked. The fountain pen struck her hand, joggling it; Ellery struck her legs, upsetting them; and the bullet struck Sergeant Velie's hat, causing it to dart from his head like a bird.

The revolver clanked to the porch.

Sergeant Velie pounced on it, mumbling incredulously: "She took a shot at me. She took a shot at me! Blame near got me in the head. In the head!" He gaped at Cornelia Potts as he rose, clutching the gun.

Ellery got up and brushed himself off. "Forgive me," he said to the furious old lady, who was struggling between Inspector Queen and Dr. Innis.

"I'll have the law on you!" she screamed.

"Let me get you inside, Mrs. Potts," murmured Dr. Innis, twisting her arm. "Quiet you down—your heart—"

"The law on you ..."

Inspector Queen smote his forehead. "*She'll* have the law on *us!*" he roared. "Flint, Piggott, Johnson! Get this maniac into her house—come out of hiding there, you yellow-bellied traitors! She'll have the law on us, will she? *Velie!*"

"Huh?" Sergeant Velie was now staring at his hat, which stared back at him with its new eye.

"Those fourteen shooting irons Thurlow bought," the old gentleman snarled. "We've got three of 'em now—the two he used in the duel this morning, and this one his mother swiped. Round up those other eleven, understand me, or don't come back to Center Street. Every last one of 'em!"

"Yes, sir," mumbled Sergeant Velie. He shambled into the house after Dr. Innis and the fighting Old Woman, still shaking his head as one who will never understand.

10

The Mark of Cain

The wake is quite all for the living, and no man eats more heartily than the butcher.

Ellery suddenly found himself craving sustenance. He was rested by his nap, Robert Potts lay irrevocably downtown on Dr. Prouty's autopsy table, and Mr. Queen was hungry, hungry. He beat a path to the dining room, one eye out for a servant; but the first living soul he met was Detective Flint, hurrying through the foyer toward the front door.

"Where's the Inspector, Mr. Queen?"

"Outside. What's wrong now, Flint?"

"Wrong!" Detective Flint mopped his face. "Inspector says 'Flint, keep an eye on this Horatio Potts,' he says. 'The one that lives in that pink popcorn shack in the court,' he says. 'I don't cotton to that billygoat,' he says, 'and a guy who'll play marbles at his age'd slip a live cartridge into his brother's rod just out of clean, boyish fun,' he says. 'Probably like to hear 'em pop good and loud,' he says—"

"Spare me," said Mr. Queen. "I'm a starving man. What's the matter?"

"So I watch Horatio," said Detective Flint. "I watch and I watch till my eyes are fallin' out of my head, and what do I see?" Flint paused to mop his face again.

"Well, well?"

"His brother's layin' downstairs dead, see? Young guy, everything to live for—dead. Murder. House full of cops. Hot hell let loose. Does Horatio get scared?" demanded Detective Flint. "Does he go around bitin' his nails? Does he dive into bed and pull the covers over his yap? Does he cry? Does he make with the hysterics? Does he yell he's gonna get revenge on whoever the bloody murderin' killer was who—"

Ellery moved off.

"Wait!" Flint hurried after him. "I'm gettin' to it, Mr. Queen."

"And so is starvation to me," said Mr. Queen gently.

"But you don't get it. What does Big Brother Horatio—cripes, what a name!—do? He sits himself down at his desk in that Valentine's box he built himself back there in the garden and he says to me—friendly, see? 'Sir,' he says 'sir, this gives me a honey of an idea for a new kiddy book,' he says. 'There is somethin' uny—uny—'"

"Versal," said Ellery, perking up.

"That's it—'unyversal in the manly code of punk-something or other—' I didn't get the word, but it sounded like Spick talk— 'and anyway,' he says, 'it's always a good theme for a child's work,' he says, 'so I'm gonna sit me down with your permission, sir, of course,' he says, 'and I'm gonna make some notes on a swashbucklin' Stevensonian romance for boys of the early teen age,' he says, 'based on two brothers who fight a dool to the death,' he says, and I'm a shyster lawyer if that big slob don't pick up one of them chicken feathers he writes with and start in writin' away like his life depends on it. Then he stops writin' and looks at me. 'Seventeenth century, of course,' he says. And he writes again. And again he stops and looks at me. 'You'll find apples and preserved ginger and cookies in the cupboard, Mr.

Flint,' he says to me." Detective Flint looked around cunningly. "Do you s'pose the wack did it to get material for a book?" he whispered. "That's what I gotta tell Inspector Queen. It's a theory, Mr. Queen, you can't break down!"

"You'll find the oldest living iconoclast out front," sighed Mr. Queen; and he hastened on.

Sheila and Charley Paxton were seated in the dining room pecking at a salad luncheon.

"No, don't go," said Sheila quickly.

"I wasn't intending to." Ellery came in. "Not with food so near."

"Oh, dear. Cuttins!" The long-shanked butler materialized, trembling. "Cuttins," said Sheila in a deadly voice, "can't decide whether to quit our service or stay, Mr. Queen. Suppose you tell him what the situation is."

"The situation," said Mr. Queen, impaling Cuttins on his glance, "is that this house and everyone in it are under surveillance of the police, Cuttins, and since you can't very well skip out without a police alarm being broadcast in your honor, you'd be well advised to get me something to eat instantly."

"Very good, sir," muttered Cuttins; and he oozed rapidly out.

"I'm still punchy," said Sheila vaguely. "I can't seem to get it through my thick head that Bob's dead. *Dead*. Not of pneumonia. Not hit by an automobile. Killed by a bullet from Thurlow's gun in a *duel*. Such a s-silly way to die!" Sheila bent suddenly over her plate. She did not look at Charley Paxton, who sat stricken.

"Something's happened between you two," said Ellery keenly, glancing from one to the other.

"Sheila's called off our engagement," murmured Charley.

"Well," said Ellery cheerfully, "don't treat it like some major convulsion of nature, Charley. A girl has a right to change her mind. And you're not the handsomest specimen roving the New York jungle."

"It isn't that," said Sheila quickly. "I still—" She bit her lip.

"It isn't?" Ellery stole a slice of bread from Charley's bread-and-butter plate. "Then what is it, Sheila?"

Sheila did not answer.

"This is no time to split up," cried Charley. "I'll never understand women! Here's a girl up to her neck in trouble. You'd think she'd want my arms around her. Instead, she pushed me away just now! Won't let me kiss her, won't let me share her unhappiness—"

"Every fact has a number of alternative explanations," murmured Mr. Queen. "Maybe you had garlic for lunch yesterday, Charley."

Sheila smiled despite herself. Then she said in despair: "There's nothing else for me to do, I tell you."

"Just because poor Bob was murdered," Charley said bitterly. "I suppose if my father had died on the gallows rather than home in bed, you'd run out on *me*, wouldn't you?"

"Cough up, sweetheart," said Mr. Queen gently.

"All right, I will!" Sheila's dimples dug hard. "Charley, I've always told you that the main reason I was holding off our marriage was because Mother would cut me off without a cent if we went through with it, and that that wouldn't be fair to you. Well, I wasn't being honest. As if I cared two cents whether Mother left me anything or not! I'd be happy with you if I had to live in a one-room shack."

"It isn't that?" The young lawyer was bewildered. "But then what possible reason, darling—?"

"Charley, *look* at us. Thurlow. Louella. Horatio—"

"Wait a minute—"

"You can't get away from the horrid truth just by ignoring it. They're insane, every one of them." Sheila's voice soared. "How do I know I haven't got the same streak in me? How do I *know?*"

"But Sheila dearest, they're not your full brothers and sisters—they're half-brothers, Louella's a half-sister."

"We have the same mother."

82

"But you know perfectly well that Thurlow, Louella, and Horatio inherited their—whatever they inherited—not from your mother but from their father, whose blood isn't in *you* at all. And there's certainly nothing wrong with Steve—"

"How do I know that?" asked Sheila stridently. "Look at my mother. Is she like other people?"

"There's nothing wrong with the Old Woman but plain, ordinary cussedness. Sheila, you're dramatizing. This childish fear of insanity—"

"I won't marry you or anybody else until I know, Charley," said Sheila fiercely. "And now with a murderer in the family—" She jumped up and fled.

"No, Charley," said Ellery quickly, as with the look of a wounded deer the lawyer started after her. "Abide with me."

"But I can't let her go like this!"

"Yes, you can. Let Sheila alone for a while."

"But it's such nonsense! There's nothing wrong with Sheila. There's never been anything wrong with the Brents—Steve, Sheila, Bob, Mac—"

"You ought to be able to understand Sheila's fears, Charley. She's in a highly nervous state. Even if she weren't a naturally high-strung girl, living here would have made her a neurotic."

"Well, then, solve this damned case so I can take Sheila out of this asylum and pound some sense into her!"

"I'll do my best, Charley." Ellery looked thoughtfully over his chicken salad, which, now that the first pangs of his hunger had been assuaged, he realized with annoyance he had always detested.

When Inspector Queen and Sergeant Velie bustled into the dining room, Ellery was low in his chair, smoking like a sooty flue, and Charlie was tormenting his nails.

"Shhh," whispered Charley. "He's thinking."

"He is, is he?" snapped the Inspector. "Then let him think about this. Velie—set 'em down."

There was a crash. Ellery looked up with a start. Sergeant

Velie had dumped an armful of revolvers and automatics on the dining-room table.

"Well, well. Thurlow's arsenal, eh?"

"Me, I found it," pouted Velie. "Don't I ever get credit for nothin'?"

"A regular Pagliacci," snarled Inspector Queen. "The fact is, son, here's the kit and caboodle of 'em, and there's two missing."

"Not fourteen?" Ellery looked distressed. In some things he had the soul of a bookkeeper; a mislaid fact irked him—two drove him mad.

"Count them yourself."

Ellery did so. There were twelve. Among them he found Thurlow's .25 Colt automatic, Robert's stubby S. & W. .38/32, and the long-barreled revolver with which Cornelia Potts had almost assassinated Sergeant Velie—a Harrington & Richardson .22-caliber "Trapper Model."

"What's Thurlow got to say?" demanded Charley.

"Can you make sense out of a pecan?" asked the Sergeant. "Thurlow says he had fourteen, and that's what the sportin'-goods store says he bought. Also, Thurlow says nobody but himself knew where he hid the guns. So I says: 'Then how come two are missin'? What did they do—pick themselves up and take a walk?' So he looks at me like *I'm* nuts!"

"Where did he have them cached, Sergeant?" asked Ellery.

"In a false closet in his bedroom along with some boxes of ammunition he'd bought."

"Oh, there," said Charley Paxton disgustedly. "Then of course everybody knew. Thurlow's been 'hiding' things in that false closet since the house was built. In fact, he had the closet installed. The whole household knows about it."

"It's a cinch the Old Woman got his Harrington & Richardson there," said Inspector Queen, sitting down and dipping into the salad bowl for a shred of chicken. "So why not Louella, or Horatio, or anybody else? Fact is, two guns are missing, and I won't sleep till they're found. Guns loose in *this* hatchery!"

Ellery studied the armory on the table. Then he produced pad and pencil and began to write.

"Inventory," he announced at last. "Here's what we now have." His memorandum listed the twelve weapons:—

1. Colt Pocket Model automatic
    Caliber: .25 } *murder weapon*
2. Smith & Wesson .38/.32 revolver
    Caliber: .38 } *Robert's weapon*
3. Harrington & Richardson Trapper
    Caliber: .22 } *Cornelia's weapon*
4. Iver Johnson safety hammerless automatic
    Caliber: .32 Special
5. Schmeisser safety Pocket Model automatic
    Caliber: .25 Automatic
6. Stevens "Off-Hand" single-shot Target
    Caliber: .22 Long Rifle
7. I. J. Champion Target single action
    Caliber: .22
8. Stoeger Luger (Refinished)
    Caliber: 7.65 mm.
9. New Model Mauser (10-shot Magazine)
    Caliber: 7.63 mm.
10. High Standard hammerless automatic Short
    Caliber: .22
11. Browning 1912
    Caliber: 9 mm.
12. Ortgies
    Caliber: 6.35 mm.

"So what?" demanded the Inspector.

"So very little," retorted his son, "except that each one of the gun is of different manufacture. Ought to make the check-back easier. Sergeant, phone Cornwall & Ritchey and get an exact list of the fourteen guns Thurlow purchased."

"Piggott's on that angle."

"Good. Make sure you locate those two missing toys of Thurlow's."

"And while we're playing detective, " put in the Inspector dryly, "we might start thinking about who had a motive to want Bob Potts six feet south. We already know who had your blasted whatchamacallit—opportunity."

"I can't imagine who'd want Bob out of the way," muttered Charley. "Except Thurlow, because Robert was always picking on him. But we know Thurlow couldn't have done it."

"Cockeyedest case I ever saw, " grumbled the Sergeant. "Guy who fires the shot *can't* be the killer. Say, this chicken salad ain't bad."

"Point is," frowned Inspector Queen, "somebody wanted Robert Potts dead, so somebody had a reason. Maybe if we find the reason we'll find the somebody, too. Any ideas, Ellery?"

Ellery shrugged. "Charley, you're attorney to the family. What are the terms of Cornelia Potts's will?"

Charley looked nervous. "Now wait a minute, Ellery. The Old Woman's very much alive, and the terms of a living testator's will are confidential between attorney and client—"

"Oh, that mullarkey," said the Inspector disgustedly.

"Come on, Ellery, we've got to talk to the old gal direct."

"Better take along a bullet-proof vest!" Sergeant Velie shouted after them through the mouthful of chicken salad.

11

"Infer the Motive from the Deed"

"But only for a few minutes, Inspector Queen." Dr. Waggoner Innis was pinch-pale, but he had recovered his stance, as it were; and here, in Cornelia Potts's sitting room, he was very much the tall and splendid Physician-in-Ordinary.

"How is she?" inquired Ellery Queen.

"Nerves more settled, but heart's fluttering badly and pulse could be improved. You've got to co-operate with me, gentle-men—"

"One side, Doctor," said the Inspector; and they entered the Old Woman's bedchamber.

It was a square Victorian room crowded with those gilded phantasms of love which in a more elegant day passed by the name of "art." Everything swirled precisely in a cold paralysis of "form," and everything was expensive and hideous. There were antimacassars on the overstuffed petit-point chairs, and no faintest clue to the fact that a man shared this room with its aged mistress.

The bed was a piece for future archeologists. Its corners were curved, the foot forming a narrower oval than the head. There was no footboard, and the headboard was a single curved piece which extended, unbroken, although in diminishing height, along the sides. Ellery wondered what was wrong with the whole production aside from its more obvious grotesquerie. And then he saw. There were no front legs; the foot of the bed rested on the floor. And since the head stood high, supported on a single thick, tapering block of wood, the sides showed a downward slant, while the spring and mattress had been artfully manufactured to maintain a level. It was all so unbelievable that for a moment Ellery had no eyes for its occupant, but only for her couch.

Suddenly he recognized it for what it was. The bed was formed like a woman's oxford shoe.

The Old Woman lay in it, a lace cap set on her white hair, the silk comforter resting on her plump little stomach. She was propped up on several fat pink pillows; a portable typewriter lay on her thighs; her claws were slowly seeking out keys and upon discovery striking them impatiently. She paid no attention to the four men. Her black eyes were intent on the paper in her machine.

"I told you, Mrs. Potts—" began Dr. Innis peevishly, raising his careful eyes ceilingward—and hastily lowering them, since they had encountered there the painful spectacle of two plaster cupids embracing.

"Shut up, Innis."

They waited for her to complete her inexplicable labors.

She did so with a final peck, ripping the sheet of white paper from the typewriter; quickly she glanced over it, made a snapping movement of her jaws, like an old bitch after flies, then reached for a thick soft-leaded pencil on the bed. She scribbled her signature, picked up a number of similar typewritten white sheets near the portable, signed those; and only then looked up. "What are you men doing in my bedroom?"

"There are certain questions, Mrs. Potts—" began Inspector Queen.

"All right. I suppose I can't be rid of you any other way. But you'll have to wait. Charles!"

"Yes, Mrs. Potts."

"These memos I've just typed. Attend to them at once."

Charley took the sheaf of signed papers she thrust into his hands and glanced through them dutifully. At the last one his eyes widened. "You want me to *sell* your Potts Shoe Company stock—*all* of it?"

"Isn't that what my memorandum says?" snapped the Old Woman. "Isn't it?"

"Yes, Mrs. Potts, but—"

"Since when must I account to you, Charles? You're paid to follow orders. Follow 'em."

"But I don't get it, Mrs. Potts," protested Charley. "You'll lose control!"

"Will I." Her lip curled. "My son Robert was active head of the company. His murder and the scandal, which I tried so hard just now to avoid—" her voice hardened—"will send Potts stock down. If I can't avoid the scandal, at least I can make use of it. Selling my stock will send the price down still further. It opened at 84 this morning. When it hits 72, buy it all back." Charley looked dazed. "Why are you standing here?" shrilled the old lady. "Did you hear what I said? Go and phone my brokers!"

Charley nodded, curtly. As he passed Ellery he muttered: "What price Mama, Mr. Q? Takes advantage of her son's murder to make a few million boleros!" And the young lawyer stamped out.

Dr. Innis bent over the Old Woman with his stethoscope, shook his head, took her pulse, shook his head, removed her typewriter, shook his head, and finally retired to the window to look out over the front lawn, still shaking his head.

"Ready for me now, Madam?" asked the Inspector courteously.

"Yes. Don't dawdle."

"Don't—!" The inspector's hard eyes glittered. "My dear Mrs. Potts," he exclaimed softly, "do you know that I could have you put in jail this minute on a charge of attempting homicide on an officer of the law?"

"Oh, yes," nodded the Old Woman. "But you haven't."

"I haven't! Mrs. Potts, I warn you—"

"Fiddlesticks," she snarled. "I'm much more use to you in my own house. Don't think you're doing me favors, Inspector Queen. I know your kind. You're all nosey, meddling, publicity-seeking grafters. You're in this case for what you can get out of it."

"*Mrs. Potts!*"

"Stuff. How much d'ye want to pronounce my son's death an accident?"

Mr. Queen coughed behind his hand, watching his father with enjoyment.

But the Inspector only smiled. "You'd play a swell game of poker, Mrs. Potts. You say and do a lot of contradictory things, all to cover up the one thing you're afraid of—that I'll call your bluff. Let's understand each other. I'm going to do my best to find out who murdered your son Robert. I know that's what you want, too, only you're full of cussedness, and you want to do it your own way. But I hold all the cards, and you know that, too. Now you can cooperate or not, as you see fit. But you won't stop me from finding out what I want to know."

The Old Woman glared at him. He glared back. Finally, she wriggled down under her silk comforter like a young girl, sullenly. "Talk or get out. What d'ye want to know?"

"What," said the Inspector instantly, with no trace of triumph, "are the terms of your will?"

Ellery caught the flash from her shoe-buttony eyes, the snick of her jaws. "Oh, that. I don't mind telling you that, if you promise not to give it to the papers."

"That's a promise."

"You, young man? You're his son, aren't you?"

Ellery glanced at her. She glanced away to Dr. Innis. The physician's back was like a wall.

"My will sets forth three provisions," she stated in a flat, cold tone. "First: On my death, my estate is to be divided among my surviving children, share and share alike."

"Yes?" prompted Inspector Queen.

"Second: My husband, Stephen Potts, gets no share at all, neither principal nor income. Cut off. Without a penny." Her jaws snicked again. "I've supported him and Gotch for thirty-three years. That's plenty."

"Go on, Mrs. Potts."

"Third: I am President of the Board of Directors of the Potts Shoe Company. On my death, a new President will have to be elected by the Board. That Board will consist of all my surviving children, and I specifically demand that Simon Underhill, manager of the factories, have one vote, too. I don't know whether this last will hold up in law," she added with the oddest trace of humor, "but I don't imagine anyone involved will take it that far. My word's been law in life, and I guess it'll be law in death. That's all, gentlemen. Get out."

"Extraordinary woman," murmured Ellery as they left Cornelia Potts's apartment.

"This isn't a case for a cop," sighed his father. "It needs the world's ace psychiatrist."

Charley Paxton came running upstairs from the foyer, and the three men paused in the upper hall. "Is Innis with her?" panted Charley.

"Yes. Does he get much of a fee, Charley?" the Inspector asked curiously.

"An annual retainer. A whopper. And he earns it."

The Inspector grunted. "She told us about her will."

"Dad went to work on her," chuckled Ellery. "By the way, Charley, where does she keep that will?"

"With her other important papers in her bedroom."

"Was that typewriting exhibition a few minutes ago something new, Charley?"

"Hell, no. We once had a difference of opinion about one of her innumerable verbal 'instructions.' She claimed she'd told me one thing, and I darned well knew she'd told me another. We had quite a row over it, and I insisted that from then on I wanted written, signed instructions. Only time she and I've agreed on anything. Since then she types out her memos on that portable, and always signs them with one of those soft pencils."

The Inspector brushed this aside. "She told us she'd cut her husband, this Stephen Brent Potts, off without a cent. Is that legal, Charley? I always thought a husband in this state came in for one third of a wife's estate, with two thirds going to the surviving children."

"That's true nowadays," nodded the attorney. "But it's been true only since August 31, 1930. Before that date, a husband could legally be cut out of any share in his wife's estate. And the Old Woman's will antedates August 31, 1930, so it's quite legal."

"Why," asked Ellery pointedly, "is Sheila's father being cut off?"

Charley Paxton sighed. "You don't understand that old she-devil, Ellery. Even though Cornelia Potts married Steve Brent, he never was and never will be a genuine Potts to her except in name."

"A convenience, huh?" asked the Inspector dryly.

"Just about. The children are part of *her,* so they're Pottses. But not Steve. You think Thurlow's got an exaggerated respect for the Potts name? Where do you suppose he got it from? The Old Woman. She's drummed it into him."

"How much is the old witch worth?"

Charley grimaced. "It's hard to say, Inspector. But on a rough guess, after inheritance taxes and so on are deducted, I'd say she'll leave a net estate of around thirty million dollars."

Mr. Queen gurgled.

"But that means," gasped the Inspector, "that when Bob Potts was alive, the Old Woman's six kids would have inherited five million *apiece?*"

"An obscene arithmetic," groaned his son. "Five million dollars left to a woman like Louella!"

"Don't forget Horatio," said Charley. "And for that matter, Thurlow. Thurlow can buy a mess of guns for five million dollars."

"And with Robert out of the way," mused the Inspector, "there's only five to split the loot, so that makes it about *six* million apiece. Robert's murder was worth a million bucks cold to each of the Potts heirs!" He rubbed his hands. "Let's see what we've got. Our active suspects are Cornelia, hubby Steve, Major Gotch, Louella, Horatio, and Mac ..."

Ellery nodded. "The only ones who had opportunity to switch bullets."

"All right, Cornelia first." The Inspector grinned. "Lord knows I never thought I'd be serious about thinking a mother'd kill her own son, but anything's possible in this family."

Charley shook his head. "It's true she hated Robert—she's always hated the three children of her marriage to Steve—but murder ..."

"I'm not impressed, either," said Ellery with a frown.

"Unless she's loco in the coco," said the Inspector.

"I think she's sane, Dad. Eccentric, but sane."

"Well, theoretically she's got a hate motive. Now how does Stephen, the husband, stack up?"

"I can't see that Steve would have any motive at all," protested Charley. "Since he's cut out of the will—"

"By the way," interrupted Ellery, "does the whole family know the terms of Cornelia's will?"

Charley nodded. "She's made no bones about it. I'm sure they do. Anyway, with Steve not getting a cent, he'd have nothing to gain financially by cutting down the number of heirs. So I can't see a motive for him."

"Let's not overlook the fact, too," Ellery pointed out, "that Stephen Brent Potts is a perfectly sane man, and perfectly sane men don't murder their sons in cold blood."

"Steve loved Bob, I think, even more than he loves Mac and Sheila. I can't see Steve for a moment."

"How about the old panhandler, Gotch?" demanded the Inspector.

"Nothing to gain financially by Bob's death."

"Unless," said Ellery thoughtfully, "he's in the pay of one of the others."

The Inspector looked startled. "You're kidding."

Ellery smiled. "By the way, I've had a fantastic notion about Gotch. It gives the man a possible motive."

"What's that?" asked both men quickly.

"I'd rather not be explicit now. I've got quite accustomed myself to the timbre of this case—the operatic timbre. I can only conjecture absurdly without intellectual conviction. But Dad, I'd like to see a report on Gotch's background."

"I'll send a couple of cables…Now Louella." The Inspector stroked his chin. "Didn't you say you heard her rant about the money she needs for her laboratory 'experiments,' and how Mama turned her down?"

"Seems to me an excellent motive for killing her mother," retorted Ellery, "not Bob. But I grant that Louella gains by Bob's death."

"Then there's Horatio, the Boy Who Never Grew Up—"

"Aaa, Horatio has no interest in money," grunted Charley. "And I don't think he's said ten words to Bob in a year. He gains, but I can't see Horatio as the one behind this."

Ellery said nothing.

"And the twin brother, Maclyn?" asked the Inspector.

Charley stared. "Mac? Kill Bob? That's ridiculous."

"He had opportunity," argued the Inspector.

"But what motive, Inspector?"

"Strangely enough," said Ellery slowly, "Mac had a sounder theoretical motive to seek Bob's death than any other."

"How do you figure that out?" said Charley belligerently.

"Don't get sore, Charley," grinned Mr. Queen. "These are speculations only. Both twins were active vice-presidents of the Potts Shoe Company, weren't they?" Charley nodded. "When the Old Woman dies—an event that, according to Dr. Innis, is imminent—who'd be most likely to take full charge of the business? The twins, of course, who seem to have been the only practical businessmen of the family." Ellery shrugged. "I toss it out for what it's worth. The death of his twin brother gives Mac a clear field when his mother yields the reluctant ghost."

"You mean," said Charley incredulously, "Mac might have been jealous enough of Bob to murder him so he could become head of the company?"

"Now that," the Inspector snapped, "is a motive that appeals to me."

Ellery opened his mouth to say something, but at this moment Sergeant Velie came plowing up the stairs, so he refrained.

"I give up," said the Sergeant in disgust. "I and the boys've turned this joint upside down and we can't find those two missing pieces of artillery. We even been in the Old Woman's rooms. She gave us hail Columbia, but we stuck it out. *I* dunno where they are."

"Did you check with Cornwall & Ritchey about what kind of guns those two missing ones were?" asked the Inspector.

Velie looked about cautiously; but the upper hall was deserted. "Get this. The thirteenth rod was a Colt Pocket Model Automatic—*a .25 caliber*—"

"But that's precisely the type of weapon Thurlow used in the duel this morning," Ellery said sharply.

"And the fourteenth was an S. & W. .38/32 with a two-inch barrel—a .38 caliber," Velie nodded.

"Like the one Bob Potts carried!" The Inspector stiffened.

"Yes, sir," said the Sergeant, shaking his head lugubriously, "it's a funny thing, but the two guns missin' are exact duplicates of the two guns used in the duel this mornin'!"

12

The Importance of Being Dead

Mac was a puzzle. For the most part he shut himself up in the room he and Robert had shared since their birth, staring at nothing. He was not dazed; he was not grim; he was simply empty, as if the vital fluid in him had drained off. At such times as he quit his room, he wandered about the house with a restless air, as if he were looking for something. Sheila spent hours with him, talking, holding his cold hand. He would only shake his head; "Go to the old man, Sheila. He needs you. I don't."

"But Mac honey—"

"You don't understand, sis."

"No, I don't! You're fretting yourself into a nervous break-down—"

"I'm not fretting myself into anything." Mac would pat her burnished hair. "Go on to Pop, Sheila. Let me alone."

Once Sheila, herself confused and conflicted, sprang to her feet with the cry: "Don't you realize what's happened? Of all the people, Mac, I thought *you*—your own twin..."

Mac raised his blue eyes. When Sheila glimpsed the fires raging there, she burst into tears and fled.

It was true: her father needed her more than her brother. Steve Potts crept about the house more timidly than ever, stuttering apologies, getting into everyone's way, and through it all with head cocked, as if he were listening for a distant voice. Sheila walked him in the garden, supervised his feeding, read the *National Geographic* to him, dialed radio programs for him, tucked him into bed. He had taken to sleeping in one of the spare rooms on the top floor; without explanation he had refused any longer to share Cornelia Potts's regal bedchamber.

Major Gotch made overtures in a clumsy way. But for once the little man found no comfort in his bulky friend. He would shake his head at sight of the worn checkerboard, squeeze his lips, squeeze and blink and, wiping his nose with an oversized handkerchief, putter off. Major Gotch spent more and more time alone in the downstairs study, raiding the cigar humidor and the liquor cabinet and brooding over the vacant board.

Then Robert Potts's body was released by the Medical Examiner's office, and it was buried in the earth of Manhattan, which is an odd story in itself, and after that neither his brother Maclyn nor his father Stephen listened for anything, since there is no finality more final than interment, not even death itself.

After that they listened for livelier voices—especially Mac.

Dr. Samuel Prouty, the peppery Assistant Medical Examiner, had known a unique intimacy with thousands of dead men. "A stiff is a stiff," he would say as he sat on the abdomen of a corpse to brace himself for a *rigor mortis* tussle, or struck a match on the sole of a mortified foot. Nevertheless, Doc Prouty showed up in a new derby at Robert Potts's funeral.

Inspector Queen was flabbergasted. "What are *you* doing here, Doc?"

"I thought you was only too glad to get rid of 'em," exclaimed Sergeant Velie, who wore a hunted look these days. "How come you're startin' to follow 'em around?"

"It's a funny thing," said Doc Prouty bashfully. "I don't usually go soft on a cadaver. But this boy's sort of taken my fancy. Nice-looking youngster, and didn't fight me one bit—"

Ellery was startled. "Didn't *fight* you, Doc?"

"Well, sure. Any undertaker'll tell you. Some corpses fight right back, and some co-operate. Most of 'em you can't get to do a blame thing you want. But this Potts boy—he co-operated every inch of the way. I suppose you might say I took a shine to him." Dr. Prouty blushed for the first time within memory of the oldest pensioner. "Least I could do was see him decently buried."

Sergeant Velie backed away, muttering.

As an afterthought, Dr. Prouty said that the autopsy had revealed nothing they did not already know about the cause of Robert Potts's death.

The other interesting element was the burial ground itself. There was a statute on the New York books which forbids interment of the dead within the confines of Manhattan. A few old city churchyards, however, predating the statute, may still inter fresh dead under certain tiresome restrictions. Usually these interments are restricted to "first families" who have owned plots from time beyond memory.

St. Praxed's had such a yard—that sunken, cramped little cloister off Riverside Drive, a few blocks north of the Potts mansion, where scattered yellow teeth of old graves still protrude from the gums of the earth, and the rest are crypts invisible. How Cornelia Potts muscled into St. Praxed's must ever remain a mystery. It was said that a branch of her New England family had burial rights there, and that she inherited them. Whatever mumbo jumbo the Old Woman performed, the fact was she had legal papers to prove her rights, and so her son Robert Potts was buried there.

Police reserves attended.

Charles Hunter Paxton was beginning to thin out. Mr. Ellery Queen was in an excellent position to observe the progressive attenuation, for the young man had taken to seeking refuge in the

Queen apartment, which he roamed like the vanishing buffalo.

"If she'd only listen to reason, Ellery."

"Well, she won't, so be a man and have another drink."

"Why not?"

"Isn't your practice suffering these days, Charley?"

"What practice? Thurlow has no suits to be pressed, and I'm not speaking sartorially. My staff is taking care of the routine Potts work. Wrestling with tax and state problems. The hell with them. I want Sheila."

"Have another drink."

"Don't mind if I do."

The two men filled the Queen apartment with smoke, Scotch bouquet, and endless chatter about the Robert Potts murder. It was maddening how few facts led anywhere. Robert was dead. Someone had stolen into his brother Thurlow's unoccupied room during the eve of the duel and had slipped a live cartridge into Thurlow's Colt .25, removing the blank. Probably the cartridge had been filched from one of the ammunition boxes from Thurlow's bedroom cache; even this was uncertain, for laboratory tests had failed to educe an unarguable conclusion. What had happened to the replaced blank cartridge was any man's guess.

"Anything," said Charley. "Down the toilet drain, or flung into the Hudson."

Ellery looked sour. "Has it occurred to you, Charley, to ask how it came about that somebody made a substitution of bullets at all?"

"Huh?"

"Well, as far as the household knew, that Colt automatic in Thurlow's bedroom the night before the duel was *already* loaded with a live cartridge. *We* know it wasn't, because I'd taken the gun downtown secretly and had Dad slip a blank into it in place of the live ammunition. *We* know that; *how did the murderer know it?* Know it he certainly did, for he subsequently stole into that room, removed the blank Dad had slipped into the magazine, and put a live shell in its place. Any ideas?"

"I can't imagine. Unless you and Sheila and the twins and I

99

were overheard by someone when we discussed the plan in the dining room."

"An eavesdropper?" Ellery shrugged. "Let's drive over to the Potts place, Charley—my head's useless today, and Dad may have turned up something. I haven't heard from him all day."

They found Sheila and her father at the Shoe on the front lawn, old Steve slumped against the pedestal in an attitude of dejection, while Sheila talked fiercely to him. When she spied Ellery and Charley Paxton, she stopped talking. Her father hurriedly swiped at his red eyes.

"Well," smiled Mr. Queen. "Out for an airing?"

"H-hello," stuttered Steve Potts. "Anything n-new?"

"I'm afraid not, Mr. Potts."

The old man's eyes flickered for an instant. "Don't c-call me that, please. My name is Brent." His lips tightened. "Never should have let C-Cornelia talk me into changing it."

"Hello," said Sheila stiffly. Charley glared at her with the hunger of advanced malnutrition. "If you'll excuse my father and me now—"

"Certainly," said Ellery. "By the way, is *my* father in the house?"

"He left a few minutes ago to go back to Police Headquarters."

"Sheila?" said Charley hoarsely.

"No, Charley. Go way."

"Sheila, you're acting like a ch-child," said Steve Potts fretfully. "Charley, I've been t-trying to get Sheila to forget this s-silliness about not marrying you—"

"Thanks, Mr. Pot—Mr. Brent! Sheila, hear that? Even your own father—"

"Let's not discuss it," said Sheila.

"Sheila, I love you! Let me marry you and take you out of here!"

"I'm staying with Daddy."

"I w-won't have it!" said old Steve excitedly. "I won't have you w-wasting your young life on me, Sheila. You marry Charley and get out of this house."

"No, Daddy."

Ellery sat down on the grass and plucked a blade, examining it studiously.

"No. You and Mac and I have to stick together now—we *have* to. I won't ruin Charley's life by mixing him up in our troubles. I've made my mind up." Sheila whirled on Charley. "I wish Mother'd discharge you, get another lawyer, or something!"

"Sheila, you're not going to get rid of me this way," said young Paxton in a bitter tone. "I know you love me. That's all I give a hoot about. I'll stick around, I'll hound you, I'll climb ladders to your window, I'll send you love letters by carrier pigeon ... I won't give up, darling."

Sheila threw her arms around him, sobbing. "I do love you, Charley—I do, I do!"

Charles, the Unhappy, was so surprised he lost his opportunity to kiss her.

Sheila put her hands on his chest and pushed, and ran to her father and took his arm and almost dragged him off to the house.

Charley gaped.

Ellery rose from the grass, flinging the dissected blade away. "Don't try to understand it, Charley. Now let's scout around and see if we can't come up with something."

13

Thurlow Potts, Terror of the Plains

Something caught their eye, and they paused in the downstairs study doorway. There was the familiar game table in the center of the study, flanked by the two inevitable chairs; on the table lay the checkerboard; a fierce game was in progress. Major Gotch sat crouched in one of the chairs, his broad black chin on a fist, studying the board with aggressive eyes. The other chair, however, was unoccupied.

Suddenly the old pirate moved a red checker toward the center of the board. He sat back and smacked his thigh, exulting. But then he jumped from his chair, dodged round the table, and sat down in the opposite chair to fall into the same dark brown study over the board. He shook his head angrily, moved a black checker, jumped up, rounded the table again, sat down in the original chair, and with every indication of triumph jumped three black checkers, his red coming to rest with a bang on the black king row. The Major leaned back and folded his thick arms across his chest majestically.

At this point Mr. Queen coughed.

Gotch's arms dropped as he looked around, his ruddy cheeks turning very dark. "Now, I don't like that," he roared. "That's spying. That's a sneaky Maori trick, that is. I mind mine, Mister—mind yours!"

"Sorry," said Ellery humbly. "Come in, Charley—we may as well have a chat with Major Gotch."

"Oh, is that you, Charley?" growled Major Gotch, mollified. "Eyes ain't so good any more. That's different. That's a technical difference, that is."

"Mr. Queen," explained Charley mystified, "is helping to find out who killed Bob, Major."

"Oh, that. Thurlow killed him." The Major spat through one of the French doors onto the terrace, contemptuously.

"Thurlow merely pressed the trigger," sighed Ellery. "There was supposed to be a blank in that Colt, Major Gotch. But there wasn't. Someone substituted a live cartridge during the night."

Major Gotch scraped his jaws. "Well, now," he said. "Wondered what all the boilin' and bubblin' was. But Thurlow thinks he killed Bobby fair and square in that shenanigan."

"I'm afraid Thurlow's still a bit confused," said Ellery sadly. "Major, did you kill Bob?"

"Me? Hell, no." Gotch spat again, calmly. "Too old, Mister. Did my killin' forty, forty-five year ago, round and about." He chuckled suddenly. "We did plenty of it, Steve and me, in our day."

"Steve?" Paxton looked skeptical.

"Well, Steve never had too much pepper for killin', I'll admit that. Sort of took after me, though. Looked up to me like a big brother. Many a time I saved his life from a brownskin's knife. Never could stomach knives, Steve. Too much blood made him sick. Hankered after guns, though."

"Uh...where did all this manslaughter take place, Major?" asked Ellery courteously.

"Nicaragua. Solomons. Java. One hitch down in Oorgawy."

"Soldiers of fortune, eh?"

The Major shrugged. "Seems to me I told you already."

"Didn't you two gentlemen spend most of your early days in the South Seas and Malaysia?"

"Oh, sure. We were all over. Raised plenty of hell, Steve and me. I remember once in Batavia—"

"Yes, yes," said Ellery hurriedly. "By the way, Major, where were you the other evening? The night before the duel?"

"Bed. Sleepin'. Charley, how about a game of checkers?"

Charley muttered something discouraging.

"And Major." Ellery lit a cigaret scrupulously. "Have you ever been married?"

The old man's jaw dropped. "Me? Hitched? Jipers, no."

"Any idea who might have murdered Robert Potts?"

"Same question that old albatross was askin' me. Nope, not a notion. I'm a man minds his own business, *Tuan*. Live an' let live, that's how I figger it. Sure you won't play a game o' checkers, Charley?"

Charley knocked on the tower door. Louella's bony face appeared behind the glass-protected grille and grinned at them. She unlocked her laboratory door quickly and welcomed them into her den of retorts with a frenetic eagerness that raised lumps on Ellery's scalp. "Come in! So glad you've come to visit me. The most wonderful thing's happened! See—here—" She kept chattering as she bustled them over to her workbench and exhibited a large procelain pan heaped with some viscid stuff of a green-gray, dead color, like sea slime. It had a peculiarly pervasive and unavoidable stench.

"What is it, Miss Potts?"

"My plastic." Louella lowered her voice, looking about. "I think I'm very near my goal, Mr. Mulqueen—I really do. Of course, I put you on your honor not to mention this to *anyone*— even the police. I don't trust police, you know. They're all in the pay of the corporations, and armed with authority as they are, they can come in here and steal my plastic and I wouldn't be able to do a *thing* about it. I know your father is that little man, the Inspector, but Charley's assured me you have no connection with the police department, and—"

Ellery comforted her. "But, Miss Potts, I understood that you needed more funds to carry on your work. I heard your mother refuse you the other evening—"

Louella's dry face twisted with rage. "She'll feel sorry!" she spat. "Oh, that's always the way—the great unselfish ones of science have to accomplish their miracles despite *every* hardship and obstacle! Well, Mother's avarice won't stop *me*. Some day she'll regret it—some day when the name of Louella Potts ..."

So Louella's tortured strivings in her smelly laboratory were run by the same dark generator that moved Cornelia Potts, and Thurlow Potts, and even Horatio Potts, to glorification and defense of the Name. The Name...Mr. Queen could wish it were lovelier.

He asked Louella several offhand questions, calculated not to alarm her. No, she had been in her laboratory, working on her plastic, the night before the duel. Yes, all night. Yes, alone.

"I *like* to be alone, Mr. Mulqueen," she said, her bony face glowing. And, as if her own statement had brought in its train a whole retinue of old black moods, she lost her enthusiasm, her eagerness palled, her face grew sullen, and she said: "I've wasted enough time. Please. If there's nothing else—I have my Work to do."

"Of course, Miss Potts." Ellery moved toward the door; Charley was already there, nibbling his fingernails. "Oh, incidentally," said Ellery lightly, turning around, "do you keep any guns up here? We're trying to round up all the guns in the house, Miss Potts, after that terrible accident to your brother Robert—"

"I hate guns," said Louella, shivering.

"No bullets, either?"

"Certainly not." Her eyes wandered to the dingy mess in the porcelain pan. "Oh, *guns*," she said suddenly. "Yes, they've been inquiring about that. That large man—Sergeant Something-or-other—he forced his way in here and turned my laboratory upside down. I had to hide my plastic under my gown ..." Her voice became vague.

They fled, depressed.

Dr. Innis was just striding out of Cornelia Potts's apartment when the two men came down from Louella's tower.

"Oh, Doctor. How's Mrs. Potts?"

"Not good, not good, Mr. Queen," said Innis fretfully. "Marked cardiac deterioration. We're doing what we can, which isn't much. I just administered a hypo."

"Maybe we ought to have a consultant in, Dr. Innis," suggested Charley.

Dr. Innis stared as if Charley had struck him. "Of course," he said icily. "If you wish it. But Mr. Thurlow Potts has every confidence in me. I suggest you discuss it with him, and—"

"Oh, come down, Doc," said Charley irritably. "I know you're doing what you can. I just don't want anyone saying we haven't gone through the motions. How about a nurse?"

Dr. Innis was slightly appeased. "You know how she is about nurses. Goes into tantrums. I really feel it would be bad to cross her in that. That old woman in the house—"

"Bridget?"

"Yes, yes. She's adequate." Dr. Innis shook his head. "These heart conditions, Mr. Paxton—we know so little about the heart, there's so little we can do. She's an old lady, and she's driven herself hard. Now this excitement of the past few days has dangerously weakened her, and I'm very much afraid her heart won't hold out much longer."

"Too bad," said Ellery thoughtfully.

Dr. Innis glanced at him in amazement, as if it had never occurred to him that anyone could rue the possible passing of Cornelia Potts. "Yes, certainly," the physician said. "Now if you gentlemen will excuse me—I must phone the pharmacy for some more digitalis." He hurried off with his elegant strides.

They made their way downstairs through the foyer to the French doors leading to the terrace and court. Ellery barely glanced into the study as they passed. He knew that Major Gotch was still hopping from chair to chair, playing checkers with himself.

"Horatio?" sighed Charley Paxton.

"None other."

"You won't get any more out of him than you got out of Louella. Ellery, we're wasting our time."

"I'm beginning to think so. Dad's been all through this, anyway, and he said he'd got exactly nowhere." They paused in the doorway, looking out across the gardens to the multi-colored cottage. "I must have been born under a very subtle curse. I live in hope always that some rationale can be applied to even the most haphazard human set-up. This time I think I'm licked...*Voici* Horatio."

The burly figure of Horatio Potts appeared from behind the little house, carrying a long ladder, his red bristles a halo in the sun. He wore filthy ducks tied about his joggled paunch with a piece of frayed rope, and tattered sandals on his broad feet. Perspiration stained his blouse darkly.

"What the devil's he *doing?*"

"Watch."

Horatio padded to the nearest tree, a patriarchal sycamore, and set the ladder against the trunk. Then he began to climb, the ladder protesting clearly all the way across the garden. He disappeared among some lower branches, his fat calves struggling upward, disembodied.

The two men waited, wondering.

Suddenly the legs began to dangle; Horatio appeared again, blowing in triumph. One hand firmly clasped the crosspiece of a kite. Carefully the fat man descended from the tree; then he ran out into the open, busily tying the broken end of the kite cord to a large ball of twine from one of his bulging pockets. In a few

107

moments he had his kite whole again, and Messrs. Queen and Paxton stood some yards away, in a doorway, enjoying the spectacle of an elephantine red-haired man racing with whoops through the gardens to let the wind catch a Mickey Mouse kite and lift it bravely into the air above Riverside Drive, New York City, the United States of America, Planet Earth.

"But I thought you wanted—" began Charley, as Ellery turned back into the house.

"No," growled Ellery. "It wouldn't do any good. Leave Horatio alone with his kites and his picaresque books and his gingerbread house. He's too immersed in the fairy tale he's living to be of any terrestrial use in the investigation of such a grown-up everyday business of murder.

"Strangest case I've ever seen," complained Ellery as they strolled back to the foyer. "Usually you get *somewhere* in questioning the people in an investigation. If they don't tell the truth, at least they tell lies, which are often more revealing than truths. But in this Potts fantasy—nothing! They don't even know what you're talking about. Their answers sound like Esperanto. First time in my life I've felt completely disheartened in such an early stage."

"Now you know why I want to get Sheila out of here," said Charley quietly.

"I certainly do." Ellery stopped short. "Now what's *that?*"

They were at the foot of the spiral staircase. Somewhere beyond the upper landing raged a bedlam of thumpings, yells and cracking furniture. There was nothing playful in these sounds. If murder was not being committed upstairs, it was at the very least assault and battery with murderous intent.

Ellery took the staircase in rejuvenated bounds: violence was an act, and acts are measurable; something had broken out into the open at last....A little way down the foyer, Major Gotch thrust a startled head out of the study. Seeing the two young men speed upstairs, and hearing the noise, the Major thundered out, tightening his belt.

Ellery followed his ears; they led him to Maclyn Potts's room.

Mac and his eldest brother were rolling over and over on the bedroom floor, bumping into the twin beds, in the débris of the overturned and splintered night table and its lamp. Mac's shirt was torn and there were four angry parallel gouges on his right cheek all bleeding. Thurlow's cheeks were gory, already turning purple in splotches. Both were screaming curses as they wrestled; and each was quite simply trying to kill the other with his bare hands. Mac, being younger, hard, and quicker, was closer to his objective. Thurlow looked forlorn.

Ellery plucked the younger man from the floor and held him fast; Charley pounced on Thurlow. Thurlow's little eyes were shooting jets of hate across the disordered bedroom through swollen blackening lids.

"You killed my brother!" shouted Mac, struggling in Ellery's arms. "You killed him in cold blood and I'll make you pay for it, Thurlow, if I have to go to the Chair!"

Thurlow deliberately rolled over, avoiding Charley Paxton's frantic clutch, and scrambled to his feet. He began to paw his baggy tweeds with blind, bleeding strokes.

Sheila and her father ran in, brushing Major Gotch aside. The Major had chosen to remain a spectator.

"Mac, what's happening?" Her eyes widened. "Did he—" Then Sheila sprang at Thurlow, and he cringed. "Did you try to kill my brother Mac, too?" she shrieked. "*Did* you?"

"Mac, y-your face," stammered his father. "It's all b-bloody!"

"His damned womanish fingernails," panted Mac. "He doesn't even fight like a man, Pop." He pushed Ellery away. "I'm all right, thanks."

Thurlow uttered a peculiar sound. Where his face was not puffed and stained, it was deadly white. His fat cheeks sucked in and out nervously; he kept trying not to lick his cracked lips. There was intense pain on his face. Slowly Thurlow took a handkerchief from his hip pocket, slowly unfolded it, grasped it by one corner and walked over to his brother. He flicked the handkerchief across Mac's wounded cheek.

As in a dream, they heard his voice.

"You've insulted me for the last time, Maclyn. I'll kill you just the way I killed Robert. This can only be wiped out in blood. Meet me at the Shoe tomorrow at dawn. I'll get two more guns—they've taken all of mine. Mr. Queen, will you do me the honor of acting for me once again?"

And, before they could recover from their astonishment, Thurlow was gone.

"I'll meet you!" Mac was roaring. "Bring your guns, Thurlow! Bring 'em, you murdering coward!"

They were holding him down forcibly—Ellery, Charley, Major Gotch. Steve Potts had dropped into a chair, to look at his writhing son without hope.

"You don't know what you're saying, Mac. Stop it, now. Daddy, do something. Charley...Mr. Queen, you can't let this happen again. Oh God," Sheila sobbed, "I'm going mad myself ..."

Her terror brought Mac to his senses. He ceased struggling, shook off their arms. Then he twisted to lie prone on his bed, face in his hands.

Ellery and Charley half-carried Sheila into the hall. "That maniac—he'll kill my Mac," she wept. "The way he killed Bobby. You've got to stop Thurlow, Mr. Queen. Arrest him—something!"

"Stop your hysterics, Sheila. Nothing's going to happen. There won't be another duel. I promise you."

When Charley had led Sheila off, still crying, Ellery stood for a moment outside Mac's room. Steve Potts was trying to soothe his son in an ineffectual murmur. Major Gotch's brassy voice was raised in a reminiscence half biography and half advice, and concerned a Borneo incident in which the artful use of knee and knife had saved his younger, more valuable life.

From Mac silence.

Ellery ran his hand desperately through his hair and hurried downstairs to telephone to his father.

14

Mac Solves the Mystery

The old woman suffered a heart attack that evening. For a few moments Ellery suspected malingering. But when Dr. Innis, hastily summoned, took over, and Ellery permitted himself an oral expression of his cynicism, without a word the physician handed him the stethoscope. What Ellery heard through those sensitive microphones banished all suspicions and gave him a respect for Dr. Innis he had not had before. If the Pasteur of Park Avenue had kept this wheezing, stopping, skipping, racing organ from ceasing to function altogether, then he was a very good man indeed.

Cornelia Potts lay gasping high on pillows. Her lips were cyanosed and her eyes, deeply socketed, in agony. With each breath she flung herself upward, as if to engulf the elusive air with her whole body.

Dr. Innis busied himself with hypodermics under Ellery's eye. After a few minutes, seeing the Old Woman's struggles for breath subside a little, he left on tiptoe. Outside the Old Woman's door he found Detective Flint.

"Old Woman kick the bucket?" Flint inquired with a hopeful inflection. When Ellery shook his head, Flint shook his. "Got a message for you from the Sarge. He's tailing Thurlow."

"Thurlow's left the house?" Ellery said quickly.

"A couple of minutes ago. Sergeant Velie's hangin' on to his tail like a tick, though."

"I suppose Thurlow's in quest of two more revolvers," mused Ellery. "Let me know when he gets back, will you, Flint?" He went into Mac's room. Major Gotch had vanished for some hole of his own in the vast building, but Stephen Potts was hovering over his son's bed, and Sheila and Charley Paxton.

"I don't know what you're all hanging around me for," Mac was saying listlessly as Ellery came in. The twin of dead Robert lay on his back, staring at the ceiling. "I'm fine. Don't treat me as if I were a baby. I'm all right, I tell you. Pop, go to bed. Let me alone. I want to sleep."

"Mac, you're planning to do something foolish." Sheila held tightly to her brother's hand.

"He wants a duel, he'll get a duel."

Old Steve made washing motions with his gnarled hands.

Ellery said: "Did you people know that Mrs. Potts has had a heart attack?"

It was cruel, but informative. Perhaps not so cruel, considering the startled hope that sprang into those faces, and the slow turn of Mac's head.

Sheila and her father ran out.

It took Charley and Ellery until past midnight to get Mac Potts to sleep. By the time they left his room and shut the door softly, Cornelia Potts not far along the hall was also in a deep sleep. They met Sheila and her father coming wearily out of the Old Woman's apartment with Dr. Innis.

"Condition's improved," said the doctor briefly. "I think she'll pull through this one. Amazing woman. But I'll stay here for another hour or so, anyway." He waved and returned to his patient.

Ellery sent Sheila and Stephen Potts to bed. They were both exhausted. Charley, who looked in hardly better case, comman-

112

deered a spare room, recommended that Ellery do the same, and trudged off after Sheila.

Mr. Queen was left alone in the upper hall. He spent much time there, smoking cigarets and pacing before the silent row of doors.

At 1:10 A.M. Thurlow Potts came home. Ellery heard him tottering upstairs. He dodged into the entrance to the turret staircase; Thurlow passed him, lurching. The elder Potts was toting a badly wrapped package. He meandered down the hall and finally wandered into his own rooms.

A moment later Sergeant Velie came upstairs, softly.

"Guns, Sergeant?"

"Yeah. Scared up some old bedbug in a hockshop down on West Street who sold 'em to him." Velie kept his eye on Thurlow's door. "Two big babies. I couldn't go in and find out what they were or I would a lost *my* bedbug. They looked heavy enough to sink a sub."

"Why so late?"

"He stopped into a row of gin mills on his way back. Got tanked to the eyeballs. For a little guy he sure can lap it up." The Sergeant chuckled. "Mr. Thurlow Potts ain't doin' any dueling tonight. I can tell you that. This is one that gets slept off, brother, unless he's been kiddin' me."

"Good work, Velie. Wait till he falls asleep. Then go in there and take that package away from him."

"Yes, sir."

Ten minutes later Sergeant Velie slipped out of Thurlow's apartment with the poorly tied package in his arms.

"Beddy-by," grinned the Sergeant. "Flopped on his flop with his clothes on, and he's snorin' away like a water buffalo. What do I do now?"

"Give me the package for one thing," replied Ellery, "and for another get some sleep. Tomorrow, I think, will be a large fat day."

Velie yawned and went downstairs. Ellery saw him stretch out in a plush chair in the foyer, tip his hat over his eyes, fold his hands on his hard stomach; heard him settle back with voluptuous sighs.

Ellery opened the package. It contained two colossal revolvers, single-action Colt .45's, the weapon that played so important a role in the winning of the West. "Six-shooters, by thunder!" He hefted one of the formidable guns and wondered how Thurlow had ever expected to handle it: its shape and the size of its grip were adapted for big brawny hands, not the pudgy little white hands of the Thurlow Pottses of this world. Both guns were loaded.

Ellery retied the package, placing it at his feet, and curled up on the top step of the spiral staircase.

At 2:30 Dr. Innis emerged from the Old Woman's apartment, yawning. "She'll sleep through the night now, Mr. Queen. This last hypo injection would put an elephant to sleep. 'Night."

"Good night, Doctor."

"I'll be back first thing in the morning. She's in no danger." Dr. Innis trudged downstairs and disappeared.

Ellery rose, clutching Thurlow's newest arsenal, and made a noiseless tour of the floor. When he had satisfied himself that everyone was asleep, or at least in his room, he hunted up an empty bedroom on the top floor, flung himself on the bed with his arms about Thurlow's package, and fell instantly asleep.

At six o'clock sharp, in the red-gold of a charming dawn, Thurlow Potts dashed out of the Potts Palace and raced down the steps to the Shoe. He stopped short. A delegation awaited him.

Inspector Queen, Sergeant Velie, Sheila and her father, Charles Hunter Paxton, a half-dozen plainclothes men, and Ellery Queen.

"My guns!" Thurlow saw the package in Ellery's hands, beaming with relief. "I was *so* alarmed," he said, wiping his forehead with a silk handkerchief. "But I might have known as my second you'd take care of everything, Mr. Queen."

Mr. Queen did not reply.

"Is everything ready for the duel, gentlemen?"

Inspector Queen spat out the end of his first cheroot of the day. "There's going to be no duel, Mr. Potts. Understand that? I'll repeat it for your benefit. There's going to be no duel. Your dueling days are over. And if you want to argue about it, there are plenty of judges available. Now how about it? Will you settle this fight with your brother sensibly or do I swear out a warrant for your arrest?"

Thurlow blinked.

"Ellery, get this boy Mac down here. You said last night over the phone he'd threatened to kill Thurlow. Get him down here and we'll settle this foolishness once and for all."

Ellery nodded and went back into the house. It was quiet; no servants stirred as yet; Dr. Innis had arrived fifteen minutes before and gone into Cornelia Potts's room with the same heavy tread which had carried him out of the house a few hours earlier.

Ellery went to Mac's door. It was a silent door.

"Mac?"

There was no answer. He opened the door.

Mac was lying on his back in bed, covered to the chin, a very peaceful young man. His eyes were open.

But Mr. Queen's eyes were open, too—wide. He ran over to the bed and pulled back the cover.

Some time during the night Maclyn Potts had solved the mystery of his brother's death. For his brother's murderer had visited him here, and he had looked with those staring eyes upon that creature, and that creature had left behind a hard reflection of his nature—a bullet in Mac's heart.

Ellery stood still, his heart pounding. He felt himself growing enraged. And then a coldness settled down on him. His eyes narrowed. The pillow on which Mac's head rested showed powder burns and one bullet hole.

There were some strange marks on Mac's face—long thin blue marks. As if the second twin had been whipped.

115

On the empty bed of departed Robert there stood a bowl of gold-spotted liquid. Ellery sniffed it, touched its bland surface with a cautious finger tip. It was cold chicken broth.

He looked around. The door through which he had just come...A little behind it lay a crop, a crop such as horsemen use to whip their mounts. And, near it, a small revolver with a familiar look.

Part Three

15

And Whipped Them All Soundly and Put Them to Bed

Dr. Samuel Prouty, Assistant Medical Examiner of New York County, squinted past his fuming cigar at the body of Maclyn Potts and said through his stained teeth: "I've seen a lot of monkey business but the Potts madness passeth understanding. I can't even bellyache any more. It's too fascinating."

"Spare me your fascinations, Prouty," snarled Inspector Queen, glaring at Mac's corpse with bitterness.

"Those marks on his face," said Dr. Prouty thoughtfully. "Very provocative. I tell you, boys, Freud's at the bottom of this."

"Who?" asked Sergeant Velie.

"Perhaps," remarked Ellery Queen, "perhaps Sigmund's dark land is, Prouty; but I do believe we can touch on nearer shores, if you're referring to the welts on poor Mac's face."

"What d'ye mean, Ellery?" frowned Doc Prouty.

"Not very much, Doc."

The Potts mansion was quiet. The mud had been roiled and beaten; now it settled into new patterns. Mac's body lay on his bed, as Ellery had found it. Nothing had been disturbed except the weapon, which had been taken downtown for ballistics examination.

The photographer, the fingerprint crew, had come and gone. These had been dutiful motions, for the sake of the record. The photographs preserved forever the visual memory of the scene; the fingerprints had no significance except to satisfy the undiscriminating appetite of routine and regulation. They told a story Inspector Queen already knew. Those who were known to have visited deceased's room since its last cleaning by the housemaids had left the marks of their hands there; of those who were not known to have visited the room, there was no fingerprint evidence. But this could have been because the murderer of Maclyn Potts wore a protective covering on the hands.

Ellery was inclined to this theory. "The fact that no prints at all have been found on the pistol, on the riding crop, or on the bowl of broth indicates gloves, or a very careful wiping off of prints afterwards." In any event, the fingerprints that were present and those that were not had no clue or evidential value.

"When was the boy murdered, Doc?" asked the Inspector.

"Between three and four A.M."

"Middle of the night, huh?" said the Sergeant, who had a passion for simplification.

"The shot was fired through the pillow." Ellery pointed to the powder burns and the bullet hole.

"That's why no one heard it," his father nodded.

"Probably," reflected Ellery, "when the killer stole in here at three or four A.M. Mac's head had either slipped off the pillow in his sleep or was resting on one corner of it, so that his murderer easily slipped it from under his head. Certainly Mac didn't wake up until a second or two before the shot was fired, otherwise there'd be signs of a tussle, and there aren't."

"Maybe the picking up of the pillow was what woke him," suggested Velie.

Ellery nodded. "Quite possibly. But he had no time to do more than stare at the face bent over him. The next moment he was dead."

Dr. Prouty shivered the least bit. "The things people do."

Inspector Queen had no mind for moralizing; upon him lay

the pressure. "Then after the shot was fired, this killer stuck the pillow back under Mac's head—"

"Neat soul," murmured Mr. Queen. "Yes, the things people do..."

"And took that riding crop and smacked the boy over the face with it? Is that the way it happened, Doc?"

"Yes," said Prouty, gazing at the thin blue welts, "the whipping was administered shortly after death, not before. I'd say within seconds. Yes, he dropped the gun and picked up the crop and whacked away. I'd say he whacked away even before he replaced the pillow, Dick."

Inspector Queen shook his head. "It's beyond me."

"But not beyond Mr. Queen," boomed the Sergeant. "This is the kind of stuff you specialize in, ain't it, Mr. Queen?"

Mr. Queen did not react to this obvious sarcasm.

"And another thing," grumbled the Inspector. "That bowl of soup. For Mike's sake, did this crazy killer bring up a midnight snack with him?"

"How d'ye know he brought it up for himself?" argued the Sergeant. "Maybe he was bringin' it up to this young guy. In case Mac woke up and said, 'What the hell are you doin' in my bedroom at four o'clock in the morning, you so-an-so?' Then he could show the bowl of soup and say: 'I figgered you might want some soup before the duel. Chicken broth is swell just before duels,' he could say. Get his confidence, see? Then— whammo! And he's killed another chicken." The Sergeant flushed in the silence. "Anyway," he said doggedly, "that's the way *I* look at it."

"When I said 'midnight snack,' Velie," said the Inspector, softly savage, "I was just trying to express in my crude way the fact that this is a wacky kill, Velie—madness—lunacy. Ellery, what are some more synonyms? Velie, dry up!"

"Okay, okay."

"The strange part of the Sergeant's theory," murmured Ellery, "is not its wrongness, but its rightness."

His father stared, and Velie looked amazed.

"Oh, it's not right," Ellery hastened to add. "It's all wrong, in fact. But it's on the right track. I mean it's a reasonable theory—it attempts to put a reasonable construction on an absurdity. And that's definitely correct, Dad."

"You're getting deluded, too, Ellery," said Doc Prouty.

"Not at all. This bowl of chicken broth was brought up here by the killer—incidentally, it *was* the killer, because the soup wasn't here when I left Mac asleep in bed last night—and, what's more, the killer brought the soup up for a completely logical reason."

"To eat it?" sneered the Inspector. "Or to have Maclyn Potts eat it?"

"No, it wasn't brought here to be eaten, Dad."

"Then why?"

"For the same reason the crop was brought...*and used.* By the way, whose riding crop is it, Dad? Have you identified it yet?"

"It belonged to Mac himself," replied the Inspector with a sort of frustrated satisfaction, as if to say: And see what you can make out of that little pearl of information!

"And the soup and bowl?"

"From the kitchen. That Mrs. Whatsis, the cook, says she always keeps chicken broth handy in the refrigerator. The Old Woman has to have it."

"So this killer," said Sergeant Velie, undaunted, "this killer, before he comes up to the future scene of his foul crime, this killer goes downstairs to the kitchen, takes a bowl, fills it up with cold soup from the icebox, and pussyfoots it upstairs here. There's even a splash or two on the staircase, where the soup slopped over as he carried it up. Cold soup," he said thoughtfully. "I've heard of jellied soup," he said, "and hot soup, but just plain cold soup..."

"Don't fret yourself into a breakdown over it, Velie," yipped Inspector Queen. "Just check back with downtown and see if they've done a ballistics yet on that rod. Ellery, come on."

Dr. Prouty left, reluctantly, saying to Mr. Queen that this was one case he wished he could follow through *ex officio*, you lucky dog, you. The body was to be picked up and carted down to the Morgue for routine autopsy, but nothing more could be expected in the way of discoveries: the mouth had shown no trace of soup, or poison, death resulted from one .38-caliber bullet in the heart, and so it was all dirty work from here on in, and he didn't even think he'd attend the funeral. (*Exit* DR. PROUTY.)

Inspector Queen and his son made a grand tour of the mansion before retiring for further conversations.

These were dreary rounds. Sheila lay on a chaise longue in her boudoir without tears, staring at her ceiling. (Mr. Queen was uneasily reminded of her brother, who lay in a similar attitude a few doors down the hall, not breathing.) Charley Paxton kept chafing Sheila's hands, his swollen eyes fixed fearfully on her expressionless face. It was Stephen Brent Potts's voice which emerged, almost without stuttering, in loving reassurance.

"There's no sense in giving in, Sheila lambie," he was saying as the Queens stole in. "Mac's dead. All right, he's dead. M-murdered. What are we supposed to do—commit suicide? Curl up and d-die? Sheila, we'll fight back. We're not alone, baby. The p-police are our friends. Charley's on our sis-side...Aren't you, Charley?" Old Steve dug Charley sharply in the ribs.

"I love you, darling," was all Charley could say as he chafed Sheila's cold hands.

"Don't lie there that way, Sheila," old Steve said desperately. "Do you want a doctor?"

"No." Sheila's voice was faint.

"If you don't snap out of this, I'll call one. I'll call two. I'll make your life miserable. Sheila honey, don't go under. Talk to me!"

"Never would have believed it of the old duck," muttered the Inspector as he and Ellery left, unobserved. "Of all these people, he's the one with guts. Where's that sucker Gotch?"

"Taking a nap in his room, Velie told me." Ellery seemed pained by the memory of that white, frozen face.

"Taking a nap!"

"Steve sent him to bed. It seems," growled Mr. Queen, "that the worm has turned and, coincidentally with the illness of his mate and the murder of his second son, has developed hair on his chest. I like that little man."

"Like—dislike!" raved his father. "Who cares how wonderful they are? I want to see this case solved and get the kit and caboodle of 'em out of my hair! What did he send Gotch to bed for?" he asked suspiciously.

"Gotchie-boy has been 'worrying' about him too much, it appears. Hasn't had his proper rest. Stephen Brent Potts version."

"Gotchie-boy has been hitting the bottle too much, that's what Gotchie-boy's been doing," rasped the Inspector. "If this ain't all a smoke screen. I don't get that old pirate at all."

"It's very simple, Dad—he found snug harbor, and he's dug in like a barnacle. By the way, have you had a report on the Major yet?"

"Not yet."

They hunted Louella in her ivory tower, they took wing and visited Horatio in his house in the clouds, they returned to the Palace and looked in on Thurlow. Louella was still creating sea slime in her porcelain pans. Horatio was still wielding a quill on the greater *Mother Goose*—wielding it even more zestfully. And Thurlow was sleeping like a just man who has offered to do the honorable thing and been absolved by forces beyond a chevalier's control. An aroma of alcohol hovered over his pillow, like angels' wings.

Nothing had changed except that, as Horatio Potts put it, looking up from his versifying, "one person less lives in the house."

The Inspector crossed lances with Dr. Innis upstairs in Cornelia Potts's sitting room. The Inspector was determined to speak with mother of deceased; Dr. Innis was equally determined that the Inspector should not speak to mother of deceased.

"Unless," said Dr. Innis stiffly, "you promise you won't mention this latest development, Inspector."

"Promise your jaundiced liver," said the Inspector. "What would I want to speak to her about if not this 'latest development,' as you put it so delicately?"

"Then I'm sorry. She's a very sick woman. The shock of another murder—another son's death—would undoubtedly kill her on the spot."

"I doubt it, Doctor," said the Inspector grumpily; but he gave up the joust and took Ellery down to the study. "Sit down, son," sighed the old gentleman. "You generally have a cockeyed slant on cockeyed cases. How about squinting at this one? I'm groggy."

"I'm a little crocked myself," admitted Ellery with a wry smile.

"Sure, but what are you thinking?"

"Of Bob. Of Mac. Of life and death and how ineffectual people really are. Of Sheila…What are *you* thinking?"

"I don't know what to think. In the past this family of drizzle-birds, while they've been mixed up in plenty of trouble, have always wound up in the civil courts. Little stuff, inflated big. But now murder! And two in a row…I'm thinking something's been smoking under the surface for a long time. I'm thinking the fire's broken through. And I'm thinking: Is it out, or isn't it?"

"You think there may be further attempts?"

The Inspector nodded. "It might be just the beginning of a plot to wipe out the lot of them. Not that that wouldn't be a good thing," he added dourly. "Except that I wish they'd started on the nuts rather than those two nice young fellas."

"Yes," said Ellery grimly.

"Is that all you're going to say—'yes?' Then there's this crazy lashing of Mac Potts's dead face. That looks to me like pure hate—psychopathic. The chicken broth certainly indicates an unbalanced mind, in spite of that fancy speechifying you made upstairs to Velie."

"But the whipping and the leaving of a bowl of chicken broth are easy, Dad," said Ellery patiently. "As I said, they were both introduced into the murder's stew for identical reasons."

"Flog a corpse—leave soup around." The Inspector shook his head. "You'll have to show me, son."

"Certainly." And Ellery paused a moment. Then he did the most absurd thing. He began to chant, with an expression of utter gravity, a nursery rhyme:—

> "There was an old woman who lived in a shoe,
> She had so many children she didn't know what to
> do.
> She gave them some broth without any bread,
> And whipped them all soundly, and put them to
> bed."

And Mr. Queen clasped his hands behind his head and gazed steadily at his father.

His father's eyes were like new quarters.

"The Old Woman," continued Ellery quietly. "She lives in a Shoe—or rather a house that the Shoe built. And there's even a nice, literal Shoe on the front lawn. She has so many children...yes, indeed. Six! That she doesn't know what to do with them I should think is evident to anyone; all her eccentricity and cruelty are masks for her frustration and helplessness."

"She gave them some *broth*," muttered the Inspector. "That chicken broth in Mac's room!"

"Without any bread," his son added dryly. "Don't overlook that precious coincidence. Or perhaps you're not aware that on Dr. Innis's orders Mrs. Potts may not eat bread, and consequently she serves none at her table."

"And *whipped* them all soundly—!"

"Yes, or at any rate whipped Mac. And the bed motif? Mac was killed in bed. You see?"

The Inspector jumped up, fire-red. "No, blast it, I don't see! Nobody could make me believe—"

"But you do believe, Dad," sighed Ellery. "You're terribly impressed. A number of people crazy, and now apparently a series of crimes following a Mother Goose pattern. Well, of course. Would crazy people commit rational crimes? No, no. Crazy people would commit crazy crimes. Mother Goose crimes...Don't you see that you're *supposed* to believe in the lunacy of these two crimes? Don't you see that a *sly brain is creating an atmosphere of madness,* or rather utilizing the one that exists, *in order to cloak the reality?* And what could madness cloak but sanity?"

The Inspector drew a grateful breath. "Well, well. And I'd have fallen for it, too. Of course, son. This is the work of a sane one, not a crazy one."

"Not necessarily."

The Inspector's jaw dropped.

Ellery smiled. "We just don't know. I was merely expounding an attractive theory. As far as logic is concerned, this might well be the work of a madman."

"I wish you'd make up your mind," said his father irritably.

Ellery shrugged. "You've got to have more than theories to bring to the District Attorney."

"Let's get on with it, let's get on with it!"

"All right, we'll proceed on the rational theory. What comes to mind immediately?"

The Inspector said promptly: "We're supposed to pin this on Horatio Potts. *He's writing a modern 'Mother Goose.'*"

Ellery laughed. "You saw that, you old fox."

"Plain as the nose on your face. If this is the work of a sane mind, then Horatio is being framed for the murders of his two half-brothers."

"Yes, indeed."

"Horatio being framed...why, the man hardly knows what's going on!"

"Don't be too sure of that," said Ellery, knitting his brows. "Horatio's a good deal of a *poseur*. He knows lots more than he lets on."

127

"*Now* what d'ye mean?"

"Just speculating, Dad. The man's not a fool. Horatio has an unorthodox slant on life and a great cowardice where adult problems are concerned, but he's aware of the score at all times. Believe me."

"You're no help at all," grumbled the Inspector. "All right, score or no score, Horatio's supposed to take the rap; we're to think he's behind all this. That means he isn't."

"Not necessarily," said Ellery.

"*Will* you stick to one point of view?" howled the Inspector, now maddened beyond reason. His face was very red indeed. "Look," he began again, desperately. "Certain things we *know*—"

"You wouldn't be referring," asked Ellery, "to the arithmetic involved?"

"Yes, the arithmetic involved! When all six children were alive, each one stood to come into five millions at the death of the Old Woman. Then Robert Potts was knocked off, leaving five. Now Mac's gone, leaving four. Four into thirty millions makes seven and a half million apiece—*so the murder of the twins means over two and a half million bucks extra* to each of the four surviving children!"

"I can't get excited over a mere two and a half million," moaned Mr. Queen. "I doubt if anyone could, where five millions are guaranteed. Oh, well, I'm probably wrong. It's your fault for having brought into the world the son of a poor man, Dad."

Providentially, Sergeant Velie came in.

Velie tramped in to ease his two hundred and twenty-five pounds into Major Gotch's favorite chair. He was yawning.

"Well?" snapped the Inspector, turning the wind of his fury on this more vulnerable vessel.

The Sergeant looked pained. "What did I do now? Don't follow orders, get bawled out. Follow orders—"

"What order are you following now?"

"The ballistics check-up."

"Well, what do you think this is, the gentlemen's lounge at the Grand Street Turkish Baths? Report!"

"Yes, sir." Velie rose with a noticeable lack of fatigue. "The Lieutenant says the gun found on the floor upstairs is the gun with which Maclyn Potts was homicidally and with murderous intent shot to death—"

"That," said the Inspector, spreading his hands to Ellery, "is news, is it not? The gun is the gun. We're certainly progressing! What else?"

"That's all," said the Sergeant sullenly. "What did you expect, Inspector—the Lieut should come up with the name of the killer?"

"Just what kind of gun was it, Sergeant?" interposed Ellery. "I didn't get a good look at it."

"It's a Smith & Wesson .38/32 revolver, 2-inch barrel, takes an S. & W. .38 cartridge—"

Mr. Queen gave voice to a strangled exclamation.

His father stared. "What's the matter? Sick?"

Ellery sprang to his feet. "Sick! Don't you recall the fourteen guns Thurlow bought at Cornwall & Ritchey's? Don't you remember that you've accounted for only twelve? Don't you remember that two guns are missing, that the missing guns are exact duplicates of the two used in the Bob-Thurlow duel—don't you remember that, according to the store's check list, *one of those two missing guns is a Smith & Wesson .38/32 with a 2-inch barrel?* And now you tell me the gun which shot Mac Potts to death last night is a Smith & Wesson .38/32 with a 2-inch barrel!"

After a long time the Inspector choked: "Velie, phone the Lieutenant at H.Q. and get the serial number of the gun in Maclyn Potts's murder. Then phone Cornwall & Ritchey and get the serial number of the missing Smith & Wesson. Right away, please."

Dazed by this politeness, Sergeant Velie staggered out. Five minutes later he returned with the information that the Smith & Wesson which had taken Mac's life was the same Smith & Wesson that appeared on the check list as unaccounted for.

One of the two missing revolvers had been found.

"Clearer and foggier," moaned Inspector Queen. "Now we know why the killer of Robert hid two of the fourteen guns

Thurlow bought—to use one of 'em, the S. & W., for a second murder."

"The murder of Mac," put in Velie, the simplifier.

"That's certainly the look of it," Ellery mumbled. "But why did he steal and hide *two* guns?"

Sergeant Velie's face fell. "You mean we ain't *through?*"

"Of course we 'ain't' through!" snarled his superior. "Two guns missing, one of 'em turns up in a murder, so what would the killer be doing with the other if he isn't planning still another killing?"

"A third murder," Ellery muttered. "Everything points to it. Not only the missing guns ..." He shook his head.

"Then we got to find that last gun—the Colt .25 automatic that didn't turn up," said the Sergeant with a groan, "or go fishin' for dreams."

"Not that finding the missing Colt would necessarily stop a third murder," Ellery pointed out. "We have no Achilles here, and there are more ways of killing than by an arrow. But finding the missing Colt might uncover a clue to the person who secreted it. By all means search for it. And at once."

"But where?" whined the Sergeant. "My gosh, we've turned this coocoo's nest upside down, and not only the house but the grounds, too. It's a pipe to hide a little bitty thing like that vest-pocket Colt in a square block of house and grounds! It would take twelve squads twenty-four weeks—"

The Inspector said: "Find that gun, Velie."

16

And Then There Were None

But Sergeant Velie did not find that gun. Nor Sergeant Velie, nor Detectives Flint, Piggott, Hesse, Johnson, and company, searching at all hours, in odd places, under irritated or indifferent or astonished noses.

There were days of this fruitless exploration in the Potts mansion and on the Potts grounds, and while some interesting exhibits were turned up—a Spanish leather chest, for instance, buried behind Horatio's cottage and filled with broad and crooked coins which Mr. Queen delightedly pronounced to be pieces of eight, at the disinterment of which Horatio went into a tantrum and howled that it had taken him years to gather an authentic Spanish "treasure" and a week of dark nights with an iron lantern and a cutlass between his jaws to bury it, and he wasn't going to stand by and see a lot of cursed policemen spoil his fun—the duplicate Colt Pocket Model .25 automatic remained in the limbo of lost things. The cursed policemen tramped off on aching feet, leaving Horatio to reinter his pirate's chest angrily.

Inspector Queen staged a mild tantrum himself, but for other reasons.

Then Mac was buried in the family plot at St. Praxed's churchyard. A section four blocks square was roped off for the ceremony, traffic was re-routed, and police cordons exercised their muscles.

Somehow Cornelia Potts, recovering from her heart attack in the big house, learned of her son's death.

The first inkling that the Old Woman knew came on the morning of her son's funeral. She sat up in bed and called for her maid, a woman almost as old as she, Bridget Conniveley by name, whom Dr. Innis detested. Old Bridget, who was a bent and sibilant crone, threw over the yoke of the Old Woman's authority and telephoned Dr. Innis. Innis came rushing over, pale and stammering. It was impossible. He could not be responsible. She must be sensible. She could do nothing more for Maclyn. He forbade her to leave her bed.

To all this the Old Woman said nothing. She calmly crept out of bed and flayed Bridget with her tongue. Bridget scurried, cowering, to draw her mistress's bath.

When the Inspector heard about it from the detective on guard outside the Old Woman's apartment, his face glowed with a dark joy. "Mustn't talk to her, huh?" he said to Dr. Innis. And he strode by into the Presence.

It was a short, bitter interview. The Old Woman spoke scarcely at all. What she did say was acrid and precise. No, nobody had told her. She just "knew." And she was going to Maclyn's funeral; the State Militia could not stop her. Get out and let an old woman dress, you fool.

The Inspector got out. "It's a cinch little Thurlow spilled the beans to Mama," he grunted. "What a bunch!"

Cornelia Potts was assisted from her Palace by Dr. Innis and Bridget Conniveley, wrapped in shawls, only the buttery tip of her nose showing. Her expression was one of gloomy interest. She shed no tears, nor would she gaze upon her son's face before the mortician's assistant closed the coffin.

At St. Praxed's Ellery kept watching her with amazement.

That aged heart, to whose stuttering and whimpering he had laid his own ear, seemed unmoved by the second death of a son within a week. She was built of granite, and sulphuric acid coursed through her veins…She did not glance at Sheila, or at Stephen her husband, or at Major Gotch, who looked pinched and confused this morning. She did not seem surprised that her other children were not present.

Back at the house, Bridget undressed her and she crawled into bed. She closed her eyes and asked Dr. Innis for "a little something to put me to sleep."

And she fell asleep and slept restlessly, moaning.

"Well," demanded the Inspector when it was all over, "where do we go from here?"

"I wish I knew, Dad."

"You're stumped?"

His son shrugged. "I can't believe this case is insoluble. There's sense in it somewhere. Our job is to spot it."

The Inspector threw up his hands. "If *you* can't see any light, I certainly can't, Ellery. All we can do is keep a close watch on these people and follow up the few clues we have. Let's go home."

A few days after Mac's funeral, Ellery Queen had two breakfast callers.

He was startled by the change in Sheila Potts. Her face seemed half its normal size, the skin gray; her blue eyes were darker and deeper blue and more liquid, their sockets underscored as by a paintbrush. She was in black, a pitiable figure of distress.

Charley Paxton looked thin and ill, too. And his eyes shared with Sheila's that burden of anxiety which Mr. Queen had come to associate with the troubled ones of this world who find themselves caught in a tangle from which there is no escape.

The Inspector had been about to leave for his office, but when he saw the haggard faces of the two young people he phoned

Police Headquarters to say he would be delayed and became mine host cunningly. "How's your mother this morning?" he asked Sheila, with an elaborate expression of concern.

"Mother?" said Sheila vaguely. "About the same."

Charley braced himself. "Now you'll see it's all stuff, darling," he said in a cheery voice. "Tell Ellery and the Inspector about it."

"It isn't stuff, Charley, and you know it," Sheila said tiredly. "Sometimes you make me sick. I know I've done an awful lot of weeping and squalling, but I'm not a child—I can add. This adds up to more, and you know it. You see," she said, turning to the Queens before Charley could reply, "I've been thinking, Mr. Queen—"

"Ellery," said Ellery.

"Ellery. I've been thinking, and I've seen—well, a dreadful design in what's been happening."

"Have you? And what design is that?"

Sheila shut her eyes. "At first I was shocked. I couldn't think at all. Murder is so...newspapery. It doesn't happen to *you*. You read about it in a paper, or in a detective story, and it makes you wriggle with disgust, or sympathy. But it doesn't *mean* anything."

"That's quite true."

"Then—it happens to you. There are police in your house. Somebody you love is dead. Somebody you've been with all your life is...a fiend of some sort. You look at the faces around you, the familiar faces, even the ones you dislike...and you die yourself. Inside. A thousand times. It doesn't seem possible. But there it is.

"And there *you* are.... When Bob died I couldn't believe anything. I was all mixed up; none of it seemed real. I just went through the motions. Then Mac ..." She put her hands quickly to her face.

Charley reached out to touch her, but Ellery shook his head

and Charley turned away to stare blindly out the Queens' window at the quiet street below.

Inspector Queen kept his hard eyes on the weeping girl.

After a while Sheila groped in her bag and took out a handkerchief. "I'm sorry," she sniffed. "All I seem to do these days is imitate a fountain." She blew her little nose with energy and put her handkerchief away, sitting back and even smiling a little.

"Go ahead, Miss Potts," said Inspector Queen. "This personal stuff is interesting."

She looked guilty. "I don't know why I wandered that way...What I began to say was—I've been thinking since Mac died. There have been two murders in the house. And who's been murdered? Robert. Mac. My twin brothers." Her blue eyes flashed. "Not one of Mother's first husband's three children—oh, no! Not one of the *crazy* ones. Only the Brents are dying. Only the Brents—*the sane ones.*"

Charley cleared his throat.

"Let me finish, Charley. It's as clear as anything. We Brents are being killed off, one by one. First Robert, then Mac...*then either my father or me.* Charley, it's true and you know it! One of us is next on the list, and if Daddy gets it, I'll be the only Brent left, and I'll get it."

"But why?" shouted Charley, out of control. "It doesn't make sense, Sheila!"

"What's the difference why? Money, hate, just plain insanity...*I* don't know why, but I know it's true, as truly as I'm sitting here this minute. And what's more, *you* know it, too, Charley! Maybe Mr. Queen and the Inspector don't know it, but you know it—"

"Miss Potts—" began the Inspector.

"Please call me Brent. I don't want ever to be called by that horrible name again."

"Of course, Miss Brent."

Ellery and his father exchanged glances. Sheila was right. It was what they themselves feared, a third murder. With even more reason: the missing automatic.

The Inspector went to one of the front windows. After a moment, he said: "Miss Brent, would you mind coming here?"

Sheila wearily crossed the room to stand beside him in the sun.

"Look down there," said the Inspector. "No, across the street. The service entrance of that apartment house. What do you see, Miss Brent?"

"A big man smoking a cigaret."

"Now look on this side, a few yards up, towards Amsterdam Avenue. What do you see?"

"A car," said Sheila, puzzled. "With two men in it."

The Inspector smiled. "The man in that areaway, and the two men in that car, Miss Brent, are detectives assigned to follow you wherever you go. You're never out of their sight. When you're in your mother's house, other detectives have their eye on you every possible moment. The same is true of your father. No one can get near you two, Miss Brent, unless the men on duty feel sure you're running no risk."

Sheila flushed. "Don't think I'm ungrateful, Inspector. I didn't know that, and it does make me feel better. And I'm happy for Daddy's sake. But—you know perfectly well if I were surrounded by a cordon twenty-four hours a day—if you put the whole police department to guarding us—sooner or later we'd be caught. A shot through a window, a hand aiming around a door—"

"Not at all," said the Inspector crossly. "I can promise you *that* won't happen!"

"Of course it won't, dear," said Charley. "Be sensible, now— let me take you out somewhere. We can have lunch at the Ritz and go to the Music Hall or some place—get your mind off things—"

Sheila shook her head, smiling faintly. "Thank you, darling. It's sweet of you." And then there was a silence.

"Sheila." She turned to Ellery very quickly. His eyes were admiring, and a little color came into her face. "You have something specific in mind—a most excellent mind, by the way," he said dryly. "What is it?"

Sheila said in a grim tone: "Have them put into an institution."

"Sheila!" Charley was appalled. "Your own mother?"

"She hates me, Charley. And she's got a sick brain. If mother had tuberculosis, I'd send her to Arizona, wouldn't I?"

"But—to put her away..." said Charley feebly.

"Don't make me sound like a monster!" Sheila cried. "But none of you knows my mother as I do. She'd cheerfully kill me if she thought it would help some 'plans' of hers. Her brain's twisted, I tell you! I won't feel safe until Mother and Thurlow and Horatio and Louella are behind bars somewhere! Now call me anything you like," and Sheila sat down and wept again.

"We've already considered that plan," said Ellery gently. She looked up, startled. "Oh, yes. We haven't overlooked any bets, Sheila. But Charley will tell you there'd be no legal grounds whatever for committing your mother to an institution. Thurlow, Louella, Horatio? It would be very difficult, as there's no doubt whatever that your mother would fight any such move with every penny of the considerable fortune she possesses. It would take a long time, with no certainty of success—they're borderline cases, I should say, if they're mentally deficient in any medical sense at all.

"Meanwhile, they could be doing...damage. No, we abandoned the idea of trying to commit anyone in the Potts family to a mental hospital. Later, perhaps, when this case is settled. Now it would be futile and even dangerous, as it might force someone's hand."

"Then there's the possibility of throwing the lot of them in jail," said Inspector Queen quietly. "We've considered that, too. We could hold them as material witnesses, maybe. Or on some other charge. Whatever the charge, I can tell you—and Charley as a lawyer will bear me out—that we couldn't hold them indefinitely. Your mother's money and pull would get them out eventually, and you'd be back where you started. We need more evidence before we can take that step, Miss Brent."

"It doesn't leave me very much except to order the latest shroud, does it?" said Sheila with a white smile.

"Sheila, please! Stop talking like that!" cried Charley.

"Meanwhile," continued the Inspector, "everything's being done that can be. Every member of your household is under a twenty-four-hour guard. We're doing all we can to dig into the background of this case, in the hope that we'll find some clue to the truth. Yes, there's always the danger of a slip. But then," added the Inspector in a peculiar tone, "you could slip on a banana peel this afternoon, Miss Brent, and break your neck."

"Now hold on, Inspector," said Charley angrily. "Can't you see she's scared blue? I know you're doing all you can, but—"

"Shut up, Charley," said the Inspector.

Ellery glanced at his father quickly. This had not been on the agendum. Charley was shocked.

"How about Charley's taking Sheila away somewhere?" asked Ellery innocently. "Out of range of any possible danger, Dad?"

The Inspector's cheeks darkened to a crimson gray. "I think not," he snapped. "No. Not out of the state, Ellery."

Ellery drew his horns in very quickly indeed. So that was it!

"I wouldn't go, anyway," said Sheila listlessly. "I won't leave Dad. I didn't tell you that my father doesn't think he ought to leave. He says he's an old man and he won't start running away at his age. He wants me to go, but of course I can't. Not without him. It's all rather hopeless, isn't it?"

"No," smiled Ellery. "There's one person who can put a stop to all this."

"Huh?" The Inspector looked incredulous. "Who?"

"Cornelia Potts."

"The Old Woman?" Charley shook his head.

"But Mr. Queen—" began Sheila.

"Ellery," said Ellery. "You see, Sheila, your mother is the lord and the law in Potts Palace. At least to the three children of her first marriage. I have the ridiculous feeling suddenly that if she could be persuaded to issue an ultimatum—"

"You saw how hard she tried to stop the duel between Bob and Thurlow," said Sheila bitterly. "I tell you she wants us Brents dead. She's been happy about it in her own perverted way. She went to poor Mac's funeral to gloat! You're wasting your time, Ellery."

"I don't know," muttered Charley. "I'm not defending your mother, darling, but that's a bit hard on her, it seems to me. I think Ellery's right. She could put a stop to all this, and it's up to us to make her do it."

"It's an idea," said the Inspector unexpectedly. But it was evident he was thinking of other fish to fry. "As long as Sheila's mother is alive, she rules that roost. They'd quit on her say-so.... Yes. It's worth a try."

17

How the Old Woman
Got Home

They met Dr. Innis in the driveway. The physician had just driven up for his daily visit to the Old Woman.

They all went in together.

The Inspector kept a sharp eye out for his men. What he saw seemed to satisfy him. He grunted and stumped on upstairs, keeping his counsel.

Sheila kept saying: "I tell you it's hopeless," in a tone appropriate to the utterance.

At the top of the spiral staircase, Ellery said to Dr. Innis: "By the way, Doctor, Mrs. Potts seems to have come through this last heart attack and the death of Mac very well indeed. What would you say is the prognosis now?"

Dr. Innis shrugged. "You can't make over a heart like hers, Mr. Queen. We don't know very much about stamina, and the will to live. But that woman's alive this moment, I'm convinced, only because she wants to be. No other reason. In fact, there's every reason to believe her heart should have given out years ago."

"We may talk to her freely? There's one question I'm anxious to ask her, Doctor, that I should have asked long ago. And then we have a rather grim job."

The physician shrugged again. "I'm through trying to make people around here do what they ought to do. Every medical sign indicates that absolute rest and freedom from excitement are called for. I can only ask that you take as little time with her as possible."

"Fair enough."

"She'll live forever," said Sheila wildly. "She'll be alive when we're all dead."

Dr. Innis glanced at Sheila oddly as they went to the door of Cornelia Potts's apartment. He began to say something, but then Inspector Queen knocked softly, so he refrained. When there was no answer the Inspector opened the door and they went into the sitting room, and Dr. Innis opened the door to the bedroom.

"Mrs. Potts," said Dr. Innis.

The Old Woman lay in her incredible bed, rather high on two fat pillows, as usual, with her eyes open and her mouth open and the lace cap a trifle askew on her head.

Sheila screamed and ran, and Charley, crying out, ran after her.

"It's the good Lord's gospel," wept old Bridget. "She rings for me not an hour and a half gone, and she says I'm not to come blunderin' in, may she rest in peace, because seein' as how she wants to be alone, poor soul—alone with the good Lord and His heavenly saints, as it turns out, but how was a miserable sinner like me to know that? That's all I know, sir, so help me God.... Dead—the Old Woman dead! It's like the end of the world, it is."

Inspector Queen said harshly: "Don't monkey with that body, Doctor."

"I'm not monkeying," shrilled Dr. Innis. "You asked me to examine her, and I am. This woman was my patient, and she died while under my care, and it's my right to examine her, any-way! I have to sign the death certificate—"

"Gentlemen, gentlemen," said Ellery in a weary voice. "Did Cornelia Potts die in the conventional manner, Dr. Innis, or was she assisted into the hereafter? That's what I want to know."

"Death from natural causes, Mr. Queen. Heart gave out, that's all. She's been dead about one hour."

"Normal death." The Inspector gnawed his mustache, eyeing that silent, pudgy corpse as if he expected it at any moment to gush blood.

"Excitement and the strain of the past week have been too much for her. I warned you this was coming." Dr. Innis picked up his hat, bowed frigidly, and left.

"Just the same, *Dr. Innis*," said the Inspector under his breath, "old Doc Prouty's going to check your findings, and Jehovah help you if you're covering something up! Ellery, what are you doing?"

"It might be called," grunted Ellery, "'looking over the scene of the crime,' except that there seems to have been no crime, so let's call it simply finding out what the hell Cornelia Potts had been writing when the Dark Angel paid her his long-overdue visit."

"Writing?" The Inspector came over swiftly.

Ellery indicated the portable typewriter on its stand, beside the bed. Its case was on the floor, as if the machine had been used and death had come before the cover could be replaced. On the night table stood a large box of varisized notepapers and envelopes, its hinged lid thrown back.

"So what?" frowned the Inspector.

Ellery pointed to the dead woman's right hand. It was almost buried in the bedclothes, and the Inspector smoothed them a little to see better. What he saw made his brows huddle together over his eyes.

In Cornelia Potts's right hand lay a large sealed envelope, undoubtedly one of the envelopes from the box by her bed.

The Inspector snatched the envelope from the stiff hand and held it up to the light. The face bore the typewritten words: LAST

WILL AND TESTAMENT. Beneath this was the scrawled signature, in the broad strokes of the soft-leaded pencils the Old Woman affected: *Cornelia Potts*.

"I've got Sheila quiet," said Charley Paxton distractedly, running. "What is it? Murder, Ellery?"

"Dr. Innis pronounces it a natural death."

"I won't believe it till Doc Prouty tells me so," said Inspector Queen absently. "Charley, here's what we just found in Cornelia's hand. I thought you said she *had* a will."

"Yes." Charley took the proffered envelope with a frown. "Don't tell me she's made a *new* will!"

"I hardly think so," said Ellery. "Tell me, Charley. Did she have possession of the original of her will?"

"Oh, yes."

"Where did she usually keep it, do you know?"

"In the night-table drawer. Right by her bed."

Ellery looked into the drawer. It was empty.

"Was it in an envelope, or loose?"

"Not in an envelope the last time I saw it."

"Well, this is a fresh one, and the typing and signature look fresh, too, so I'd say she felt herself going, took the old will from the drawer, pulled over the portable, typed an envelope, scrawled her signature, and sealed the will in the envelope just before she died."

"I wonder why," mused the Inspector.

Ellery raised his brows.

The Inspector raised his shoulders. "Well, we'll find out when the will's opened after the funeral." He handed Charley Paxton the sealed envelope for safekeeping, and they left the Old Woman alone in her bed.

And so Cornelia Potts was dead, and that was the end of the world, as old Bridget Conniveley had sobbed, for a number of servants, many of whom had never known another mistress; it was the end of a dynasty for certain others whose memories were yellow-tinged; and for those who had been closest to the stiffly dead it was ... as nothing.

This was the remarkable thing about the Old Woman's death. It seemed to concern none of her children—not those she loved, nor Sheila whom she hated. Sheila after that first scream had felt a weight slip from her heart. She was ashamed, and frightened— and relieved.

Sheila remained in her quarters, resting and alone. Outside her door Detective Flint smoked a five-cent panatela and read a racing form.

As for the bereaved husband, he called quietly to his crony, Major Gotch, and the two men went into Steve Brent's room with two virgin fifths of Scotch and two whiskey glasses and shut themselves firmly in. An hour later they were singing Tahitian beach songs at the tops of their voices, uproariously.

18

Who'll Be Chief Mourner? "I!" Said the Dove

Dr. Prouty said that this was getting to be a personal affair and perhaps he had better resign from the Medical Examiner's office and become private mortician to the Pottses. "I'm getting to know 'em intimately," said Doc Prouty to Ellery, on the morning when he handed Inspector Queen his official post-mortem finding *in re* Cornelia Potts, deceased. "Now take the Old Woman. A fighter. She gave me a battle all the way. Not like those two fine sons of hers, Bob and Mac. She was a hell-raiser, all right. Could hardly do a thing with her."

Ellery, who was at breakfast, closed his eyes and murmured: "But the report, Prouty."

"Aaaa, she died of natural causes," said the Inspector before Prouty could reply. "At least that's what this old poop's report says."

"What are you so grumpy about, you cantankerous fuddy-duddy?" demanded Doc Prouty. "Haven't you had enough murders at that address? Are you disappointed?"

"Well, if she had to die," grumbled Inspector Queen, "I wish she'd done it in such a way as to leave some clue to this screwy business. Natural death! Go on, get back to your boneyard."

Dr. Prouty snarled and went out, muttering something about O base ingratitude thou are a viper's fang.

Now you must believe a wonderful thing, you who have read of the Pottses and their Shoe and their duels and their laboratories and their boys who never grew up and the improbable house they all lived in.

You must believe that this woman, this Old Woman, who had once inexplicably been a child and a girl and who married a dark character named Bacchus Potts and was thereafter bewitched by his name, who had founded a dynasty and built a pyramid and lived on its apex like a queen, who had spawned three dark children and lived to defend them with her considerable cunning against their own dark natures and so defend herself against the pricks of conscience—you must believe that this Cornelia Potts, who had lived only for those three, who had built and been ruthless only for those three, who had lied and scratched and spent her substance upon those three, who had cuffed them and nurtured them and kept them out of public institutions—you must believe that she went to her grave in St. Praxed's churchyard unattended by any of them, to lie by her sons whom she did not love and whose violent death meant no more to her than the violation of her sacred precincts—if indeed that much.

Mr. Ellery Queen took the astonishing census before and during the last rites. Mr. Queen was not interested in the details of the Old Woman's interment. She was dead of natural causes; *requiescat in pace*. But the three troglodytes of her womb—ah, Confusion!

Check them off, Mr. Queen:—*Louella*...The mother was an old pink goddess whose claws held the lever of life. She punished, she denied, she ruled. Yes, she endeavored to love. But what is love to Louella? A mating of guinea pigs (a most interesting experiment which Louella can watch tirelessly, and does). Love is an impediment: a wall, a wood of black and tangled depths standing between Louella and the temple, where the stuff of life may be played with in ritual worship. Good riddance, love.

Louella remains faithful to the sexless god of knowledge. In its fane there is no room for sentiment. Like all eunuchs, it is stern, and cruel, and above mankind... Louella could have seen the cortege making its way up Riverside Drive to St. Praxed's from her tower window, but Ellery doubted if she even bothered to straighten up from her packing cases.

For in the three days between her mother's death and funeral, Louella, the scientist, truly went mad of her science. Went mad with the relaxation of those biting claws of motherhood. Now there was no old pink goddess to say her nay, or even yea. Now there was a many-armed telephone, and the riches of all the laboratory supply houses of the world within its genie's reach.

Equipment poured in: an electric oven, retorts, racks of brilliant new test tubes, motors, a refrigerator, chemicals in blue, and brick, and yellow, and silver, and magenta—lovely colors, lovely colors... Louella was unpacking crates, clambering over boxes, in her tower all that day when her mother was borne up the Drive to eternity.

Horatio... Horatio fascinates Ellery Queen. Horatio is a phenomenon to Ellery, a mythological figure. Ellery was unceasingly astonished to see Horatio caper about the Potts estate in the quivering flesh. It was like seeing Silenus on Times Square grinning down from the moving news sign on the Times Building. It was like having Vulcan change your tire at Ye Olde Garage.

Horatio and Death have no *simpatico*. Horatio is above Death. Horatio is Youth, when Death is inconceivable, even the death of the old.

Informed by Ellery and Charley Paxton of his mother's death, Horatio scarcely turned a hair. "Come, come, gentlemen. Death is an illusion. My mother is still in that house, in her bed, being

147

crotchety about something." Horatio tossed a bean-bag frog into the air and caught it clumsily in its descent. "Always being crotchety about something, Mother," he boomed. "Good scout at heart, though."

"For heaven's sake, Horatio," cried Charley, "will you try to realize that she *isn't* in the house any more? That she's lying on a slab in the Morgue and that she'll be buried six feet deep in a couple of days?"

Horatio chuckled indulgently. "My dear Charley. Death is an illusion. We're all dead, and we're all living. We die when we grow up, we live when we're children. You're dead right now, only you haven't sense enough to lie down and be shoveled under. Same with you, sir," said Horatio, winking at Ellery. "Lie down, sir, and be shoveled under!"

"Aren't you even going to the funeral?" choked Charley.

"Gosh, no," said Horatio. "I've got a swell new kite to fly. It's simply super!" And he seized a large red apple and ran munching out into the gardens, joyously.

When the cortege passed, Horatio saw it. He must have seen it, for he was perched on the outer wall disentangling the cord of his swell new kite from the branches of an overhanging maple. He must have seen it, because instantly he turned his meaty back and jumped off the wall, abandoning his kite. He capered off towards his sugarloaf house, whistling *Little Boy Blue Come Blow Your Horn* bravely. Horatio didn't believe in Death, you see.

Thurlow... Thurlow, the Terror of the Plains, is a bold bad man this day. His not to display unmanly grief before the vulgar. His to mourn in the solitude of his apartment, hugging a bottle of cognac to his plump bosom. This is the way of men who are masculine. The mother is dead—God rest her, gentlemen. But let the son alone; he mourns.

Ellery suspected other Thurlovian thoughts, in the light of subsequent events. Ellery suspected that among Thurlow's thoughts ran one like a Wagnerian leitmotif: The Queen is dead; long live the King. Ellery suspected royalist thoughts because it

148

was evident shortly after the funeral that Thurlow had planned—during his manly, solitary session with the cognac—to seize his mother's ermine and seat himself upon her throne instanter.

No, Thurlow the Killer did not attend his mother's funeral. He had too many affairs of state to think through.

So, Old Woman, this is your final bitterness, that the children you loved turned their backs on you, and the child you hated came to weep at your grave.

Sheila wept without explanation, with Charley Paxton supporting her on one side and Stephen Brent on the other. Sheila wept, and Stephen Brent did not. He followed the coffin with his eyes into the grave, whiskey-reddened eyes without expression.

Major Gotch wore an old jacket of Horatio's, the only member of the household with a commensurate girth. The Major sneezed frequently and carried himself with great dignity. He seemed to regret the Old Woman's passing in a bibulous sort of way. As the earth clumped on the coffin, he was actually seen to shed a tear, at which he swiped surreptitiously with the back of Horatio's sleeve. But then a reporter was so unwise as to ask the Major what he was Major of, and where he had been honored with his Majority. Whereupon Major Gotch did an unmilitary thing: he kicked the press. There were some moments of confusion.

Another was there, a stranger both to Ellery Queen and to his father. He was an elderly gentleman with a pointed Yankee face and mild, observing eyes, dressed plainly but correctly, whom Sheila addressed as "Mr. Underhill." Mr. Underhill had the hands of a workman. Charley Paxton presented him to the Queens as the man who managed the Potts factories.

"Knew Cornelia when she was a young woman, Inspector," Mr. Underhill said, shaking his head. "She was always one to stand on her own two feet. I'm not saying she didn't have faults, but she always treated me fine, and I'm darned sorry to see her go." And he blew his nose exaggeratedly in the way men do at funerals.

No photographers allowed. No windy eulogy. Just a funeral

with a handful of curious passers-by and, beyond, the police cordon.

"So that's how the Old Woman got home," mumbled Mr. Queen as the last shovelful of earth was patted into place by the gravedigger's spade.

"How's that?" The Inspector was absently searching the faces of those beyond the cordon.

"Nothing. Nothing, Dad."

"Thought you said something. Well, that's over." The Inspector pulled his jacket more tightly about him. "Let's go back to the house and listen to the reading of the will." He sighed. "Who knows? There may be something there."

19

The Queen Wills It

Thurlow came downstairs grasping the bottle of cognac by the neck like a scepter. "In the library?" he squeaked, stepping high. "Yes, in the library. Very nice. Nice and proper." He paused gallantly to permit Sheila to precede him into the study. "I trust everything went off nicely at the funeral, my dear?" asked Thurlow.

Sheila swept by him with a noble loathing. Thurlow clucked, narrowed his eyes into a leer, and then, gravely, stepping higher, he crossed the threshold and waded into the study.

"Aren't the others c-coming?" asked Steve Brent.

"I've sent for them twice," replied Charles Hunter Paxton.

"What good would it do?" cried Sheila. Then she looked down and took a seat, flushing a little.

"Send for them again," suggested Inspector Queen.

Cuttins was summoned. Yes, he had delivered Mr. Paxton's message in person to Miss Louella and Mr. Horatio.

"Deliver it again," said Charley irritably. "We're not going to wait forever. Five minutes, Cuttins."

The butler bowed and drifted off.

No one spoke as they waited.

It was late afternoon and the westering sun was being coy above the Palisades. It sliced its blades into the library through the French doors, cutting the gilt of book titles, flicking Sheila's hair, stabbing at the dregs of gold in Thurlow's bottle. Ellery, looking about, thought he had never beheld Nature in such an undiplomatic mood. There should be no sharp sparkle in this place; it should be all browns and glooms and dullnesses.

He turned his attention to Thurlow. Thurlow's eyes were still narrowed in that absurd leer. I am master here, he seemed to say. Beware my wrath, for it is terrible. The Queen is dead—long live the King, and you'd better be good subjects! Read, read the will, slave; your master waits.

And Thurlow beamed upon them all: upon Sheila; upon Steve Brent, a haggard man ill at ease and out of place; upon quiet, watching Mr. Underhill; upon Major Gotch, who also sat uneasily, but in a corner, as if he felt himself tied to this house and these people only by the slenderest of Minoan threads; upon harassed Charley Paxton, who stood behind the small kneehole desk in one of the angles of the library, which he had used frequently to transact the Old Woman's business, and tapped a nervous tattoo upon the sealed envelope Inspector Queen had entrusted to his care; upon the Queens, who stood together near the door, forgotten, watching everything.

And no one spoke, and the mahogany grandfather clock which Cornelia Potts had hauled from her first "regular" house up north pick-picked away at the silence, patiently.

Cuttins reappeared in the doorway. "Miss Louella cannot be disturbed for anything," he announced to the opposite wall. "I am to say that she is engaged in a very important experiment. Mr. Horatio regrets that he cannot attend; I am to say that he is composing a verse and may lose his inspiration."

Sheila shuddered.

"All right, Cuttins. Close the door," said Charley.

Cuttins backed away; the Inspector made sure the door was shut. Charley picked up the sealed envelope.

"Just a moment," said Inspector Queen. He advanced to the desk and turned to face Thurlow. "Mr. Potts, you understand why I'm here?"

Thurlow blinked, looking uncertain. Then he beamed. "As a friend, of course. A friend in our sad troubles."

"No, Mr. Potts. As the officer in charge of the investigation of two murders which occurred in this house. I admit they're posers, and that we know very little about them, not even the motive...for sure. That's why I'm interested in your mother's will. Do you grasp that?"

Thurlow shrank a little. "Why do you tell me these things?" he asked in frightened tones. The King had run to cover.

"You're head of the family now, Mr. Potts, the eldest." Thurlow swelled again. "I want you to be sure everything's aboveboard. This envelope—" the Inspector took it from Charley— "was found in your mother's dead hand upstairs. The flap was pasted down tight, as you see it. We have not opened the envelope. It says it's Cornelia Potts's will, and it has her signature on it, but we've no way of knowing until it's opened for the first time, here in this room, whether it's her old will, which was made out many years ago, or a new will which she typed and signed just before she died.

"The odds are it's the old will, because we can find no one in the house who witnessed her signature the other day, as would have had to be done if your mother had made a new will. But new or old, this is her will, and I want you to be satisfied that nobody's putting one over on you or anybody else who might be mentioned in it. All clear, Mr. Potts?"

"Of course, of course," said Thurlow grandly, waving his bottle. "Very kind of you, I'm sure."

The Inspector grunted, tossing the envelope onto the desk. "Make sure you don't forget it, Mr. Potts," he said mildly. "Because there are a lot of witnesses in this room who won't." And he returned to Ellery's side and made a sign to Charley Paxton. Charley picked up the envelope again and ripped off an edge. He shook the envelope out. A blue-backed document fell to the desk.

"It's the old will, Inspector," said Charley, seizing it. "Here's the date and the notary's seal. You were right—she just put it into this envelope to get it ready for us…What's this?"

A smaller envelope, bearing a few typewritten lines, had fallen out of the folds of Cornelia Potts's will. Charley read the legend on the envelope aloud:—

To be opened after the reading of my will and the election of a new President of the Potts Shoe Company.

He turned the smaller envelope over; it was sealed. Charley stared inquiringly at the Queens.

Father and son came forward eagerly and examined the small envelope.

"Same typewriter."

"Yes, Dad. Also the same make of envelope as the larger one. There were both sizes in that box of stationery on her night table upstairs."

"So that's why she typed out a large envelope before she died."

"Yes. She wrote something on the portable, enclosed it in this smaller envelope, then enclosed envelope and the will from her night table in this large envelope." Ellery looked up at his friend. "Charley, you'd better get on with the formal reading. The sooner we can open this small envelope officially the sooner we'll find out what I feel in my bones is a vital clue in the case."

Charley Paxton read the will rapidly aloud. There was nothing important in it that the Queens had not heard from the Old Woman's own lips the day the Inspector had demanded she tell him the terms of her will.

There were, as she had said, three main provisions:—Upon her death her estate, after all legal debts, taxes, and expenses of the funeral had been paid, was to be divided "among my surviving children" share and share alike. Stephen, "my husband by my second marriage," was to get no share whatever, "either in real or personal property." The election of a new President of the Board of Directors of the Potts Shoe Company was to be held immediately upon her death, or as soon after the funeral as possible.

The Board, as currently constituted, comprised the Potts family (except for Stephen Brent Potts). The new Board was to be the same, plus Simon Bradford Underhill, superintendent of the factories, who was, like the others, to have one vote.

"While the enforcement of this provision is not strictly speaking within my powers as testatrix" (Charley Paxton read), "I nevertheless enjoin my children to obey it. Underhill knows the business better than any of them."

There were certain minor provisions:—The Potts property on Riverside Drive was to remain the joint property of "my designated heirs." "All of my clothing is to be burned." "My Bible, my dental plates, my wedding rings" were bequeathed to "my daughter Louella."

That was all. No bequests to charity, no bequests to old Bridget or the other servants, no endowments to universities or gifts to churches. No specific mention of her daughter Sheila or of her sons Robert and Maclyn. Or of Major Gotch.

Thurlow Potts listened with an indulgent expression, his eyes nearly closed and his head nodding benevolently with every sentence, as if to say: "Quite so. Quite so."

"Dental plates," muttered the Inspector.

Charley finished reading and began to put the will down. But then he looked startled and picked it up again. "There's a...codicil at the bottom of this last sheet, under the signatures of testatrix and witnesses," he exclaimed. "Something typed in and typesigned 'Cornelia Potts'..." He scanned it quickly, his eyes widening.

"What is it?" demanded Ellery Queen. "Here, let me see that, Charley."

155

"I'll read it to you," said Charley grimly. That forbidding tone sat Thurlow upright in his chair and brought the others half out of theirs.

"It says: 'Hold the Board of Directors meeting right after the reading of the will. As soon as a new President of the Potts Shoe Company is elected, open the enclosed sealed envelope—'"

"But we know that," said Ellery with a trace of impatience. "That's practically the same thing she typewrote on the small envelope itself."

"Wait. This message attached to the will isn't finished." Charley was tense. "It goes on to say: *The statement inside the small envelope will tell the authorities who killed my sons Robert and Maclyn.*'"

20

The Old Woman's Tale

Inspector Queen bounded across the room. "Give me that envelope!" He snatched it and held it fast, glaring about as if he expected someone to try to take it away from him.

"She knew," said Sheila in a wondering voice.

"She knew?" cried her father.

Major Gotch rubbed his jaw agitatedly.

Thurlow grasped the arms of his chair.

At the door Mr. Queen had not stirred.

"Hold that blasted Board meeting right now!" the Inspector yapped. "Can't do a thing without that Board meeting. Come on, get it over with. I want to open this envelope!" He chuckled and peered at the envelope. "She knew," he chortled. "The old harridan knew all along, bless her." Then he growled to Charley: "Did you hear what I said? Get it over with!"

Charley stammered something ridiculously like "Y-yes, sir," and then he shook his head. "I've got nothing to do with the Board, Inspector. No power and no authority."

"Well, who has? Speak up!"

"I should imagine if anyone has to take charge, it's Thurlow.

Cornelia was President—she's dead. Bob and Mac were Vice-presidents—and they're dead. Thurlow's the only officer left."

Thurlow rose, frightened.

"All right, Mr. Potts," said the Inspector testily. "Don't just stand there. Call your Board to order and start nominating, or whatever it is you're supposed to do."

Thurlow drew himself up. "I know my duties. Charles—I'll sit at that desk, *if* you please."

Charley shrugged and went over to sit with Sheila, who took his hand in hers but did not look at him.

Thurlow edged behind the desk, picked up a paperweight, and rapped with it.

"The meeting will come to order," he said, and harrumphed. "As we all know, my dear mother has passed on, and—"

"Kindly omit flowers," said Inspector Queen.

Thurlow flushed. "You make this difficult, Inspector Queen, most difficult. Things must be done decorously, decorously. Now the first question is the question of—" Thurlow paused, then continued in an acid, querulous tone, "Simon Bradford Underhill. He has not been a member of this Board—"

"Least I can do, Thurlow." The speaker was Underhill, and he was smiling very sadly. "Cornelia's request, you know."

Thurlow frowned. "Yes. Yes, Underhill, I know." He cleared his throat again. "Wouldn't dream of having it otherwise." He sat down suddenly in the chair behind the desk; it might almost be said that he fell down. He looked longingly at the bottle of cognac, which he had left behind him in the other chair. Then he harrumphed a few more times and said sternly: "I believe we have a quorum. I will accept nominations for the Presidency of the Board of Directors of the Potts Shoe Company." And now Thurlow did an extraordinary thing: he rose, circled the desk, faced the unoccupied chair, said: "I nominate myself," nodded defiantly, then went round the desk again and reseated himself. "Any other nominations?"

Sheila sprang to her feet, her dimples plunging deep. "This is

158

the last straw! Everybody here knows you haven't the ability to manage a peanut stand, let alone a business that earns millions every year!"

"What's that? What's that?" said Thurlow excitedly.

"You'd ruin the company in a year, Thurlow. My brothers Bob and Mac *ran* this business, and you've never had a single constructive thing to do with it! All you ever did was make ridiculous mistakes. And you've got the nerve to nominate yourself President!"

"Now Sh-Sheila," stuttered her father. "Don't upset yourself, d-dear ..."

"Dad, you know yourself that if the twins were alive, one of them would have become the new head of the firm to take Mother's place. You *know* it!"

Thurlow found his voice. "Sheila, if you weren't a female—"

"I know, you'd challenge me to a duel," said Sheila bitterly. "Well, your dueling days are over, Mr. Potts. And you're not going to ruin the company. I'd nominate Daddy if he were a member of the Board—"

"Stephen?" Thurlow gazed with astonishment at his stepfather, as if he had never contemplated the possibility of such a watery character's usurping his prerogatives.

"But since I can't I nominate Mr. Underhill," cried Sheila. "Mr. Underhill, please. At least you know the business, you know how to make shoes, you're the oldest employee, you own stock in the company—"

Thurlow now turned his astonishment upon the lean old Yankee.

But Underhill shook his head. "I'm very grateful, Sheila. But I can't accept the nomination. I'm an outsider. You know how set your mother was about keeping the firm in the family—"

Thurlow nodded vigorously. "That's right. Underhill's got no business sticking his nose in at all. I won't let him be President. I'll discharge him first—"

Color stained the old man's cheeks. "Now that makes me

mad, Thurlow. That makes me real mad. Sheila, I've changed my mind. I'll accept that nomination, by Godfrey!"

The Inspector stamped. "My envelope!" he cried. "For Joe's sake, get this musical comedy over with!"

Thurlow looked desperate. Suddenly he shouted: "Wait!" and scuttled out of the library.

The delay caused by Thurlow's disappearance almost reduced the Inspector to tears. He kept looking at the sealed envelope piteously, looking at his watch, sending Sergeant Velie "to see what that oakum-headed fool Thurlow's up to," and occasionally berating Ellery in a bitter undertone for standing there and doing nothing.

"Play it out, Dad," was all Ellery would reply.

Eventually Thurlow returned, and the meeting was resumed. Thurlow looked smug. Something bulged in his breast pocket which Sergeant Velie, who had followed him, whispered to the Inspector was "papers, some kind of papers. He's been racin' all over the joint wavin' papers."

"Meeting will come to order again," said Thurlow briskly. "Any other nominations? No? Then we will proceed to a vote by the showing of hands. The nominees are Simon Bradford Underhill and Thurlow Potts. All those in favor of Mr. Underhill who have a legal vote on this Board please signify by raising your hands."

Two hands went up—Sheila's, and Underhill's.

"Two votes for Mr. Underhill." Thurlow smacked his lips. "Now. I have here," and he brought out of his pocket two envelopes, unsealed, "the absentee votes of the other members of this Board, Louella Potts and Horatio Potts. I have their votes by proxy."

Sheila paled.

"Louella Potts." Thurlow drew from one of the envelopes a signed statement. "Votes for Thurlow Potts." He threw down Louella's paper with a disdainful gesture and took up the second envelope. "Horatio Potts. Votes for Thurlow Potts." And

Thurlow Potts held up one pudgy hand triumphantly. "Tally—two votes for Underhill, three for Thurlow Potts. Thurlow Potts is elected President of the Board of Directors of the Potts Shoe Company by a plurality of one."

Thurlow rapped on the desk. "The meeting is adjourned."

"No," said Sheila in a voice full of hate. "No!"

Charley gripped her shoulder.

"Finished?" Inspector Queen strode forward. "In that case, we'll get down to business. Ellery, open this smaller envelope!"

Ellery wielded a letter knife on Cornelia Potts's envelope, slowly. This letter was going to do something final to the Potts murder case: it would name the murderer. Why this should annoy him Mr. Queen did not quite know, except the patently outlandish reason that the naming of murderers had always been a Queen specialty.

They had forgotten the small envelope in their absorption with the Board election. Now they watched him unfold a single long typewritten sheet, and scan it, and there was no sound of anything but the pick-picking of the grandfather clock.

"Well?" cried the Inspector.

Ellery replied in a quite flat voice: "This is the letter Cornelia Potts wrote. It is dated the afternoon of her death, the time specified being 3.35 P.M. The message goes:—

I, Cornelia Potts, being of sound mind and in full possession of my faculties, and knowing that I am shortly to die of my heart ailment, and in prayer that I may be forgiven in Heaven for what I have done, make this statement:

I ask not the world to judge me, for what I have done will be condemned by the world as if it were a fixed jury and I know that its judgment will be prejudiced.

Only a mother knows what motherhood is, how the mother loves the weak and hates the strong.

I have always loved my children Thurlow, Louella, and Horatio. Their weaknesses cannot be laid to them. They are what they

161

are because of their father, my first husband. This I came to know shortly after he disappeared; and I have never forgiven him for it. May he rot. I took his name and made something of it; it is more than he ever did for me or mine.

My first children have always needed me, and I have always been their strength and their defender. The children of my second marriage have never needed me. I hated the twins for their independence and their strength; I hate Sheila for hers. Their very existence has been a daily reminder to me of the folly and tragedy of my first marriage, to Bacchus Potts. I have hated them since their childhood for their health, for their laughter, for their cleverness, for their sanity.

I, Cornelia Potts, killed my twin sons Robert and Maclyn.

It was I who substituted the bullet for the blank cartridge the police had put into Thurlow's weapon. It was I who took the Harrington & Richardson revolver from Thurlow's hiding place with which I held up the newspaper people and made them leave my estate. Later it was I who stole one of Thurlow's other guns and hid it from the police and went with it into my son Maclyn's bedroom in the middle of the night and shot him with it—yes, and whipped him.

I will be called a monster. Perhaps. Let the world cast stones at me—I shall be dead.

I confess these crimes of my own free will, and let this be an end to them. I will answer for them before my Creator.

"The letter," continued Ellery Queen in the same even voice, "is signed in the usual soft-pencil scrawl, 'Cornelia Potts.' Dad," he said, "let's have a look at the Old Woman's other two written signatures—the one on the big envelope and the one on the will."

It was still in the room.

Ellery looked up. "The signature on this confession," he announced, "is the authentic handwriting of Cornelia Potts."

Sheila threw back her head and laughed and laughed.

"I'm glad," she gasped. "I'm glad! Glad she was the one. Glad she's dead. Now I'm free. Daddy's free. We're safe. There won't be any more murders. There won't be any more murders. There won't be any ..."

Charley Paxton caught her as she crumpled.

The Inspector very carefully pocketed Cornelia Potts's will, her confession, and the two envelopes.

"For the record," he grunted. The Inspector looked tired, but relaxed. He glanced about the empty study, the overturned chair in which Sheila had been sitting, the desk, the books twinkling their titles in the playful sun. "That's that, Ellery. Case of Potts and Potts *kaput*, killed off like a case of Irish whiskey at a wake." He sighed. "A nasty business from beginning to end, and I'm glad to be rid of it."

"If you are rid of it," said Ellery fretfully.

The Inspector stiffened. "If? Did you say 'if,' son?"

"Yes, Dad."

"Don't go highfalutin on me, for cripe's sake," groaned the Inspector. "Aren't you ever satisfied?"

"Not when there's a ragtag end."

"Talk English!"

Ellery lit a cigarette. He blew smoke at the ceiling without relish, swinging his leg idly against the desk on which he was perched. "One thing bothers me, Dad. I wish it didn't but it does." He frowned. "I don't think I'll ever be able to sweep it out of my skull."

"What's that?" asked his father, almost with fear.

"There's still a gun missing."

Part Four

21

The Uneasiness of Heads

Now was the winter of their discontent, and that was strange, for the Potts case was solved. Wasn't there a confession? Hadn't the newspapers leaped upon it with venal joy? Weren't old cuts of Landru lifted from morgues the length and breadth of the land? Didn't the tabloids begin to serialize still again that old standby of circulation joggers, *Famous Murders of Fact and Fiction?* Was not Herod evoked, and Lady Macbeth?

One tabloid printed a cartoon of the Old Woman, smoking gun in hand, sons writhing at her feet, with the witty inscription: "He that spareth his *rod* hateth his son. (PROVERBS, XIII, 24.)" A more dignified journalist résumé began with the quotation: "Innocent babes writhed on thy stubborn spear…(P. B. SHELLEY, *Queen Mab*, VI)."

But Ellery Queen thought the Order of the Bloodstained Footprint should have been awarded to the wag who resurrected the old labor-capital cartoon of the Old Woman in the Shoe, with her six children tumbling out, across two of whom however he now painted large black X's, and composed to explain it the following quatrain:—

167

There was an Old Woman who lived in a Shoe,
She had so many children she didn't know what to do,
She started to slaughter them, one child by one,
Only Death overtook her before she was done.

Work was begun in the studio of a Coney Island waxworks museum on a tableau, showing Maclyn Potts lying agonized in a bed weltering in thick red stuff, while the chubby figure of his mother, clad in voluminous black garments and wearing a black shawl and bonnet tied under the chin, gloated over the corpse like some demonized little Queen Victoria.

Several eggs, coming over the wall from Riverside Drive, splashed against the Shoe the afternoon the newspapers announced the discovery of the Old Woman's confession.

A stone broke Thurlow Potts's bedroom window, sending him into a white-lipped oration on the Preservation of Law and Order; a charge of criminal mischief went begging only because of Thurlow's failure to identify the miscreant.

Various detectives of Inspector Queen's staff went home for the first time in days to visit with their children. Sergeant Velie's wife prepared a mustard bath for his large feet and tucked him into bed full of aspirin and love.

Only in the apartment of the Queens were there signs that all was not well. Usually at the conclusion of a case Inspector Queen made jokes and ordered two-inch steaks which he devoured with the gusto of one who has labored well and merits appropriate reward. Now he scarcely ate at all, glowering when spoken to, was grumpy with Ellery, and fell back into the routine of his office without enjoyment.

As for Ellery Queen, it could not be said that his spirits soared above sea level. There was no taste in anything, matter or music. He went back to a detective novel he had been composing when the case of the Old Woman and her six children had thrown it into eclipse; but the shadow was still there, hanging heavily over the puppets of his imagination and making the words seem just

168

words. He went over the Potts case in his mind endlessly; he fell asleep to the scudding of far-fetched theories.

But the days came and went, the house on Riverside Drive gradually became just a house, the newspapers turned to fresh sensations, and it began to appear that the Potts case had already passed into criminal history, to be no more than a footnote or a paragraph in some morbid reference book of the future.

One morning, three weeks after the disclosures in Cornelia Potts's confession had officially closed the dossier on the case, Inspector Queen was about to leave for Police Headquarters—he had already grunted "Toodle-oo" to his son, who was still at breakfast—when suddenly he turned back from the door and said: "By the way, Ellery, I got a cable yesterday afternoon from the Dutch East Indies."

"Dutch East Indies?" Ellery absently looked up from his eggs.

"Batavia. The prefect or commissioner of police there, or whatever they call him. You know, in reply to my cable about Major Gotch."

"Oh," said Ellery. He set down his spoon.

"The cable says Gotch has no record down there. I thought you'd like to know...just to clear up a point."

"No record? You mean they haven't anything on him?"

"Not a thing. Never even heard of the old windbag."

The Inspector sucked his mustache. "Doesn't mean much. All I could give them was the name and description of a man forty years older than he'd been if he'd ever been there, and what's in a name? Or else Gotch is just a liar—a lot of these old-timers are—even though he swore he'd raised Cain in the Dutch East Indies in his time."

Ellery lit a cigaret, frowning over the match. "Thanks."

The Inspector hesitated. Then he came back and sat down, tipping his hat over his eyes as if in shame. "The Potts case is a closed book and all that, son, but I've been meaning to ask you—"

"What, Dad?"

"When we were talking over motives, you said you'd figured out that this old Major had a possible motive, too. Not that it's of any importance now—"

"I also said, I believe, that it was impossibly fantastic."

"Never mind knocking yourself out," snapped his father. "What did you have in mind?"

Ellery shrugged. "Remember the day we went over to the Potts house to ask the Old Woman to use her authority to stop the killings, and found her lying dead in bed?"

"Yes?" The Inspector licked his lips.

"Remember on the way upstairs I said to Dr. Innis that there was one question I'd been meaning to ask Mrs. Potts?"

"I sure do. What was the question?"

"I was going to ask her," said Ellery deliberately, "whether she'd ever seen her first husband again."

Inspector Queen gaped. "Her *first* husband? You mean this Bacchus Potts?"

"Who else?"

"But he's dead."

"Dead in law, Dad. That's quite another thing from being dead in fact. It struck me at one point in the case that Bacchus Potts might be very much alive still."

"Hunh." The Inspector was silent. Then he said: "That hadn't occurred to me. But you haven't answered my question. What did you have in mind when you said Major Gotch had a possible motive, too?"

"But I have answered your question, Dad."

"You…mean…Bacchus…Potts…Major Gotch—" The Inspector began to laugh, and soon he was wiping away the merry tears. "I'm glad the case *is* over," he choked. "Another week and you'd have been measured for a restraining sheet yourself!"

"Amuse yourself," murmured his son, unruffled. "I told you it was fantastic. But on the other hand, why not? Gotch *might* be Potts the First."

"And I might be Richard the Second," chuckled his father.

"Fascinating speculation at the time, as I recall it," murmured Ellery. "Cornelia Potts has her husband declared dead after he's been absent seven years. She marries Steve Brent. He has a companion, 'Major Gotch.' Many years have passed since she last saw hubby number one, and the tropics change physiognomies wonderfully. Suddenly Cornelia discovers that Major Gotch is none other than Bacchus Potts! Makes her a bigamist, or does it? Anyway, it's an embarrassing situation."

"Rave on."

"And the worst of it is, 'Major Gotch' has found himself a comfortable nest. Sees no point in waving farewell. Pals with the new husband, and all that. New husband defends him. Cornelia's trapped...That theory appealed to me, Dad, wild as it was. Charley Paxton, in telling me the story of the Old Woman's life, had been vague—as well he might be!—about Cornelia's reason for permitting Gotch to live in her household. Mightn't that have been the reason? A hold Gotch had on her? That she wasn't legally married to Brent and therefore her children—her reputation—her business—?"

"Hold it," said the Inspector testily. "I'm an idiot for listening to this fairy tale, but suppose Gotch *is* Potts the First. What motive for murdering the twins would that give him?"

"The two husbands, inseparable companions," said Ellery dreamily, "living in the same house, playing endless checker tournaments with each other...What? Oh, his possible motive. Well, Dad, we agreed at the time that the Potts clan may have been going through a process of liquidation, one member at a time. And who were liquidated? Sheila Brent spotted it immediately. Only the sane ones were dying. The Brents."

"So?"

"So suppose the first Potts *had* come back in the person of 'Major Gotch'? Mightn't he come to hate his successor, the second Potts—no matter how fast their friendship had been in the atolls of the South Seas?"

"Aaaa," said the Inspector.

"Mightn't he come to hate the three additional children Cornelia and Steve Brent brought into the world? Mightn't he resent the shares of Sheila, Bob, and Mac in what would seem to him *his* millions? Mightn't he reason, too, that their very existence jeopardized the security of his own children, the Three Goons—Thurlow, Louella, and Horatio? And because of all this, mightn't Bacchus Potts's 'Gotch' brood and plan and finally go over the deep end and begin to eliminate those not of his blood?—one by one?—Robert, Maclyn, then Sheila, and finally Steve Brent himself? Don't forget, Dad, if Gotch is Potts, he's insane. Potts's three children are proof enough of *that*."

The Inspector shook his head. "I'm glad the Old Woman's confession spared you the embarrassment of having to spout *that* theory!"

"The Old Woman's confession…" echoed Ellery in a queer tone.

"What's the matter with the Old Woman's confession?" The Inspector sat up straight.

"Your tone—"

"Did I say anything was the matter with it?"

"It's my gout, Father," smiled Mr. Queen. "My gout? I must remember to take the waters."

The Inspector threw a cushion at him. "And I must remember to send that will and confession back to Paxton. We've got photostatic copies for the files, but the pay-off is that Thurlow—Thurlow!—wants the confession for 'the family records'!…Oh, son." The Inspector stuck his head back through the doorway, grinning. "I promise not to tell a soul about that Gotch-is-Potts theory of yours."

Ellery threw the cushion back.

For Ellery Queen the path of literature this morning was paved merely with good intentions. He scowled at his typewriter for almost an hour without pecking a word. When he finally did begin to write, he found the usual digital difficulties insuperable. He had developed a mysterious habit of shifting the position of his hands one key to the left, so that when he thought he had written the sentence: "There were bloody stripes on Lecky's right elbow," he found that it actually read—more interestingly but less comprehensibly—"Rgwew qwew vkiist areuowa ib Kwzjt&a eufgr wkviq." This he felt would place an unfair burden upon his readers; so he ripped the sheet out and essayed a new start. But this time he decided that there was no special point to putting bloody stripes on Lecky's right elbow, so there he was, back at the beginning. Curse all typewriters and his clumsiness with them!

Really ought to have a stenographer, he brooded. Take all this distracting mechanical work off his hands. A stenographer with honey-colored hair...no, red hair. Small. Perky. But sensible. Not the kind that chewed gum; no. A small warm package of goodies. Of course, purely for stenographic purposes. No reason why a writer's stenographer shouldn't also be inoffensive to the eye, was there? In fact, downright pleasant to look at? Like Sheila Brent, for instance. Sheila Brent ...

Ellery was seated before his reproachful machine a half hour later, hands clasped behind his head and a self-pitying smile on his face, when the doorbell rang. He started guiltily when he saw who his caller was. "Charley!"

"Hullo," said Charley Paxton glumly. He scaled his hat across the room and dropped into the Inspector's sacred armchair. "Have you got a Scotch and soda? I'm pooped."

"Of course," said Ellery keenly. As he busied himself being host, he watched Charley out of the corner of his eyes. Mr. Paxton was looking poorly. "What's the matter? Strain of normal living proving too much for you, Charley?"

Charley grinned feebly. "It's a fact there hasn't been a murder in almost a month. Tedious!"

"Here's your drink. Why haven't I seen you since confessional?"

"Conf—Oh. *That* day." Charley scowled into his glass. "Hands full. Keeping the mobs of salesmen away from the Potts Palladium, as you call it. Handling a thousand legal details of the estate."

"Is it as large as you estimated?"

"Larger."

"I suppose a niggardly million or so?"

"Some pittance like that."

"How's Sheila?"

Charley did not answer for a moment. Then he raised his hollow eyes. "That's one of the reasons I came here today."

"Nothing wrong with Sheila, I hope?" Ellery said quickly.

"Wrong? No." Charley began to patrol the Queen living room.

"Oh. Things aren't going so well between you and Sheila—is that it?"

"That's putting it mildly."

"And I thought," murmured Mr. Queen, "that you'd come to invite me to the wedding."

"Wedding!" said Charley bitterly. "I'm further from the altar now than I ever was. Every time I say: 'When are we going to take the jump?' Sheila starts to cry and say she's the daughter of a two-times killer, and she won't saddle me with a murderess for a mother-in-law, even if she *is* dead, and a lot of similar hooey. I can't even get her to move out of that damned house. Won't leave old Steve, and Steve says he's too decrepit to start bumming again.... It's hopeless, Ellery."

"I can't understand that girl," mused Ellery.

"It's the same old madhouse, only worse, now that the Old Woman's not there to crack down. Louella's filling it with useless, expensive apparatus—I swear she'll blow that place up some night!—buying on credit, and of course she's getting all she wants now that the Old Woman's dead and the trades-people know what a lulu of a fortune Louella's coming into.

"Thurlow's lording it over them all—cock of the roost, Thurlow is. Sits at the head of the table and makes with the lofty cracks to Steve and Major Gotch, and is otherwise a complete pain in the—"

"As I was saying," said Ellery, "Sheila baffles me. Her attitude strikes me as inconsistent with my conception of the whole

174

woman. Charley, there's something wrong somewhere, and it's up to you to find out what."

"Of course there's something wrong. She won't marry me!"

"Not that, Charley. Something else...Wish I knew...Might make..." Mr. Queen stopped guillotining his sentences in order to think. Then he said crisply: "As for you, my dear Gascon, my advice is to stick to it. Sheila's worth fighting for. Matter of fact," he sighed, "I'm inclined to be envious."

Charley looked startled.

Ellery smiled sadly. "It won't come to a duel at dawn, I promise you. You're her man, Charley. But just the same—"

Charley began to laugh. "And I come here to ask your advice. John Alden stuff!" His grin faded. "Say, I'm sorry as hell, Ellery. Although as far as I can see, anybody's got a better chance with Sheila than I have."

"She loves you. All you have to do is be patient and understanding, now that the case is closed—"

Charley stopped pacing. "Ellery," he said.

"What?"

"That's another reason I came to see you today."

"What's another reason you came to see me today?"

Charley lowered his voice. "I don't think the case *is* closed."

Ellery Queen said "Ah," and turned around like a dog seeking a place to settle. Instead, he freshened Charley Paxton's drink and mixed one for himself. "Sit down, Brother Paxton, and tell Papa all about it."

"I've been thinking—"

"That's always salutary."

"Two things still bother me. So much I can't sleep—"

"Yes?" Ellery did not mention his own insomnia of the past three weeks.

"Remember the Old Woman's confession?"

"I think so," said Ellery dryly.

"Well, one statement the Old Woman made in it strikes me as pretty peculiar," said Charley slowly.

"Which statement is that?"

"The one about the guns. She wrote she was the one who swiped the Harrington & Richardson revolver from Thurlow with which she held up the reporters the day of the first murder—the gun she almost killed Sergeant Velie with—"

"Yes, yes."

"Then she said: 'Later it was I who stole one of Thurlow's other guns and hid it from the police and went with it into my son Maclyn's bedroom in the middle of the night and shot him with it.'"

"Yes?"

"'*One* of Thurlow's other guns'!" exclaimed Charley. "But Ellery, *there were two guns missing.*"

"Indeed," said Ellery, as if he had never thought of that. "What do you make of it, Charley?"

"But don't you see?" cried the young lawyer. "What happened to that second gun, the one that's still missing? Where is it? Who has it? If it's still in the house, isn't Sheila in danger?"

"How's that?"

"Thurlow, Louella, Horatio! Suppose one of those poppy-eaters takes it into his head to continue the Old Woman's massacre on the Brent part of the family? Anything is possible with those three, Ellery. They hate Sheila and Steve as much as the Old Woman—maybe more. What do you think?"

"I've concocted more fantastic theories myself," murmured Mr. Queen. "Go on talking, Charley. I've been pining to discuss the case for three weeks now, but I haven't dared for fear I'd be disowned."

"I've been bursting, too! I can't get these thoughts out of my mind. I've had another—theory, suspicion, whatever you choose to call it. This one's driving me wild."

Ellery looked comforted. "Talk."

"The Old Woman knew she was going to die, Ellery. She said so in her confession, didn't she?"

"She did."

"Suppose she thought one of her precious darlings had killed the twins! She knew she was dying, *so what did she have to lose by taking the blame on herself?*"

"You mean—"

"I mean," said Charley tensely, "that maybe the Old Woman's confession was a phony, Ellery. I mean that maybe she was covering up for one of her crazy gang—*that there's still an active killer in that house.*"

Ellery swigged deeply. When he set his glass down, he said: "My dear fraternal sleuth, that was the first thought I had when we opened the envelope and read the Old Woman's confession."

"Then you agree it's possible?"

"Of course it's possible," said Ellery slowly. "It's even probable. I just can't see Cornelia Potts killing those two boys. But—" He shrugged. "My doubts and yours, Charley, won't stand up against that confession bearing Cornelia Potts's signature.... By George!" he said.

"What's the matter?"

Ellery jumped up. "Listen to this, Charley! The Old Woman was dead an hour or so at the time we found her body. Suppose someone had gone into her bedroom during that hour she lay there dead? The door wasn't locked. And anyone could have typed out that confession right there—on the portable which was standing conveniently by the bed!"

"You think someone, the real killer, *forged* that confession, Ellery?" gasped Charley. "I hadn't thought of that!" But then he shook his head.

"I didn't say I think so. I said it's possible," said Ellery irritably. "Possible, possible! That's all I do in this blasted case—call things 'possible'! What are you shaking your head for?"

"The Old Woman's signature, Ellery," said Charley in a depressed tone. "You compared it yourself with the other signatures—the one at the end of the will, the one on the large envelope. And you pronounced the signature genuine."

"There's the rub, I admit," muttered Ellery. "On the other

hand, it was only a quick examination. It might be an extremely clever forgery that only the most minute study will disclose. The traps one's sense of infallibility sets! Stop feeling sorry for yourself, Mr. Queen, and start punching!"

"We've got to go over the signatures again?"

"What else?" Ellery clapped Charley on the shoulder. Then he fell into a study. "Charley. Remember when we visited the Old Woman early in the case to question her about the terms of her will? At that time, I recall, she handed you a slough of memorandums. I saw her sign them myself with the same soft pencil she apparently used always. What happened to those memos?"

"They're at the house, in that kneehole desk in the downstairs study."

"Well, those memos bear her authentic signature; that I'll swear to. Come on."

"To the house?"

"Yes. But first we'll stop at Headquarters and pick up the original of the confession, Charley. Maybe *one* theory in this puzzle will come out right side up!"

22

Mene, Mene, Tekel, Upharsin

They found no one about but the servants, as usual. So they made directly for the library, and Ellery shut the door, rubbing his palms together, and said: "To work. Those signed memos, please."

Charley began rummaging through the drawers of the knee-hole desk. "Got the shakes," he muttered. "If it's only...Here they are. What do we do now?"

Ellery did not reply at once. He riffled the sheaf of memorandums with an air of satisfaction. "Employ the services of a rather large ally," he said. "Nice sunny day, isn't it?"

"What?"

"Silence, brother, and reap 'the harvest of a quiet eye,' as Wordsworth recommends."

"Seems to me you're in an awfully good humor," grumbled Charley Paxton.

"Forgive me. This is like a breath of forest air to a man who's been shut up in a dungeon for three weeks. It's hope, Charley, that's what it is."

"Hope of what? More danger for Sheila?"

"Hope of the truth," cried Ellery. He went to the nearest window. The sun, that "large ally," made the window brilliant; by contrast, the study was in gloom.

"Perfect." Ellery took the topmost memorandum of the sheaf and held it flat against the pane with his left hand. The sunshine made the white paper translucent.

"The confession, Charley. Wasn't Dad curious!"

Ellery placed the confession over the memorandum on the windowpane, shifting it about until its signature lay superimposed upon the signature of the memorandum, visible through it. Then he studied the result. "No."

The signatures were obviously written by the same hand, but minor variations in the formation and length of certain letters caused a slight blurry effect when the two signatures were compared, one upon the other.

Ellery handed the memorandum to the lawyer. "Another memo, Charley."

Charley was puzzled. "I don't understand what you're doing."

"No," said Ellery again. "Not this one, either. *And* the next, Mr. Paxton."

When he had exhausted the pile of memorandums, he said to Charley in an assured voice: "Would you mind handing me again that memo which instructed you to sell all the Potts Shoe Company stock and buy back at 72?"

"But you've examined it!"

"Nevertheless."

Charley located it in the heap and handed it to him. Ellery once more placed it over the confession against the window.

"Look here, Charley. What do you see?"

"You mean the signatures?"

"Yes."

Charley looked. And then he said in an astonished voice: "*No blurriness!*"

"Exactly." Ellery took the papers down. "In other words, the

Cornelia Potts signature on this stock-selling memorandum and the Cornelia Potts signature on the confession *match perfectly.* There are no slightest variations in the formation and size of characters. Line for line, curve for curve, the two signatures are exact duplicates. Twins, like Bob and Mac. Even the dot over the *i* is in the identical spot."

"And the signature on the stock-selling memo is the *only* memo signature that does match exactly?" asked Charley hoarsely.

"That's why I went through the entire batch—to make sure. Yes, it's the only one."

"I think I see where all this leads ..."

"But it's so clear! No one ever writes his name in precisely the same way twice—that's a scientific fact. There are invariably minor differences in the same person's signature, and there would be if you had a million samples to compare. Charley, we've established a new fact in the Potts case!"

"*One of these two signatures is a forgery.*"

"Yes."

"But which one?"

"Come, Charley. The Old Woman signed this stock-selling memo in our presence. Therefore the memo signature must be genuine. Therefore the signature on the confession is the forgery."

"Somebody got hold of this memo, typed out that phony confession, and then traced the signature of the memo off of the bottom of the confession?"

"Only way it could have produced an identical signature; yes, Charley. The stock memo's been in the desk in this study since the day the Old Woman typed out all these instructions—"

"Yes," mumbled Charley. "After I made the various phone calls necessary that day, I put the memos in this desk, as usual...."

"So anyone in the house could have found them and used this one to trace off its signature. It was probably done just the way I've illustrated—by slapping the stock memo against the sunny windowpane, placing the typed confession over the memo, and then tracing the memo signature onto the confession by utilizing the sunlight-created translucence of both sheets."

"And the house is full of those soft pencils the Old Woman used—"

"And it would have been child's play to slip into the Old Woman's bedroom and use her portable typewriter for the typing of the 'confession' and that note at the bottom of the will. The whole operation was undoubtedly done between the time the Old Woman died alone in her bed and the time we all came back to the house—you, Sheila, Dad, and I—and found her body with the large sealed envelope in her hand. There was about an hour for the criminal to work in—and a few minutes would have been ample."

Ellery went to the telephone.

"What are you going to do?"

"Bring joy to my father's heart." He dialed Police Headquarters.

"What?" repeated the Inspector feebly.

Ellery said it again.

"You mean," said the old gentleman after another pause, "you mean…it's open again?"

"What else can it mean, Dad? The confession signature is now patently a tracing job, so Cornelia Potts never wrote the confession. Therefore she didn't confess to the murders at all. Therefore we still don't know who killed the Potts twins. Yes, I'm afraid the case *is* open again."

"I might have known," muttered the Inspector. "All right, Velie and I will be up there right away."

When Ellery turned from the telephone, there was Sheila, her back against the door. Charley was licking his lips.

"I heard you tell your father," said Sheila.

"Sheila—!"

"Just a minute, Charley." Ellery advanced across the study

with outstretched hands. Hers were cold, but steady. "I think you know, Sheila, that I'll—"

"I'm all right, thanks." She was tightly controlled. She slipped her hands from his, and clenched them. "I'm past being shocked or surprised or sent into hysterics by anything, Ellery."

"You sensed this all along."

"Yes. Instinct, I guess." Sheila even laughed. She turned to Charley Paxton, her face softening. "That's why I refused to leave the house, darling. Don't you see now?"

"No, I don't see," muttered Charley. "I don't see anything any more!"

"Poooor Charley."

Ellery was quite suffused in admiration.

Sheila kissed her troubled swain. "You don't understand so many things, lambie-pie. I've been a coward long enough. Nobody can make me afraid any more." Her chin tilted. "Somebody's out for my blood, is he? Well, I won't run away. I'll see this through to the bitter end."

23

The Fruit of the Tree

Now the house of Potts bore palls once more, shadows that shrank in stealth from them, like cats.

It became intolerable. They walked out onto the terrace overlooking the inner court to be rid of it. Here there was some graciousness in the flagged floor, the Moorish columns, the ivies and flowers and the view of grass and tall trees. The sun was friendly. They sat down in warm-bottomed steel chairs to wait for Inspector Queen and Sergeant Velie. Sheila sat close to Charley; their hands clasped, and after a moment her head dropped, defeated, to his shoulder.

It was interesting, Ellery thought, how from the terrace one could view all the good and all the evil in this manmade scene. Directly before him, at the end of a path bordered not unpleasantly with geraniums and cockleshells, stood Horatio's Ozzian house, a distortion of a dream, but with the piquancy of all sugar-coated fantasy. Surrounded as it was by civilized lawn and serene and healthy trees, it could not offend; in certain moods, Ellery agreed as he tried not to look at Sheila and Charley, it might even charm.

The tower of Louella was another thing. It cast its squat shadow over the gracious garden, its false turret crenelated as if against a besieging army, a flag (which Ellery noticed for the first time) whipping sullenly above the mock battlements. He watched the fluttering pennant curiously, unable to make out its design. Then the breeze straightened it for a moment, and he saw it whole. It bore a picture of a woman's oxford, and across it the words, simply: THE POTTS SHOE.

"It isn't even the grotesquerie," Ellery thought to himself impatiently. "It's the downright bad taste. This flag, the bronze Shoe on the front lawn."

He turned to glower at it, for its gigantic toe box was visible from where he sat, the rest cut off by the angle of the house. THE PO he read, backwards. In neon tubing!

Ellery wondered how Cornelia Potts had neglected in her will to leave instructions for her tombstone. Perhaps, he thought uncharitably, the Old Woman had foreseen the reluctance of St. Praxed's to permit erection of a Vermont marble lady's oxford, tombstone size, within its hoary yard.

Stephen Brent and Major Gotch were raptly playing checkers under a large green table umbrella to one side of the court lawn. They had not even noticed in their absorption the appearance of Sheila, Charley Paxton, and Ellery. Birds sang ancient melodies, and Ellery closed his eyes and dozed.

"Sleeping!"

Ellery awoke with a jerk. His father stood over him, in the scowling mood of frustration. Behind him bulked Sergeant Velie, belligerent. Sheila and Charley were on their feet. On the lawn, where old Steve and the Major had been bent over their checkerboard, stood merely an umbrella table and two iron chairs.

"Are we boring you, Mr. Queen?" asked the Inspector.

Ellery jumped up. "Sorry, Dad. It was so peaceful here—"

"Peaceful!" The Inspector was red of face, and Sergeant Velie perspired freely; it was evident the two men had rushed uptown from Center Street. "I can think of other words. Blasted case busted wide-open again!"

185

"Now I suppose I got to start lookin' for the missing rod all over again," growled Sergeant Velie in his basso profundo. "I was only tellin' the wife last night how the whole thing seemed like a bad dream—"

"Yes, yes, the gun, Sergeant," said Ellery absently.

Velie's anvil jaw swelled. "I searched this house, I dug up practically this whole square block—I tell you, Maestro, if you want to find that gun, go look for it yourself!"

"Stop it, Velie." Inspector Queen sat down with a groan. "Who's got that confession and stock memo? Hand 'em over."

The Inspector superimposed the signatures, as Ellery had done, and held them up to the sun for a squint. "No doubt about it. They're identical." He jammed both papers into his pocket. "I'll keep these. They're evidence now."

"Evidence against who?" grumbled Sergeant Velie, making up in scorn what he lacked in grammar.

At this moment Horatio Potts, in character, chose to enter the scene. That is to say, he appeared from the other side of his improbable dwelling, bearing the now familiar ladder. He waddled to a tall sycamore tree between his cottage and the umbrella table, set the ladder against the bole, and began to climb.

"Now what in the name of thunder is *he* doing?" asked Inspector Queen.

"It's his kite again," said Sheila grimly.

"Kite?" Ellery blinked. "Still at it, eh?"

"While you were napping here, he came out of his shack and began to fly one of 'em," explained Charley. "It got snarled in that big tree, so I suppose he's going after it."

The ladder was shaking under Horatio's weight.

"That Horatio's going to take a mighty tumble one of these days," said Charley critically. "If only he'd act his age—"

"Stop!" shouted Ellery Queen. They were thunderstruck. Ellery had cried out in a sort of terror, and now he was streaking across the lawn towards the sycamore with all the power of his long legs. "Stop, Horatio!" he shouted.

Horatio kept climbing.

The Inspector began to run after his son; Sergeant Velie began to run after the Inspector with a mine-not-to-reason-why expression; and so Sheila and Charley ran, too.

"Ellery, what the devil are you yelling 'Stop!' for?" cried the Inspector. "He's only—climbing—a—tree!"

"Mother Goose!" Ellery roared back over his shoulder, not slackening his pace for an instant.

"What?" screamed the Inspector.

"Suppose the ladder's been tampered with? Horatio's big—and fat—he'd fall—'Humpty Dumpty—had a great—fall ...'"

The Inspector gurgled and dug his tiny heels into the turf for traction. Ellery continued to shout at Horatio, and Horatio continued to ignore him. By the time the great man had reached the base of the sycamore, Horatio was almost invisible among the branches overhead. Ellery could hear him puffing and wheezing as he struggled to free the half-torn kite that was impaled above him. "Be careful, Mr. Potts!" Ellery yelled up.

"Ellery, are you coocoo?" panted the Inspector, coming up. Velie, Sheila, Charley were a few steps behind him. They were all frightened; but when they saw Horatio in motion in the tree, the ladder intact, and nothing amiss save the excitement on the Queen countenance, their concern changed to bewilderment.

"Mr. Potts, be careful!" Ellery roared again, craning.

"What's that?" Horatio's jovial face peeped redly down from between two leafy branches. "Oh, hullo there, nice people," beamed Horatio. "Darned kite got stuck. I'll be right down."

"Watch your step on the way down," implored Ellery. "Test each rung with one foot before you put your whole weight on it!"

"Oh, nonsense," said Horatio a little crossly. "As if I'd never climbed a ladder." And, the kite in one paw, he brought his right foot crashing down on one of the uppermost rungs.

"The fool will break his neck," said Ellery angrily. "I don't know why I even bother."

"What *are* you babbling about?" demanded his father.

"Hey, he stopped," said Sergeant Velie. "What's the matter up there, Horatio?" the Sergeant called up. "Gettin' cold feet? A great big boy like you!"

Horatio had paused in his descent to reach far over and thrust his fat hand into the foliage of a lower branch. The ladder rocked precariously, and Ellery and Velie in panic grabbed to steady it.

"Bird's nest," said Horatio, straightening. "Lots of fun, birds' nests." The kite in one hand, a starling's nest in the other, he continued his descent, pressing against the ladder's sides with his enormous forearms. "Just noticed it on that branch," he said, reaching the ground. "Nothing I like better than a good old bird's nest, gentlemen. Sets me up for the whole day."

"Beast," said Sheila; and she turned away from the nest clutched in his paw.

"Now, sir," said Horatio, beaming at Ellery, "you were saying something about being careful? Careful about what?"

Ellery had taken the ladder down and, with the Inspector and Velie, was examining it rung by rung. As he looked over the last rung, his face grew very red indeed.

"I don't see anything wrong," said the Sergeant.

"Well." Ellery laughed and tossed the ladder aside.

"Mother Goose—Humpty Dumpty," snarled his father. "This case has got you, son. Better go home and call a doctor."

"What's the matter, Horatio?" asked Charley.

Sheila turned quickly.

Horatio stood there, a large enigma, one hand plunged into the starling's nest.

"What is it, Mr. Potts?" demanded Ellery.

"Of all things!" guffawed Horatio, recovering. "Imagine finding *this* in a starling's nest." And he withdrew his great paw. On his palm lay a small, snub-nosed automatic pistol a little patchy with bird slime. It was a Colt .25.

"But that's the gun Bob Potts was plugged with," said Sergeant Velie, staring.

"Don't be a *schtunk* all your life, Velie!" cried Inspector Queen, grabbing for the automatic. "The murder gun's in the Bureau files—they all are!"

"Then this," said Ellery in a low voice, "this is the duplicate Colt .25—the missing weapon."

Later, when the lawn was empty, Ellery took his father by the arm and steered him to the umbrella table. "Sit down, Dad. I've got to think this out."

"Think what out?" demanded the old gentleman, nevertheless seating himself. He glanced at the Colt; it was loaded with a single cartridge. "So we've found the missing gun. Whoever's been pulling these jobs hid the Colt in that nest—blast that Velie for not looking in the trees!—and I suppose had the duplicate S. & W. .38/32 hidden up there, too, in preparation for the Maclyn Potts kill. But so what? The way things stand now—"

"Please, Dad."

The Inspector sat back. Ellery sat back, too, to stare with eyes that at first saw, and later did not see, the automatic in the Inspector's lap. And after a long time he smiled, and stretched, and said: "Oh, yes. That's it."

"Oh, yes, what's it?" asked his father petulantly.

"Would you do something right away, Dad? Spread the word through the house that the finding of the last gun in that bird's nest this afternoon has solved the case."

"Solved the case!" The Inspector rose and the automatic fell to the grass. Mechanically he stooped to retrieve it. "Solved the case?" he repeated faintly.

"Make sure they all understand clearly that *I know who murdered Cornelia's twin sons.*"

"You mean...you really do know? On the level, son?" The Inspector licked his lips.

But Ellery shook his head cryptically. "I mean I want everyone to think I do."

24

Queen Was in the Parlor

The time: evening. The scene: the downstairs study. As Curtain rises, we see the study in artful dim light, creating full-bodied shadows on the walls of books. Most of the furniture lies within the aura of the gloom. Only in right foreground near the French doors is there illumination, and it is evident that this concentration of light has been deliberately effected. It emanates from a standing lamp which throws its rays chiefly upon a straight-backed, uncomfortable chair which stands before a leather-topped occasional table. The boundary of brightness just touches an object lying upon the table—a .25 Colt automatic spotted with bird slime and lying half out of a raped starling's nest.

Ellery Queen leans against the lintel of one of the open French doors immediately outside the illuminated area, a little behind and to one side of the table. All the doors are open, for it is a warm evening (but we may suspect, knowing the chicanery potential of the Queen mind, that the barometer is not the sole, or even the principal reason). Ellery faces the straight-backed chair beyond the table; he also faces the door from the foyer, off left.

The terrace, which lies behind him, is in darkness. Offstage, from beyond the terrace, we hear the vibrant songs of crickets.

In the shadows of the study, well out of the light's orbit, sit Sheila Brent and Charles Hunter Paxton, still, expectant, and baffled spectators.

Ellery looks around in a last survey of his set, nods with a self-satisfied air, and then speaks.

ELLERY (*sharply*): Flint! (*Detective Flint pokes his head into the study from the foyer doorway.*)

FLINT: Yes, sir, Mr. Queen?

ELLERY: Thurlow Potts, please. (*Detective Flint withdraws. Thurlow Potts enters. The foyer door swings shut behind him; he looks back over his shoulder nervously. Then he advances into the scene, pausing uncertainly just outside the circle of lamplight. In this position the chair and the table with the gun and the bird's nest on it are between him and Ellery. Ellery regards him coldly.*)

THURLOW: Well? That detective said—(*He stops. Ellery has suddenly left his position at the French window and, without speaking, comes downstage and around the table to turn and pause so that he faces Thurlow, forcing him to follow him with his eyes.*)

ELLERY (*sternly*): Thurlow Potts!

THURLOW: Yes, Mr. Queen? Yes, sir?

ELLERY: You know what's happened?

THURLOW: You mean my mother?

ELLERY: I mean your mother's confession!

THURLOW: No. I mean yes. I mean I can't understand it. Well, that's not quite true. I don't know quite how to say it, Mr. Queen—

ELLERY: Stop pirouetting, Mr. Potts! Do you or don't you?

THURLOW (*sullenly*): I know that man—your father—told us Mother's confession was forged. That the case is opened again. It's very confusing. In the first place, I shot Robert to death in the duel—

ELLERY: Come, come, Mr. Potts, we've been all through your Dumasian career and you know perfectly well we substituted a blank cartridge for your lethal one to keep you from doing a very silly thing, and that someone managed to slip into your bedroom the night before the duel and put a live cartridge back into the automatic so that when you fired, Bob would die—as he did, Mr. Potts, as he did.

THURLOW: (*touching his forehead*): It's all very confusing.

ELLERY (*grimly*): Is it, Mr. Potts?

THURLOW: Your tone, sir!

ELLERY: Why do you avoid looking at this table, Mr. Potts?

THURLOW: I beg your pardon?

ELLERY: This table, Mr. Potts—t-a-b-l-e. This handsome little piece just beyond the end of your nose, Mr. Potts. Why haven't you looked at it?

THURLOW: I don't know what you mean, and what's more, Mr. Queen, I won't stand here and be insulted—

ELLERY (*suddenly*): Sit down, Mr. Potts.

THURLOW: Uh?

ELLERY (*in a soft tone*): Sit down. (*Thurlow hesitates, then slowly seats himself in the uncomfortable chair beside the table, knees together and pudgy hands in his lap. He blinks in the strong light of the lamp, wriggling. He still has not glanced at the weapon or the bird's nest.*) Mr. Potts!

THURLOW (*sullenly*): Well? Well?

ELLERY: Look at the gun, please. (*Thurlow licks his lips. Slowly he turns to stare at the table. He starts perceptibly.*) You recognize it?

THURLOW: No! I mean it looks just like the gun I used in my duel with Robert....

ELLERY: It *is* just like the gun you used in your duel with Robert, Mr. Potts. But it isn't the same gun. It's a duplicate, the duplicate you bought from Cornwall & Ritchey. Remember?

THURLOW (*nervously*): Yes. Yes, I seem to recall there were two Colt .25's among the fourteen I purchased—

ELLERY: Indeed. (*He steps forward suddenly, and Thurlow makes an instinctive backward movement. Ellery picks up the automatic from its nest, removes the magazine, bending over to let the light catch the cartridge inside. Thurlow follows his movements, fascinated. Suddenly Ellery rams the magazine back into place and tosses the automatic into the nest.*) Do you know where we found this missing loaded gun of yours today, Mr. Potts?

THURLOW: In—in the sycamore tree? Yes, I've heard about that, Mr. Queen.

ELLERY: Why did you put it there?

THURLOW (*gasping*): I never did! I haven't seen this weapon since the day I bought it with the other thirteen!

ELLERY (*with a cynical smile*): Really, Mr. Potts? (*Then sharply.*) That's all! You may go.

(*Thurlow blinks, hesitates, rises, openly surprised and upset by this peremptory dismissal. Then, without a backward glance, he hurries from the scene.*)

ELLERY: Flint! Louella Potts.

And now it became evident that Mr. Queen's scene with Thurlow Potts was a deliberate design for the scenes that followed. For when Louella Potts swept in, a violently self-assured Louella, quite altered from that sullen and sour spinster who had been under her mother's thumb, Ellery's script adapted itself to the unpredictable dialogue of this second character smoothly and with scarcely an emendation.

Again Ellery put the preliminary questions, again they led to the gun on the table, again he picked it up, fiddled with its magazine, displayed its cartridge, replaced the magazine, tossed the automatic back on the table, and asked the last question. "Why did you hide this loaded gun of Thurlow's in the starling's nest, Miss Potts?"

Louella sprang from the straight-backed chair, her saffron features convulsed. "Is it for this childish nonsense I've been dragged away from my important experiments? I never saw this weapon before, I didn't put it in the nest, I know nothing about it, and I'll ask you, Mr. Queen, to stop interfering with the progress of science!" And Louella strode out, all bones and indignation.

But Mr. Queen only smiled to Sheila and Charley Paxton and summoned Horatio Potts.

Horatio was immense in more ways than one. For purposes of this scene he had become a completely reasonable man. If the truth were known, the sudden sanity of his answers and a certain unexpected acuteness of insight into the trend of Mr. Queen's questions rather took the spotlight away from that great man and focused it brilliantly upon his victim.

"Very interesting, sir," said Horatio indulgently at one point. "I never did believe my mother murdered the twins. Too gory, you know. Madame Tussaud stuff. No, indeed. That confession, though. Very clever. Don't you think so, Mr. Queen?"

Mr. Queen thought so.

"And now you know who did it all," said Horatio at another point. "At least that's what I heard."

Ellery pretended to be angry at the "leak."

"I wish you'd enlighten me," continued the fat man, chuckling. "Sounds like good material for a book."

"You don't know, of course."

"I?" Horatio was astonished.

"Come, Mr. Potts. You hid this loaded automatic in the starling's nest, didn't you?" And again Ellery went through the business of opening the gun, displaying its cartridge, and closing it again.

"I hid it in the nest?" repeated Horatio. "But why?"

Ellery said nothing.

"As a matter of fact," continued Horatio reflectively, "the very idea's silly. If I hid Thurlow's gun in the tree and wanted it to stay hidden, would I have found it under your nose this afternoon, Mr. Queen? No, no, sir, you're on the wrong track."

Ellery could only wave Horatio Potts feebly out and call for Stephen Brent.

With Sheila's father the script resumed its character. The old man was nervous, and while Ellery was gentle with him Brent's nervousness was not allayed.

194

He denied with bewilderment having known anything about the gun in the tree, and left in a trot.

His stuttering had been pronounced.

Sheila began to examine Ellery with an ominous grimness. Charley had to restrain her from jumping up and running after her father.

With Major Gotch Ellery was severe. The old pirate showed his teeth at once. "I've taken a lot of berserker nonsense in this house, Mister," he roared, "but you've no call to speak to me this way. I don't know a cursed thing, and that's a fact you can't deny!"

"I thought you were well-known in the Dutch East Indies," said Ellery, departing from the script.

Gotch snorted. "One of its notorious characters, Mister. Bloomin' myth. Left my mark, I did."

"They never heard of you, Major."

He looked aghast. "Why, the muckin' liars!"

"Ever use another name, Major?"

The man sat still. Then he said: "No."

Ellery, lightly: "We can find out, you know."

"Find and be damned to you!"

"Don't have to, as it turns out. This is the last round-up, Major. Our friend the killer hasn't much grace left. Why'd you put the gun in the bird's nest?"

"You're barmy," said the Major, shaking his head; and he left as Ellery opened the automatic for the fifth time and played with the cartridge.

"Well, Mr. Queen?" asked Detective Flint from the foyer doorway. "Where do we go from here?"

"*You* exit quietly, Flint."

Flint shut the foyer door with a huffy bang.

Sheila jumped out of the shadows at once. "I don't see why you had to drag my father into this," she said tartly. "Treating him like the others—!"

"Smoke screen, Sheila."

"Yes?" she said suspiciously.

"I had to go through the motions of treating all the suspects equally."

Sheila did not seem convinced. "But why?"

"I can't imagine what you're driving at, Ellery," said Charley gloomily, "but whatever it is, you haven't learned a darned thing as far as *I* can see."

"Grilling Daddy!" said Sheila.

"It's all part of a plan, part of a plan," said Ellery cheerfully. "It hasn't quite worked out yet—"

"Shhh," whispered Sheila. "Someone ..."

"On the terrace ..." Charley whispered.

Ellery waved them back into the gloom imperiously. He himself darted out of range of the light, flattening against a wall. There was no sound but the beating of the grandfather clock. Then they heard a quick cautious step from the terrace darkness. In his shadow, Ellery crouched on the balls of his feet.

Inspector Queen stepped into the study through one of the French doors.

Ellery shook his head, chuckling. "Dad, Dad."

The Inspector peered about the dimly lit room, trying to locate the source of his son's voice, moving uncertainly.

"Ellery, you fox!" cried Charley, jumping forward. "Darned if I don't get the point!"

"But Ellery, if that's it," cried Sheila, running forward too, "you *mustn't*. It's dangerous!"

"What is this?" demanded Inspector Queen, blinking at them. "Mustn't do what, Ellery?"

"Nothing, nothing, Dad." Ellery came out of his shadow quickly. "Out of the light, Dad. We're waiting."

"Waiting for what? All right, I spread the word and stayed out of sight, but I'm not going to wait all night—"

Ellery pulled his father into the shadows.

"I don't like it," grumbled the Inspector. "What's going on here? Why were you so tense when I came in? So quiet?" And then he spied the Colt automatic in the nest on the table.

Ellery nodded.

"So that's it," said the Inspector slowly. "That's why you wanted the kit and caboodle of 'em to think you knew who the killer was. It's a trap."

"Of course," said Sheila breathlessly. "He's just interviewed everybody, asking a lot of useless questions—"

"Just so he could show them this gun on the table," said Charley, "right near the terrace!"

"Ellery, you can't do it," said the Inspector with finality. "It's too dangerous."

"Nonsense," said the great man.

"Suppose one of them sneaked onto the terrace. You mightn't hear him. You certainly couldn't see him." The Inspector went to the table. "All he'd have to do would be to stick his hand in here from the terrace, grab the gun, and fire at you point-blank."

"It's loaded, too, Inspector!" said Sheila. "Ellery, your father's right."

"Of course it's loaded," said Charley, frowning. "He went to an awful lot of trouble to show 'em it's loaded."

"You wouldn't have a chance, Ellery," said the Inspector. "You've set a trap, all right—they all think you know who did it and here's a loaded gun within easy reach—you've set a trap, but if you think I'm going to let you use yourself as live bait—"

"I've taken a few precautions," said Ellery lightly. "Come over here, the three of you."

The Inspector followed Ellery into the heavier shadows, away from the windows. "What precautions?"

Charley and Sheila backed off from the windows, joining them. "You'd better get out of here, Sheila—"

"Just a minute, Charley," snapped the Inspector. "*What* precautions, Ellery?"

Ellery grinned. "Velie's posted outside on the terrace behind one of those Moorish pillars. He'll nab whoever comes in before—"

"Velie?" The Inspector stared. "*I* just came in from the terrace and Velie didn't see or hear *me*. It's dark as a coal passer's glove out there—he couldn't have known it was me—so why didn't he nab me before I stepped through the French door?"

Ellery stared back at his father. "Something's gone wrong," he muttered. "Velie's in trouble. Come on!" He took two strides toward the open French door behind the occasional table, the others following. But then he stopped. On the very edge of the circle of lamplight.

A slender thing had darted in from the black terrace, a snake. But it was not a snake; it was a human arm. Even this was the impression of an instant, for it all occurred so quickly that they could only halt, Ellery included, and glare, powerless to move, unable to comprehend its nature or its purpose.

The hand was gloved, a gloved blur. It snatched the .25 automatic from the bird's nest on the table, brought it to a level in an amazingly fluid extension of its original movement, and for the fragment of a second poised the snub nose of the weapon on a direct line with Ellery's heart.

In that instant several things happened. Sheila screamed, clutching Charley. Ellery's hand came up from his side, defensively. With a snarl the Inspector dived head-first at Ellery's legs.

But one thing happened before any of the other three got fairly started...The gloved finger squeezed the trigger of the Colt and smoke and flame enveloped it. Ellery toppled to the floor.

"Sissy," he growled. "Letting me knock the wind out of you. You'd never make a cop."

"And talking about cops," said Charley, "what happened to Sergeant Velie?"

"Velie!" exclaimed Ellery. "Knocked my brains out, too, Dad. Gangway!"

"Be careful, Ellery! Whoever that was took the gun with him!"

"Oh, *that* character's made his exit from the script long ago," snapped Ellery; and he dived through the nearest French door. "Sheila, turn the lights on out here, will you?" he called back.

Sheila ran for the foyer. A moment later the terrace was flooded with light.

"No sign of whoever it was," panted Charley Paxton.

"Here's the gun," cried the Inspector. "Dropped it on the terrace just outside the study. Velie! Where are you, damn your idiot's hide?"

"Velie!" shouted Ellery.

Detective Flint stamped out of the house by way of the foyer, his big hand on Sheila's arm. "I caught this gal in the foyer, Inspector. Monkeying with the light switch."

"Start looking for the Sergeant, you dumb ox," snarled the Inspector. "Ellery sent Miss Brent!"

"Yes, sir," said Flint startled, and at once he began to search among the empty chairs of the terrace, as if he expected Sergeant Velie to materialize in one of them.

"Here he is." Ellery's voice was faint. They found him at the far end of the terrace. He was kneeling by the Sergeant's still, supine figure, slapping the big man's cheeks without mercy. As they ran up, Velie gurgled deep in his throat and blinked his eyes open.

"Glug," said Sergeant Velie.

"He's still dizzy." Inspector Queen bent over him. "Velie!"

"Huh?" The Sergeant turned glassy eyes on his superior.

"Are you all right, Sergeant?" asked Ellery Queen anxiously. "What happened?"

"Oh," Velie groaned and sat up, feeling his head.

"What happened, Velie?" roared the Inspector.

"Take it easy, will ya? Here I am hidin' behind one of these pillars," rumbled Velie, "and—ouch! The roof comes down on my conk. Say," he said excitedly, "I'm wounded. I got a lump on the back of my head!"

"Slugged from behind," said Ellery, rising. "Sees nothing, hears nothing, knows nothing. Come along, Sergeant. It's a miracle you're alive."

There was no clue to Velie's assailant. Detective Flint had seen nothing. They agreed it was the same person who had attempted to assassinate Ellery.

"It was a good trap while you set it," laughed Charley as they returned to the library. Then he shook his head.

"Smart," said Ellery through his teeth. "And quick. Slippery customer. Have to use grappling hooks." He fell into a fierce study. The Inspector examined his clothes while Sergeant Velie groped in the liquor cabinet for first aid.

"Funny," mumbled the Inspector.

"What?" Ellery was scarcely paying attention.

"Nothing, son."

The Inspector then examined the room under full light. The longer he searched, the more perplexed he seemed. And finally he stopped searching and said, "It's impossible."

"What's impossible?" asked Sergeant Velie. He had administered two glasses of first aid and was himself again.

"What are you talking about, Dad?"

"You're still slug-nutty from that fall you took," said the Inspector, "or you'd know without my having to tell you. A shot was fired in this room, wasn't it?"

"The bullet!" cried Ellery. "You can't find it?"

"Not a sign of it. Not a mark on the walls or the furniture or, as far as I can see, the floor or ceiling. No bullet, no shell, no nothing."

"It must be here," said Sheila. "It was fired point-blank into the room."

"Ricocheted off, most likely," said Charley. "Maybe took a funny carom and flew out into the garden."

"Maybe," grunted the Inspector. "But where are the marks of the ricochet? Bullet doesn't ricochet off empty space, Charley. It just isn't here."

"My vest!" said Ellery. "If it's anywhere, it's in my bulletproof vest. Or at least some mark of it, if it bounced off." He opened his shirt again and he and his father together examined the steel vest covering his torso. But there was no indication of a bullet's having struck—no dent in the fabric, no powder burns, no glittering line of abrasion. Moreover, his shirt and jacket were clean and whole.

"But we heard the shot," cried Inspector Queen. "We saw it fired. What is this, another magic trick? Another gob of Mother Goose nonsense?"

Ellery buttoned his shirt slowly. Sergeant Velie was frowning in a mighty, dutiful effort at concentration, a bottle of Irish whisky in his fist. The Inspector was glaring at the Colt which he had recovered from the terrace floor. And then Ellery chuckled. As he was buttoning the top button of his shirt. He chuckled: "Of course. Oh, of course."

"What are you patting yourself on the back about?" demanded the Inspector peevishly.

"That confirms everything."

"*What* confirms everything?"

Sergeant Velie set the whisky bottle down and began to shuffle toward the Queens, a curious look on his rocky face.

"Dad, I know who killed Robert and Maclyn Potts."

Part Five

26

The Identity of the Sparrow

"You really know?" said Inspector Queen. "It's not guesswork?"

"I really know," said Ellery with wonder, as if he were surprised himself at the simplicity of it all.

"But how can you?" cried Sheila. "What's happened so suddenly that tells you?"

"Who cares what's happened?" said Charley Paxton grimly. "I want to know who it is!"

"Me, too," said Sergeant Velie, feeling his head. "Put the finger on him once and for all, Maestro, so we can stop shadow-boxin' and get in there and punch."

Inspector Queen was regarding his eminent son with suspicion. "Ellery, is this another 'trap' of yours?"

Ellery sighed, and sat down in the straight-backed chair to lean forward with his elbows on his knees. "It rather reminds me," he began, "of *Mother Goose*—"

"Oh, my gosh," groaned the Sergeant.

"Who killed Robert and Maclyn? 'I,' said the Sparrow," murmured Mr. Queen, unabashed. "Wonderful how those jingles which were originally political and social satires keep cropping up in this case. I don't know if the Cock Robin thing was one of those, but I do know the identity of the Sparrow. Except,

Charley, that I can't tell you the 'who' without first telling you the 'how.' You wouldn't believe me otherwise."

"Tell it any way you please," begged Sheila. "But tell it, Ellery!"

Ellery lit a cigaret slowly. "Thurlow bought fourteen guns when he launched his dueling career. Fourteen…Sergeant, how many of those did you manage to round up?"

Velie started. "Who, me? Twelve."

"Yes. Specifically, the two used in the duel with Bob Potts, the one the Old Woman stole from Thurlow's hoard in that false closet of his, and the nine you found there afterwards, Sergeant. Twelve in all. Twelve out of the fourteen we knew Thurlow had purchased from the small-arms department of Cornwall & Ritchey. So two were missing."

Ellery looked about absently for an ashtray. Sheila jumped up and brought him one. He smiled at her, and she ran back to her chair. "Two were missing," he resumed, "and subsequently we discovered which two. They were exact duplicates in manufacture and type of the two guns Thurlow had produced for his duel with Bob: a .25-caliber Colt Pocket Model automatic, and a Smith & Wesson number known as the S. & W. .38/32 revolver, with a 2-inch barrel.

"That struck me as a curious fact. For what were the first twelve weapons?" Ellery took his inventory from his wallet. "A Colt .25 automatic, Pocket Model; a Smith & Wesson .38—the .38/32 revolver with 2-inch barrel; a Harrington & Richardson .22, Trapper Model; an Iver Johnson .32 Special, safety hammerless automatic; a Schmeisser .25 automatic, safety Pocket Model; a Stevens .22 Long Rifle, single-shot Target pistol; an I. J. Champion .22 Target single action; a Stoeger Luger, 7.65 millimeter, refinished; a New Model Mauser of 7.63 millimeter caliber with a ten-shot magazine; a High Standard hammerless automatic Short, .22 caliber; a Browning 1912 of 9-millimeter caliber; and an Ortgies of 6.35-millimeter caliber."

Ellery tucked away his memorandum. "I even remarked at the time that every one of the twelve guns listed was *of different manufacture.* I might have added what was evident from the list itself: that not only were the twelve utterly different in manufacture, but they were as nearly varied in caliber and type as one could reasonably gather in a gun shop.

"*Yet the thirteenth and fourteenth weapons—the two missing ones—were exact duplicates of the first two on the list; not merely similar, but identical.*" Ellery stared at them. "In other words, there were two *pairs* of guns in the fourteen items Thurlow bought at Cornwall & Ritchey's. Why? Why *two* Colt .25 automatics of the Pocket Model type, whose overall length is only four and a half inches, as we pointed out at the time? Why *two* S. & W. .38/32's, whose overall length is only six and one-quarter inches? Hardly dueling pistols, by the way!—although of course they could serve that purpose. There were much larger and longer pistols in Thurlow's arsenal for such romantic bravura as a duel at dawn. Why *those*, and such little fellows, too?"

"Coincidence?" asked Sheila.

"It might have been coincidence," admitted Ellery. "But the weight of logic was against it, Sheila. Because what happened? In giving Bob his choice of weapons at the dinner table the evening before the duel, Thurlow didn't offer Bob one of a *pair* of guns—one of the pair of Colt .25 automatics we know he had at that time, or one of the pair of Smith & Wessons—which would have been the natural thing to do in a duel. No, Thurlow offered Bob his choice of two quite *dissimilar* weapons. Coincidence? Hardly. I could only say to myself: There must have been some purpose, some motive, some plan behind this."

"But what?" Inspector Queen frowned.

"Well, Dad, what was the effect of Bob's choosing one of the two dissimilar guns Thurlow offered him? This: *that no matter which weapon Bob chose—*whether he chose the Colt automatic or the Smith & Wesson revolver—*Thurlow was left not with one gun for himself, but a pair.*"

"A pair!" exclaimed Charley. "Of course! Since Bob picked the Smith & Wesson, Thurlow was left with two identical Colts!"

"And it would have been the same if Bob had selected the

Colt," nodded Ellery. "Thurlow couldn't lose, you see—he *had* to be left with a pair of identical weapons. The question was: What was the advantage to Thurlow in this? I couldn't answer it then; but I can now!"

"Wait a minute, son," said the Inspector irritably. "I don't see what difference it would have made if Thurlow'd been left with a dozen identical guns."

"Why not?"

"Why not? Because Thurlow couldn't have murdered Bob Potts, that's why not. From the time you left that Colt .25 in Thurlow's bedroom with a blank in it till you handed Thurlow that same gun the next morning at the duel, Thurlow couldn't possibly have touched it. You said so yourself!"

"That's right, Maestro," said Sergeant Velie. "He never could of got into his bedroom during the night to take the blank out and put the live bullet in the gun—he was with Miss Brent and Charley Paxton, and later you, all the time."

"Either here in the study with us," nodded Charley, "or in Club Bongo, where all four of us went that night after you came downstairs from putting the blank-loaded gun in Thurlow's room, Ellery."

"Not only that," added Inspector Queen, "but you told me yourself, Ellery, that the only ones who positively did *not* have opportunity to switch bullets in that gun in Thurlow's room were Charley, Miss Brent, and Thurlow."

"From the facts, Maestro," chided the Sergeant. "From the facts."

Ellery smiled sadly. "How you all belabor the 'facts'! Although I shouldn't cast the first stone—I did a bit of belaboring myself. I agree: Thurlow could not have replaced the blank cartridge with the live one in that Colt I left on his highboy."

"Then what are you talking about?" expostulated his father.

"Just this," said Ellery crisply. "*Thurlow murdered his brother Bob deliberately nevertheless.*"

"Huh?" Sergeant Velie reamed his right ear doubtfully.

"Thurlow murdered—" Sheila stopped.

"But Ellery," protested Charley Paxton, "you just got through admitting—"

"That Thurlow couldn't have replaced the blank with the live cartridge, Charley? So I did. And I still do. But don't you people see that by having two identical guns, Thurlow not only prepared a colossal alibi for himself but pulled off a seemingly impossible murder, too? Look!" Ellery jumped up, grinding out his cigaret. "We all assumed that the killer replaced the blank in the Colt with a live bullet; we all assumed that this was the only possible way in which Bob Potts could have been murdered. *But suppose that blank had never been replaced?*"

They gaped at him.

"*Suppose the blank-loaded Colt was not used in the duel at all, but the other Colt was used—the duplicate Colt?*"

At that the Inspector groaned and clapped his palms to his gray head in an agony of realization.

"Very fundamental," said Mr. Queen, lighting a fresh cigaret. "Thurlow didn't use the Colt .25 we'd put the blank cartridge in. He simply used the other Colt .25, loaded with a live bullet. The attack on me a few minutes ago proved this—proves that *Thurlow switched the two Colt .25's just before his duel with Bob,* switched them right under our noses. How does the attempt on my life in this room prove this?

"Well, ever since Bob's death, the Colt that killed him—the one we know had a live bullet in it *because* it killed him, the Colt that Thurlow aimed at him—has been in your possession, Dad, as the murder weapon, the vital piece of evidence. Today Horatio Potts found the *duplicate* Colt .25 in the sycamore tree on the estate. A few minutes ago that duplicate Colt was fired at me at point-blank range. Yet there was no mark on me, no bullet hole, no abrasion on my steel vest, no powder burn; and no bullet or bullet hole or sign of ricochet anywhere in this room. Only possible explanation: That duplicate Colt fired at me tonight *was loaded with a blank cartridge.* But we'd loaded a Colt .25 with a blank cartridge for Thurlow to use in his duel with Robert!

"Conclusion: The weapon fired at me tonight *was that first gun*, the gun that had been on Thurlow's highboy the whole night before the duel, the gun I'd run up to fetch for him, the gun I'd handed him at dawn and which he immediately put, you'll recall, into the right-hand pocket of his tweed jacket...The gun he did *not* take out of that pocket a few moments later! Yes, Thurlow switched guns on us under our eyes; and how he did it becomes childishly apparent once you recognize the basic fact that he *did* switch guns. The fact that, having *two* guns, he had no need to switch *bullets* was the strongest and wiliest part of Thurlow's plan. It made it possible for him to create an unassailable alibi. He must have eavesdropped and overheard our plan to replace the live bullet with a blank in the only Colt .25 we knew at the time he possessed. But *he* knew he had a duplicate Colt. So why not let us go through with our plan to draw the death out of the first Colt, give himself that powerful alibi, and still manage to kill Robert? Moreover, under such circumstances that he'd seem the witless tool of some mysterious other person?

"Thurlow snatched his opportunity. Sheila, he permitted you to get him 'out of the way.' Charley, he welcomed your joining him and Sheila here in the study later. And he must have been beside himself with delight when I came down, too, to join the party. Then what did he do? If you'll recall, it was *Thurlow* who suggested going to Club Bongo; it was *Thurlow* who managed things so that we stayed out all night and didn't get back until it was time for the duel—whereupon it could never be said that he'd had opportunity to switch bullets in that gun in his room at any time after I placed the blank-loaded weapon there. How were we to know that all the previous evening, all that night at Club Bongo, all the early morning coming back to the grounds, Thurlow had the duplicate Colt .25, loaded with a lethal bullet, in his right-hand pocket?

"And now observe how cunning he is. We get back, and he sends *me* upstairs to his room to fetch the blank-loaded Colt, under the 'artless' pretense that I'm his second! For it must not be said afterwards that Thurlow Potts for even two minutes was alone with that gun ...

"I fetched the gun, playing the dupe, handed it to Thurlow in sight of numerous witnesses, and he slipped it at once into his coat pocket.

"The dueling silliness began. Thurlow took a Colt .25 from that pocket. How were we to know that it was not the same weapon, loaded with a blank? How were we to know that the Colt he took out of that pocket was a duplicate of the one I had just handed him, a weapon identical in shape and size and appearance, and that the one just handed him was still in his pocket? And remained there?"

Inspector Queen groaned. "Who'd ever think to search the nut? We didn't even know at the time that there *were* duplicate Colt .25's!"

"No, we did not. And Thurlow knew we didn't. He was running no risks. Later, he simply disposed of the first Colt—hid it in that starling's nest in the sycamore tree, the blank cartridge still in it."

"And then, of course," muttered the Inspector, "he pulled that second challenge—to Mac—as a fake and a cover-up. By that time we were sure to pass his part in the killing off as irresponsible craziness. So he murders Mac in an ordinary way during the night, while we're expecting a duel in the morning. Clever is right."

"But *why'd* he kill the twins?" demanded Sergeant Velie.

Sheila said: "Because he hated them," and began to cry.

"Stop it, darling," said Charley, putting his arms about her. "Or I'll take you out of here."

"It's just that it's the same old story—hate, insanity—" Sheila sobbed.

"Not at all," said Mr. Queen dryly. She looked up quickly; they were all startled. "There's no insanity in Thurlow's murder plan, believe me. It was cold, brutal, logical, criminal ruthlessness."

"Now how do you figure that?" demanded Paxton.

"Yes, what in time did he gain by killing the twins?" echoed the Inspector.

213

"What did he gain?" Ellery nodded. "Very pointed question, Dad. Let's explore it a bit. But first let's state an interesting fact: This is not a case of one murder; it's a case of two. ALL RIGHT. Who gained most by the deaths of *both* Bob and Mac?"

They were silent.

"Thurlow, and only Thurlow," Ellery answered himself. "Let me show you why I say that.

"What would have happened if Bob and Mac had not been murdered? When the Old Woman died, there'd automatically be an election to determine the new President of the Board of Directors of the Potts Shoe Company. Seven people would have the right to vote in that election, as everyone knew from her will, which we were told was a matter of common knowledge in the household for years.

"With Robert and Maclyn alive, one of them would necessarily have been nominated to take full charge of the huge shoe enterprise. This was brought out at the actual election the day after the Old Woman's death; you said it yourself, Sheila, rather bitterly." Sheila nodded in a puzzled way. "Now suppose the twins had not been murdered? Suppose at your mother's death, Sheila, the twins were still alive? One of them would have been nominated, and he would have been sure of the following votes: his own, his twin's, Sheila's, and Mr. Underhill's. Neither Louella nor Horatio had the desire or capacity to head the business. Thurlow, then, would have been the opposing candidate. Now, who would have voted for Thurlow?

"Well, who did vote for Thurlow—in the election that was held? Louella, Horatio and Thurlow himself. In other words, had the twins remained alive, *one of them would have been elected over Thurlow by a vote of four to three.*"

"That's it," said Charley softly.

"By a plurality of one," exclaimed Velie.

"Thurlow would have lost ..." mused the Inspector.

"Yes, Thurlow would have lost by a vote of four to three," murmured Ellery. "Knowing Thurlow's sensitivity, what

214

wouldn't this have meant to him! Deflated, 'disgraced' in his own eyes, forced to take a back seat to the two younger men when all his adult life he had been waiting for his mother to die so that he could reign supreme in the family! Yes, defeat in the election would have been the supreme insult of Thurlow's life. And not only that. He knew that as soon as his mother passed on, Sheila and the twins and their father intended to take back Steve's real name, Brent. This meant that the Potts business might eventually lose even its name. At best, it would be in the hands of those whom Thurlow had always considered outsiders—not true Pottses.

"Knowing to what lengths Thurlow has gone in the past to avenge fancied insults and ridicule where the name of Potts was concerned, it's easy to believe that his intensely concentrated ego dictated a plan whereby he would seize control of the business on his mother's hourly expected death (page Dr. Innis) and avert the 'catastrophe' of seeing the Potts name possibly lost to a grieving posterity. And what was the only way he could accomplish this? The *only* way? By eliminating the two brothers who stood in his path, the two who not alone controlled two vital votes but who, both of them, were logical candidates to head the firm on the Old Woman's death.

"And so—Bob and Mac died by Thurlow's hand, and in the election, instead of losing by a vote of four to three, he won by a vote of three to two. Oh, no," said Mr. Queen, shaking his head, "there was no madness in Thurlow when he hatched this little mess of eggs. Or should I say the crime was sane if the criminal was not....Granted Thurlow's obsession with the name of Potts, everything he planned and executed afterwards was severely logical."

"Yes," said Sheila slowly. "I was stupid not to have seen it. Louella, Horatio—why should they care? All they've ever asked was to be let alone. But Thurlow—he's been a frustrated little shadow of my mother all his life."

"What do you think, Dad," asked Ellery, "of my Sparrow?"

"I buy it, son," the Inspector said simply. "But there's one little detail you haven't supplied."

"What's that?"

"Proof. Proof that District Attorney Sampson'll cock an eye at," continued the Inspector, "and say: 'Dick, we've got a case for the courts.'"

And there fell upon them the long silence.

"You'll have to dig up the proof yourself, Dad," said Ellery at last, uncoiling his long legs. "All I can do is supply the truth."

"Yeah. The trouble is," said Sergeant Velie, dryly, "they ought to fix up a new set o' laws for you, Maestro. The kind of case you make out—it puts the finger on murderers but it don't put 'em where they can get a hot foot in the seat."

Ellery shrugged. "Not my province, Sergeant. Ordinarily at this stage I'd say to hell with it and go home to my orphaned typewriter. But I must admit—" his eye wandered to Sheila Brent— "in this case I'd feel better seeing Thurlow safely behind bars before I retire, like his sister Louella, to my ivory tower."

"Wait," said Charley Paxton. He was shaking his head. "I think I can supply one important fact that'll tie Thurlow up to at least one of the murders—Bob's. I'm a fool!"

"Two-times killer isn't any the less dead for being burned for only one," said the Inspector. "What have you got, Charley?"

"I should have told you long ago, Inspector, only it didn't mean anything to me till Ellery just explained about the duplicate guns. Some time ago—you'll be able to check the exact date—Thurlow asked me the name of my tailor."

"Your tailor!" Ellery's brows rose. "Never a dull moment. What about it, Charley?"

"I gave it to him, assuming he wanted to order a suit. Next thing I knew, I got a bill from the tailor—I still have it somewhere, and that's evidence for the D.A.—charging me for repairs made on 'a tweed suit jacket.'"

"*Tweed?*"

"I never wear tweeds, so I knew there was a mistake. Then I remembered Thurlow's quizzing me about my tailor. So I asked

Thurlow about the tweed jacket my tailor'd billed me for and he said, yes, it must have been his jacket the man meant, because he'd had my tailor make some repairs on it and hadn't received a bill. So Thurlow asked me to pay for the repairs and said he'd reimburse me. He did, too," added Charley grimly, "in cash, the cagey devil!"

"Repairs," exclaimed Ellery softly. "What kind of repairs, Charley, did Thurlow say?"

"No, Thurlow didn't say," retorted the lawyer. "But I smelled a little mouse, I can't tell you why. I asked my tailor when I paid the bill. And he said Mr. Potts had asked him to change the right-hand outside pocket of the tweed jacket into a double pocket—"

"*Double pocket!*" The Inspector leaped to his feet.

"With a partition lining between."

"Charley, that's it," whispered Sheila.

"Double pocket," grinned the Sergeant, "double guns, double bye Mr. Potts!"

"If that won't establish premeditation, I don't know what will," said the Inspector, rubbing his hands briskly. "Charley, I thank you."

"Yes, that's it," said Ellery. "I should have seen it myself. Of course he'd have to take the precaution of preventing a mix-up in the two guns during the short time he had them both in the same pocket. But with a double pocket, he could put the live-loaded Colt in one half, say the half at the front of the pocket; and the Colt with the blank in the half at the back. That made it easy to locate the live-loaded Colt with his fingers when the time came to withdraw the gun for the duel."

"Better get hold of that coat immediately, Inspector," advised Charley. "Thurlow thinks he's safe, so he's done nothing about it. But if he suspects you're looking for evidence, he'll burn the coat and you'll never have a case for Sampson."

A dark figure flung itself through one of the French doors off the terrace and stumbled into the study.

It was Thurlow Potts.

One glimpse of his contorted features was proof enough that Thurlow had overheard every word of the analysis by which Ellery Queen had relegated him to the Death House, and of the testimony of Charley Paxton's which was to provide the switch.

For the second time that evening they were paralyzed by the inhuman quickness of Thurlow's appearance. This was a Sparrow possessed of demons. Before any of them could stir, he had flung himself at Charley Paxton's throat.

"I'll kill you for telling them about that pocket," Thurlow shouted, digging his fingers into Charley's flesh. The young lawyer, taken completely by surprise, had not even had time or presence to rise from his seat; the force of Thurlow's assault had sent him hurtling over backward, and his head had struck the floor with a soggy thud. Thurlow's fingers dug deeper. "I'll kill you," he kept screaming. "That pocket. I'll kill you."

"He's unconscious," Sheila was shrieking. "He hit his head. Thurlow, stop it! Stop, you dirty butcher—*stop!*"

The Queens, father and son, and Sergeant Velie hit the little man simultaneously from three directions. Velie scooped up Thurlow's legs, which instantly began kicking. Ellery grabbed one arm and yanked, and the Inspector the other. Even so, they found it difficult to pluck him from Paxton's throat. It was only by main force that Ellery was able to tear those stubby, suddenly iron fingers away.

Then they had him loose, and Sheila dropped hysterically by Charley's side to chafe his swollen neck, where the bite of Thurlow's fingers was deep and clear.

Sergeant Velie got Thurlow's throat from behind in the crook of his arm, but the little man kept kicking viciously even as his eyes bugged from his head. They were red, wild eyes. "I'll kill him," he kept screaming. "I killed the twins, and I'll kill Paxton, too, and I'll kill, I'll kill, kill…"

And suddenly he went soft all over, like a rag doll. His head draped itself over the Sergeant's arm. His legs stopped kicking.

"On the davenport," said Inspector Queen curtly. "Miss Brent, is Charley all right?"

"I think so, Inspector! He's coming to. Charley, Charley darling..."

Velie picked up the little man and carried him to the studio couch. He did not drop Thurlow; he laid him down carefully, almost tenderly.

"Cunning as they come," grunted the Inspector. "Well, son, you heard him say he did it. So you're right, and we've got plenty of witnesses, and Thurlow's a gone rattlesnake."

Ellery brushed himself off. "Yes, Dad, premeditated purchase of two pairs of guns, premeditated manufacture of a double pocket, premeditated build-up of a perfect alibi, a clear motive—I think you've got a case for the District Attorney."

"He won't need it," said Sergeant Velie. There was something so sharply strange in Velie's tone that they looked at him in inquiry. He jerked his big jaw in the direction of the man on the couch.

Thurlow Potts lay quiet, with a stare at right angles to sanity. There was nothing in his eyes now, nothing. They were lifeless marbles. The face was putty patted into vertical lines. He was staring up at Sergeant Velie without resentment or hatred, without pain—without recognition.

"Velie, call Bellevue," said Inspector Queen soberly.

Ave atque vale, Thurlow, thought Ellery Queen as he looked down at that stricken flesh of the Old Woman's flesh. For you there will be no arrest, no arraignment, no Grand Jury, no trial, no conviction, no electric chair. For you there will be a cell and bars, and green fields to watch with eyes that see crookedly, and jailers in starched white uniforms.

27

The Beginning of the End

It cannot be stated that Ellery Queen was satisfied to the point of exaltation with his role in the Potts murder case.

Heretofore, Ellery's pursuit of truth in the hunt of human chicanery had been attended by a sort of saddle irritation which magically disappeared when the hunter returned to his hearth. But now, a week after Thurlow Potts had confessed his crime and lapsed into burbling insanity, Ellery's intellectual seat still smarted.

He wondered at himself, thinking over the horrid fantasy of the past week. That he had succeeded, there could be no question. Thurlow Potts had murdered Robert Potts with his own hand. Thurlow Potts had murdered Maclyn Potts similarly. Logic had triumphed, the miscreant had confessed, the case was closed. Where, then, had he failed?

King James had said to the fly, "Have I three kingdoms and thou must needs fly into my eye?"

What was the nature of the fly?

And suddenly, at breakfast with his father that morning, he saw that there were two flies, as it were, in his eye. One was Thurlow Potts himself. Thurlow was still a conundrum, logic and confession notwithstanding. Mr. Queen was uncomfortably aware that he had never known the true nature of Thurlow, and that he still did not know it. The man had been too rich a mixture of sense and nonsense, a mixture too thoroughly mixed. But the recipe for Thurlow was preponderantly madness, and for some reason this annoyed Mr. Queen no end. The man had been mostly mad, and his crime had been mostly sane; perhaps this was the source of the smart. And yet there could be no doubt whatever that Thurlow had murdered his twin brothers, knowing exactly what he was doing.

Ellery gave it up.

The other fly was equally obvious, and equally pestiferous. It had dimples, and its name was Sheila. At this point, Ellery quickly resumed the attack on his breakfast under his father's inquiring eye. Sometimes it is wiser, he thought, not to probe too deeply into certain branches of entomology.

By coincidence Sheila and Charley Paxton dropped into the Queen apartment before that uneasy breakfast was concluded; and it must be said that Mr. Queen rose heroically to the occasion, the more so since the young couple had come to announce their approaching marriage.

"The best of everything," he said bravely, pressing their hands.

"If ever two snooks deserved happiness in this world," said the Inspector, shaking his head, "it's you two. When's it coming off?"

"Tomorrow," said Sheila. She was radiant.

"Tomorrow!" Mr. Queen blinked.

Charley was plainly embarrassed. "I told Sheila you'd probably be pretty busy catching up on your book," he mumbled. "But you know how women are."

"Indeed I do, and I'd never have forgiven you if you'd taken any such silly excuse for not dropping in."

"There, you see, dear?" said Sheila.

Charley grinned feebly.

"Tomorrow," smiled Inspector Queen. "That's as fine a day as any."

"Then we're going on a honeymoon," said Sheila, hugging

Charley's arm, "and when we get back—work, and peace."

"Work?" said Ellery. "Oh, of course. The business."

"Yes. Mr. Underhill's going to manage the production end—he's far and away the best man for it, and of course the office staff will keep on as before."

"How about the executive set-up?" asked the Inspector curiously. "With Thurlow out of circulation—"

"Well, we've tried to get Sheila's father to change his mind about taking an active part in the business," said Charley, "but Steve just won't. Says he's too old and wants only to live the rest of his life out playing checkers with that old scalawag Gotch. So that sort of leaves it up to Sheila. Of course, Louella and Horatio are out of the question, and now that Thurlow's gone, they'll do as Sheila says."

"We've had a long talk with Louella and Horatio," said Sheila, "and they've agreed to accept incomes and not stand in the way of the reorganization. They'll live on at the old house on the Drive. But Daddy and Major Gotch are taking an apartment, and of course Charley and I will take our own place, too." She shivered the least bit. "I can't wait to get out of the house."

"Amen," said Charley in a low voice.

Ellery smiled. "Then from now on I'm going to have to address you as Madam President, Sheila?"

"Looks that way," retorted Sheila. "Actually, I'll be President only for the record. With Mr. Underhill handling production and Charley the business end—he insists on it—I won't have anything to do but clip coupons."

"What a life," groaned the Inspector.

"And of course," said Sheila in an altered tone, gazing at the floor, "of course, Ellery, I can't tell you how grateful I am for everything you've done for us—"

"Spare me," pleaded Ellery.

"And Sheila and I sort of thought," said Charley, "that we'd be even more grateful if you sort of finished the job—"

"Beg pardon?"

"What's the matter with you two?" laughed Sheila. "Charley, can't you even extend a simple invitation? Ellery, Charley would like you to be best man tomorrow, and—well, I think you know how thrilled I'd be."

"On one condition."

Charley looked relieved. "Anything!"

"Don't be so rash, Charley. I'd like to kiss the bride." That'll hold you, brother! thought Mr. Queen uncharitably.

"Sure," said Charley with a weak grin. "Help yourself."

Mr. Queen did so, liberally.

Now this was strange, that even in the peace of the church, with Dr. Crittenden smilingly holding his Book open before him, and Sheila standing before him straight and still and tense to the left, her father a little behind and to one side of her, and Charley Paxton standing just as solemnly to the right, Ellery behind him...even here, even now, the flies buzzed about Ellery's eye.

"Dearly beloved, we are gathered together here in the sight of God, and in the face of this company ..."

Inspector Queen stood behind Ellery. With his father's quiet breathing in his ear, the son was suddenly seized with an irrelevance, so unpredictable is the human mind in its crises of desperation. He slipped his hand into his coat pocket to feel for the ring of which he was honored custodian, and also to finger absently the three documents that lay there. The Inspector had given them to Ellery that morning.

"Give them back to Charley for his files, or hold them for him," the Inspector had said. "Lord knows I can't get rid of 'em fast enough."

One was the Old Woman's will. His fingers knew that by the thickness of the wrapper. The Old Woman ...

"... to join together this Man and this Woman in holy Matrimony; which is an honorable estate, instituted of God ..."

The Old Woman's confession. Her notepaper. Only one left, anyhow, so it must be. He found it outside his pocket, in his hand. Now how did that happen? Ellery thought innocently. He glanced down at it.

"*... and therefore is not by any to be entered into unadvisedly or lightly ...*"

Forged confession. Never written by the Old Woman. That signature—traced off in the same soft pencil...Ellery found himself turning the closely typed sheet over. It was perfectly clean. Not a pencil mark, not the sign of an erasure.

"*... but reverently, discreetly, advisedly, soberly and in the fear of God.*"

Something clicked in the Queen brain. Swiftly he took the slip of flimsy from his pocket, the stock memorandum from which he had decided—how long ago it seemed!—the signature of Cornelia Potts had been traced onto the "confession."

He turned it over. On the back of the memorandum he now noticed, for the first time, the faint but clean pencil impression in reverse of the words "Cornelia Potts."

He shifted his position so that he might hold the memorandum up to a ruffle of sunlight skirting Charley's arm. The pencil impression on the reverse of the memorandum lay directly over the signature on the face, with no slightest blurring.

"*Into this holy estate these two persons present come now to be joined.*"

Ellery turned, groped for his father's arm.

Inspector Queen looked at him blankly. Then, scanning Ellery's face, he leaned forward and whispered: "Ellery! Don't you feel well? What's the matter?"

Ellery wet his lips.

"*If any man can show just cause, why they may not lawfully be joined together, let him speak now—*"

"Damn it!" blurted Ellery.

Dr. Crittenden almost dropped the Book.

Ellery's face was convulsed. He was pale and in a rage, the two documents in his hand rustling like rumors. Later, he said he did not remember having blasphemed.

"Stop," he said a little hoarsely. "Stop the wedding."

28

The End of the Beginning

Inspector Queen whispered: "El, are you crazy? This is a wedding!"

They'll never believe me, thought Ellery painfully. Why did I get mixed up in this fandango? "Please forgive me," he said to Dr. Crittenden, whose expression of amazement had turned to severity. "Believe me, Doctor, I'd never have done this if I hadn't considered it imperative."

"I'm sure, Mr. Queen," replied the pastor coldly, "I can't understand how anything could be more important than a solemnization of marriage between two worthy young people."

"What's happened? What's the matter, Ellery?" cried Charley. "Dr. Crittenden, please—would you be kind enough to leave us alone for five minutes with Mr. Queen?"

Sheila was looking fixedly at Ellery. "Yes, Doctor, please."

"B-but Sheila," began her father. Sheila took old Steve's arm and took him aside, whispering to him.

Dr. Crittenden looked appalled. Then he left the chapel with agitated steps to retire to his vestry.

"Well?" said Sheila, when the vestry door had closed. Her tone was arctic.

"Please understand. This can't wait. You two can always be married; but this can't wait."

"What can't wait, Ellery?" demanded Charley.

"The undoing of the untruth." Ellery cleared his throat; it seemed full of frogs and bulrushes. "The telling of the truth. I don't see it clearly yet, but something's wrong—"

His father was stern. "What are you talking about? This isn't like you, son."

"I'm not like myself—nothing is as it should be." Ellery shook his head as he had shaken it that night on the floor of the Potts study after Thurlow had shot at him. "We've made a mistake, that's all. I've made a mistake. One thing I do see: *the case is still unsolved.*"

Sheila gave voice to a little whimper, so tired, so without hope, that Ellery almost decided to say he had slipped a gear somewhere and that this was all, all a delusion of a brain fallen ill. Almost; not quite.

"You mean Thurlow Potts is *not* our man?" cried the Inspector. "But that can't be, Ellery. He admitted it. You heard him admit the killings!"

"No, no, that's not it," muttered Ellery. "Thurlow did commit those murders—it was his hand that took the lives of Bob and Mac Potts."

"Then what *do* you mean?"

"There's someone else, Dad. *Someone behind Thurlow.*"

"Behind Thurlow?" repeated his father stupidly.

"Yes, Dad. Thurlow was merely the hand. Thurlow pulled the triggers. But he pulled them at the dictation, and according to the plan, of a brain, a boss—the real murderer!"

Major Gotch retreated into a corner of the chapel, like a cautious bear, and it was curious that thenceforth he kept his old puff eyes fixed upon the pale blinking eyes of his crony, Stephen Brent.

"Let me analyze this dreary, distressing business aloud," continued Ellery wearily. "I'll work it out step by step, Dad, as I see it now. If I'm wrong, call Bellevue. If I'm right—" He avoided looking at the others. Throughout most of what followed, he kept addressing his father, as if they had been alone with only the quiet walls of the chapel to keep them company.

226

"Remember how I proved the Old Woman's signature on that typewritten confession we found on her body was a forgery? I placed the stock memorandum against a windowpane; I placed the confession over the stock memorandum; and I worked the confession about on the memo until the signature of the one lay directly over the signature of the other. Like this." Ellery went to a clear sunny window of the chapel and with the two documents illustrated his thesis.

"Since both signatures were identical in every curve and line," he went on, "I concluded—and correctly—that one of the signatures had been traced off the other. No one ever writes his name exactly the same way twice."

"Well?" The Inspector was inching toward the chapel door.

"Now since the stock memo was handed to Charley Paxton in our presence by the Old Woman herself—in fact, we saw her sign it—we had every right to assume that the signature on the *memorandum* was genuine, and that therefore the signature on the *confession* had been traced from it and was the forgery.

"But see how blind I was." Ellery rapped the knuckles of his free hand against the superimposed documents his other hand held plastered against the window. "When a signature is traced off by using light through a windowpane, in what position must the genuine signature be in relation to the one that's to be traced from it?"

"You've got to put the document being forged *above* the genuine signature, of course," replied the Inspector. He was looking around, restlessly.

"Or in other words, first you lay down on the windowpane the genuine signature, then you place the document to be forged *over* it. Or to put it still another way, it's the genuine document that lies against the glass, and the fake document that lies against the genuine one. Therefore," said Ellery, stepping back from the window, "if the signature on the confession was the traced one, as we believed, then the confession must have been lying *upon* the stock memo, and the stock memo must have been lying against the windowpane. Is that clear so far?"

"Sure. But what of it?"

"Just a minute, Dad. Now, all the Old Woman's signatures were written with a heavy, softleaded pencil." The Inspector looked puzzled by this irrelevance.

"Such pencils leave impressions so thick and soft that when they are pressed on and written over, as would have to be done in the tracing of a signature written by one of them, *they necessarily act like a sheet of carbon paper*. That is, when two sheets are pressed together, one on top of the other, and a soft-pencil signature on the bottom sheet is traced onto the top sheet, the very act of tracing, the very pressure exerted by the tracing agent, *will produce a faint pencil impression on the back of the top sheet*, because it's that back surface on the top sheet which is *in direct contact* with the soft lead of the original signature on the bottom sheet. Is *that* clear?"

"Go on."

"I've already shown that, in order to have been a forgery, the confession must have been the top sheet of the two. But if the confession was the top sheet, there should be a faint pencil impression of Cornelia Potts's signature (in reverse, of course, as if seen in a mirror) *on the back of the confession sheet*."

"Is there?"

Ellery walked over to his father, who by this time was standing, alert, against the chapel door. "Look, Dad."

The Inspector looked, quickly. The reverse side of the confession was clean, without smudge.

"That's what I saw a few moments ago, for the first time. There is not the slightest trace of a pencil mark on the back of this confession. Of course, there could have been such an impression and for some reason it might have been erased; but if you examine the surface sheet carefully, you'll find no signs of erasure, either. On the other hand, look at the back of the stock memorandum! Here—" Ellery held it up—"here is the clear, if light, impression of the signature 'Cornelia Potts' on the back of the memo, in reverse. And if you'll hold it up to the light, Dad, you'll see—as I saw—that the reverse impression of the signature lies directly behind the signature on the face of the memo, proving that the impression was made at the same time as the forgery.

"What does all this mean?" Ellery tapped the stock memorandum sharply. "It means that *the stock memo was the top sheet* of the two employed in the forgery. It means that *the confession was the bottom sheet,* lying flat against the windowpane.

"But if the confession was the bottom sheet, *then it was the signature on the confession which was being used as a guide* and it was the signature on the stock memo which was traced from it!

"But if the signature on the confession was being used as a guide then that signature was the *genuine* one, and the one on the stock memo was the forgery. Or, to put it in a capsule," said Mr. Queen grimly, "*the Old Woman's confession was not a forgery as we believed, but was actually written and signed by her own hand.*"

"But El," spluttered the Inspector, "that would make the Old Woman the killer in this case!"

"One would think so," said his son. "But strangely enough, while Cornelia Potts actually wrote that confession of guilt, and signed it, she did *not* murder her two sons, nor could she have been the person behind Thurlow who used Thurlow as a tool in the commission of the murders."

"How can you know that?" asked the Inspector in despair.

"For one thing, Dad, we now know that there never was a substitution of *bullets* in that first Colt .25—we know that there was a substitution of *guns.* Yet in her confession the Old Woman wrote—" Ellery consulted the confession hastily—"the following: 'It was I who substituted a lethal bullet for the blank cartridge the police had put into Thurlow's weapon.' But no bullet *was* substituted! In other words, the Old Woman thought the same thing we thought at the time—that a substitution of bullets had been made. So she didn't even know how the first murder was really committed! How, then, could she have been in any way involved in it?

"And look at this." Ellery waved the confession again. "'Later it was I who stole one of Thurlow's other guns and hid it from the police and went with it into my son Maclyn's bedroom in the

229

middle of the night and shot him with it,' and so on. Stop and think, Dad: Cornelia Potts couldn't have done that, either! Dr. Innis told me, just before he left the Old Woman's bedside that night—shortly before Mac was shot to death—that he had given the Old Woman a sedative by hypodermic injection *which would keep her asleep all night.*

"No, the Old Woman didn't have a thing to do with the murder of the twins, even though she wrote out a confession of guilt and signed it with her own hand. So apparently, knowing she was about to die and had nothing more to lose in this life, she wrote out a false confession to protect whichever whelp of her first litter was guilty. She was a wonderfully shrewd woman, that old lady; I shouldn't be surprised that she suspected it was Thurlow, her pet. By confessing on her deathbed, she believed the case would be officially closed and, with its close, Thurlow would be safe."

The Inspector nodded slowly. "That makes sense. But if it wasn't the Old Woman who was masterminding Thurlow, who was it, son?"

"Obviously, *the person who made us believe the signature on the confession was false when it wasn't.* And, by the way, that was a very clever piece of business. It was necessary to make us think the confession was false, for reasons I'll go into in a moment. In order to accomplish that, what did our criminal require? A signature which would be identical with the signature on the confession. No true signature of Cornelia's could possibly be *identical* with the confession signature, so our criminal had to manufacture one. In doing so, he could only use for tracing purposes the confession signature itself. He chose the stock memo he knew we remembered having seen the Old Woman sign, typed off its message exactly on similar paper, destroyed the genuine memo, and then traced the confession signature onto the spurious stock memo. Very clever indeed."

"But who was it, Ellery?" The Inspector glared about. They were all so quiet one would have thought them in the grip of a paralyzing gas.

"We can get to that only obliquely, Dad. Having established that the real criminal, the brains behind Thurlow, wanted us to believe the Old Woman's confession a forgery, the inevitable question is: Why?

"The reason must be evident. It could only be because he did not want us to accept the Old Woman as the killer, he did not want the case closed—he wanted someone other than Cornelia Potts to be arrested and convicted for the murder of the twins.

"When I proved the case against Thurlow, I thought the series of crimes had come to an end. Well, I was wrong. One more puppet in the play had to be eliminated—*Thurlow himself*." The Inspector looked befogged. "Yes, Dad, Thurlow was a victim, too. Oh, this is as fancy a plot as any that ever came out of Hollywood. It's not double murder, it's triple murder. First Bob, then Mac—and now Thurlow. For, as we know now, Thurlow was the instrument of the crime, and his being caught doesn't solve it. There's still the person behind him. Then since we see that the criminal wanted someone other than Cornelia to be caught and tried and convicted for the murders, and we've actually pinned it on Thurlow—isn't it clear that *Thurlow's capture, too, was part of the criminal's plan?*"

The Inspector blinked. "You mean—he wanted to get not only the twins, but Thurlow, whom he used to kill 'em, out of the way?"

"Exactly. And here's why I say that. Ask the question: Who benefits most by the elimination of the twins *and* Thurlow? Can you answer that?"

"Well," muttered the Inspector, "the twins were killed for control of the Potts Shoe Company—as a result of their murder, Thurlow became President and got control ..."

"*But with Thurlow out of the way as well, who has control now?*"

"Sheila."

It was not the Inspector's voice which answered Ellery.

It was Stephen Brent's.

Stephen Brent was staring at his daughter with the feeble error of a parent who sees his child, for the first time, as others see her.

29

The End of the End

"Yes, Sheila," said Ellery Queen, in the saddest voice imaginable.

And now he looked at her, with remorse, and with pity, and with something else that was neither. Sheila was glaring from her father to Ellery in a jerky arc, her lips parted and her breath jerky, too.

Major Gotch made a little whimpering noise in his corner.

Charley was glaring, too—glaring at Ellery, his hands beginning to curl into fists. "Idiot!" he shouted, lunging forward. "The Potts craziness has gone to your head!"

"Charley, cut it out," said Inspector Queen in a tired voice.

Charley stopped impotently. It was plain that he dared not glance at Sheila; he dared not. And Sheila simply stood there, her head jerking to and fro.

The Inspector asked quietly: "You mean this girl with the dimples is the brains behind this nasty business? *She* used Thurlow as a tool? *She*'s the real killer?" He shook his head. "Charley's right, Ellery. You've gone haywire."

And then Ellery said an odd thing. He said: "Thank you, Dad. For Sheila." And at this they were still with wonder again.

"Because, from the facts, it couldn't be Sheila," Ellery went on in a faraway voice. "All Sheila wants to be is...somebody's wife."

"Somebody's wife?" Charley Paxton's head started the pendulum now—from Ellery Queen to Sheila, from Sheila to Ellery.

Mr. Queen looked full upon Mr. Paxton. "This was all planned by the man who missed a brilliant career in criminal law—you told me that yourself, Dad, that very first morning in the Courthouse. The man whose every effort has been to get Sheila to marry him. The man who knew that, married to Sheila and with her twin brothers and Thurlow out of the way, he could control the rich Potts enterprises. That's what was behind your 'insistence,' as Sheila said only yesterday, Charley, on 'running the business' in the reorganization, while she sat back to be your figurehead—wasn't it?"

Charley's skin turned claret.

"Don't you see?" Ellery avoided Sheila's eyes. "Charley Paxton planned every move, every countermove. Charley Paxton played on Thurlow's susceptible mind, on Thurlow's psychopathic obsession with the honor and name of Potts. Charley Paxton convinced Thurlow that he had to murder the twins to protect himself, the business, and the family name. Charley Paxton planned every step of the crime for Thurlow—showed him how to commit two daring murders with safety, planned the scene before the Courthouse, the purchase of the fourteen guns, the duel—everything, no doubt rehearsing Thurlow patiently. A furiously vacillating brain like Thurlow's might have conceived murder, but Thurlow scarcely possessed the cunning and the application necessary to have planned and carried it out as these subtle crimes were planned and carried out. Only a sane mind could have planned these crimes. And that was why I was dissatisfied with Thurlow as the criminal even though all the evidence indicated that his hands and his person had performed the physical acts required to pull the crimes off...No, no, Charley, I can assure you you wouldn't stand a chance. Just

233

stand still and refrain from unnecessary movements."

The Inspector took a small police pistol from his shoulder holster and released its safety mechanism.

Ellery continued in a murmur: "You'll recall I conjectured that Thurlow had found out by eavesdropping that we intended to substitute a blank cartridge for the live one in the first Colt automatic. But now perceive. Who suggested the device of substituting a blank? Whose plan was it? *Charley Paxton's.*"

Sheila's eyes grew wider; she began to tremble.

"So now we have a much more reasonable answer to how Thurlow knew about the blank. *Charley, his master, told him.* Paxton waited for me or someone else to suggest the ruse, and when none of us did, he jumped in himself with the suggestion. He had to, for he'd already told Thurlow that was what was going to happen—he'd see to it.

"All along this fine, smart young lawyer who had missed a brilliant career in criminal law set traps—in particular for me. If I fell into them—excellent. But if I hadn't seen the significance of the two pairs of Colts and Smith & Wessons, if I hadn't worked out Thurlow's motive, if I hadn't deduced just how Thurlow switched the guns before our eyes on the lawn that morning—if I hadn't seen through all these things, you may be sure Mr. Charles Hunter Paxton would have managed to suggest the 'truth' to me.

"Think. How closely Paxton clung to me! How often he was there to put in a word, a suggestion, to lead me along the path of speculation he had planned for me to take! I, too, have been a pawn of Counsellor Paxton's from the beginning, thinking exactly what he wanted me to think, eking out enough of the truth, point by point, to pin it on Thurlow and so accomplish the final objective of the Paxton campaign—the elimination of Thurlow."

"You can't be serious," said Charley. "You can't really believe—"

"And that isn't all. When he needed proof against Thurlow—when you specifically asked for it, Dad—who told us about the

234

tailor and the double pocket in Thurlow's tweed jacket?"

"Mr. Paxton."

"And when Thurlow came tearing into the study from the terrace, whom did he attack—me? The man who had worked out the solution? Oh, no. He jumped for *Charley's* throat, mouthing frenzied threats to kill. Isn't it obvious that Thurlow went mad of rage because he had just heard Charley *double-cross* him? The man who had planned the crimes and no doubt promised to protect Thurlow—now giving the vital evidence that would convict him! Luckily for Counsellor Paxton, Thurlow's last link to sanity snapped at that point, or we should have heard him pour out the whole story of Paxton's complicity. But even this was a small risk for Paxton to take, although from the ideal standpoint it was the weakest part of his plot...that Thurlow would blab. But Paxton must have thought: 'Who'd believe the ravings of a man already well established as a lunatic in face of the incontrovertible evidence against him?' "

"Poor Thurlow," whispered Sheila. And for the first time since the truth had come from Ellery's lips she turned and regarded the man she had been about to marry. She regarded him with such loathing that Steve Brent quickly put his hand on her arm.

"Yes, poor Thurlow," said Ellery grimly. "We broke him before his time—although no matter what had happened, Thurlow would have come to the same end—a barred cell and white-coated attendants....It's Sheila I was most concerned about. Seeing the truth, I had to stop this wedding."

And now Sheila turned to look upon Ellery, and he flushed slightly under her gaze.

"Of course, that's it," said Charley Paxton, clearing his throat. His hand came up in a spontaneous little gesture. "You see what's happened, Inspector, don't you? This son of yours—he's in love with Sheila himself—he practically admitted as much to me not long ago—"

"Shut up," said the Inspector.

235

"He's trying to frame me so he can have her himself—"

"I said shut up, Paxton."

"Sheila, you certainly don't believe these malicious lies?"

Sheila turned her back on him.

"Anything you say—" began the Inspector.

"Oh, don't lecture me!" snarled Charley Paxton. "I know the law." And now he actually smiled. "Stringing a lot of pretty words together is one thing, Mr. Queen. Proving them in court's another."

"The old story," growled the Inspector.

"Oh, no," said Mr. Queen, returning smile for smile. "Quite the new story. There's your proof, Dad—the forged stock memorandum and the Old Woman's confession."

"I don't get it."

"I told you he's talking through his hat," snapped Paxton. He shrugged and turned to the clear window of the chapel. "Dr. Crittenden will be getting impatient, waiting in the vestry," he remarked, without turning. "Sheila, you can't give me up on this man's unsupported word. He's bluffing, because as I said—"

"Bluffing, Paxton?" cried Ellery. "Then let me disabuse that clever mind of yours. I'll clear up a few untouched points first.

"If no one had interfered with this chap's original plans, Dad, Paxton would have got away with the whole scheme. But someone did interfere, the last man in the world Paxton had dreamed would interfere—his own creature, Thurlow."

Charley Paxton's back twitched, and was still.

"Thurlow did things—and then one other did things—which Mr. Paxton in his omniscience hadn't anticipated and therefore couldn't prepare counter-measures against. And it was this interference by others that forced our clever gentleman to make his only serious mistake."

"Keep talking," said Charley's voice. But it was a choked voice. "You always were good in the gab department."

"The first interference wasn't serious," Ellery went on, paying no attention to the interruption. "Thurlow, flushed with his success in getting away with the murder of his brother Robert, began to think for himself—dangerous, Mr. Paxton, dangerous, but then your egocentric type of mind is so blind that it overlooks the obvious in its labor toward the subtle.

"Thurlow began to think. And instead of following his master's instructions in the second murder, he was so tickled with himself that he decided to add a touch or two of his own.

"In reconstructing what happened, we can ascribe these things to Thurlow because they are the kind of fantastic nonsense an addled brain like Thurlow's would conceive and are precisely not the things a cold and practical brain like Paxton's would conceive."

"What are you referring to?" The Inspector's pistol was pointed at Paxton's back.

"Thurlow shot Mac Potts in his bed in the middle of the night," replied Ellery with a curl and a twist to his tone that snapped Paxton's head up as if he had been touched with a live wire. "Shot him, whipped him with his riding crop, and left a bowl of chicken broth near by. Why? Deliberately to make the murder look like a Mother Goose crime. How sad!" said Mr. Queen mockingly. "How sad for master-minding Mr. Paxton. Upset the orderly creation, you see…"

"I d-don't understand that," stuttered Steve Brent. His arm was about Sheila's shoulders; she was clinging to him.

"Well, sir," retorted Ellery in a cheerful way, "all your late wife's first brood have been fed Mother Goose nonsense ever since she was first dubbed the Old Woman Who Lived in a Shoe. Mother Goose squatted on your rooftree, as it were, Mr. Brent, and her shadow was heavy and inescapable. Thurlow must have said to himself, in the ecstasy following his first successful homicide: 'I'm safe, but a little more safety can't do any harm. No one even suspects me for the murder of Robert in the duel. If the police and this fellow Queen see these Mother Goose clues—the whipping, the broth—they'll think of my brother Horatio, the Boy Who Never Grew Up. They'll certainly never think of *me!*'"

"It was precisely the murky sort of smoke screen a psychopathic personality like Thurlow's would send up. But it had a far greater significance for Paxton than for us. For it warped Charley's plot, which had been planned on a straight, if long, line. Charley Paxton didn't *want* suspicion directed toward Horatio. Charley Paxton wanted suspicion directed toward, and to land plumb and squarely upon, chubby little Thurlow. How annoyed you must have been, Charley! But I'll hand it to you: the foolishness being done, you took the wisest course—did nothing, hoping the authorities wouldn't recognize, or would be thrown off the scent by, the Mother Goose rigmarole. When I spotted it, you could only hope I'd dismiss it and get back on the Thurlow spoor."

"You said something about proof," said Paxton in crisp tones.

"Mmm. In good time, Charley. You're a patient animal, as you've proved.

"The next unanticipated interference came from what must have been a shocking source, Charley—the Old Woman. And here's where we hang you...no, burn you, to use the more accurate vernacular of the State of New York.

"What did the Old Woman do? She wrote out a confession of guilt, which was untrue. Most unreasonable of her, Charley; that *was* a blow to your plans. So serious a blow that it forced you into activities which you couldn't control, which controlled *you*. Oh, you made the most of your material, I'll give you that. You were ingenious and versatile, you overlooked no bet—but that false confession of Cornelia Potts's controlled you, Charley, and what it made you do is going to make you pay for your crimes by due process of law."

"Talk," sneered Paxton. But then he added: "And what did it make me do, Mr. Queen?"

"It made you say to yourself: 'If the police believe that meddling Old Woman's confession, my whole scheme is shot. They won't pin it on Thurlow, and Thurlow will take the reins of the Potts enterprises, and I'll never get to control them through

238

Sheila.' Very straight thinking, Charley; and quite true, too. So you had to do something, or give up all hope of eating the great big enormous pie you'd set your appetite on."

"Get on with it!" snarled Mr. Paxton.

"You were clever. But cleverness is not wisdom, as Euripides said a couple of thousand years ago; you'd have been better advised to be wiser and less clever, Charley."

"How long do I have to listen to this drivel?"

"You couldn't destroy the large sealed envelope containing the Old Woman's will and smaller envelope with the confession in it, for the absurd reason—"

"That we all saw the envelope in the dead woman's hand," snapped the Inspector. "Go on, son!"

"Nor could you destroy the confession itself—"

"Because," said the Inspector, "the Old Woman had typed at the bottom of the will a paragraph saying that in the smaller sealed envelope was a paper which would tell us who'd murdered the twins."

"Nor could you destroy the will which contained that paragraph—"

"Because we knew it existed and after I gave it to you to hold till the formal reading," snapped the Inspector, "you were responsible for it, Paxton!"

"Nor could you substitute another revelation," Ellery's monotone persisted, "for if you had, the revelation to further your plans could only accuse Thurlow, and no one would believe that the Old Woman, on her deathbed, would accuse her favorite son of murder—she, who had shielded him from the consequences of his aberrations all his life.

"No, indeed," continued the great man, "you were trapped by the trap of circumstance, Charley. You did the only possible thing: *you tried to make us believe the Old Woman's confession was untrue.* The simplest way to do that was to make it appear a forgery. If we could be led to believe it was a forgery then logically we'd conclude the Old Woman had not been the killer at all, we would continue the investigation, and eventually, following the trail you were so carefully laying down, we would arrive at Thurlow."

And now Charles Hunter Paxton turned from the window and stood black and stormy against it, rocking a little on the balls of his feet and glaring at the revolver in the Inspector's hand which was aimed steadily at his belly.

"I referred a few moments ago," said Ellery amiably, "to the only serious mistake you made, Charley my boy—the mistake that gives the D.A. his evidence and will bring your career to a fitting climax.

"What was your mistake? You had to prove the Old Woman's confession a forgery. To accomplish this, two series of actions on your part were mandatory:—

"One: You had to get hold of some document which the authorities knew of their own knowledge had been signed by Cornelia Potts. You remembered the stock memorandum, the signing and discussing of which had taken place before our eyes and ears. That would serve admirably, so you decided to get the original stock memo—"

"Sure!" said the Inspector. "It was in that kneehole desk in the Potts library Paxton always used for business."

"Yes. You had to get hold of it, Charley, prepare an exact duplicate on the Old Woman's portable, and then you had to trace onto the duplicate memo the signature at the bottom of the Old Woman's confession."

"Just a minute, Ellery." The Inspector seemed troubled. "Since the original stock memo was in this fellow's desk in the library, anybody in the house could have got to it. It doesn't necessarily pin anything on Paxton."

"How true," said Paxton.

"Yes, Dad," said Ellery patiently, "but what was the second thing Professor Moriarty had to do? He had to get hold of the *confession* in order to trace its signature onto the faked stock memo. *And who had access to the Old Woman's confession?* One person. Of all the people in the world, one person only. And that's

240

how I know Charles Hunter Paxton forged the stock memorandum. That's why I say there's evidence to convict him."

"Only Paxton had possession of Cornelia's confession?" muttered the Inspector.

"It's a tight little question of knowledge and opportunity," smiled his son. "All capable of confirmation. First, the confession in its envelope lay in the larger sealed envelope which also contained the will. When we found that large sealed envelope in Cornelia's hand, not only *didn't* we know that it contained a confession, we *couldn't* have known. It was just a large sealed envelope with the words on it: *Last Will and Testament*, and signed *Cornelia Potts*.

"Second step: You, Dad, hand that large sealed envelope, contents thought to be only a will, to Mr. Paxton. The envelope is still sealed; it hasn't been opened or tampered with. You hand it to him in that bedroom, over the still warm corpse of old Cornelia, only a few minutes after we found it in her dead hand. And you ask Mr. Paxton to hold that large sealed envelope containing what we can only think is the dead woman's will—to hold it until the formal reading after the funeral."

Mr. Paxton began to breathe quickly, and the Inspector's weapon waved a little.

"Third: At the formal reading Mr. Paxton produces the large sealed envelope. It is opened, we discover the confession as well as the will...and from that instant you, the officer in charge of the case, Dad, take possession of that confession as important new evidence in the case. It becomes part of an official file.

"Now we know," said Ellery with a cold smile, "we can prove, that some time *before* the opening of that envelope at the formal reading of the will, the envelope had been secretly opened by someone, because we have proved that the Cornelia Potts signature on the confession had been used as a guide to forge a signature on the fake stock memorandum, and it couldn't possibly have been done *after* it got into your possession, Dad, and the police files. When, then, specifically, could that envelope have been opened? *Only in the interim between the finding of it in the dead woman's hand and the opening of it before us all in the library for purposes of the will reading.* Who could have done it in that interim? *Only the person who had possession of the large sealed envelope.*

"Who had possession of the large sealed envelope during that interim? *Only one person: Charles Hunter Paxton.* Mr. Paxton, who when you originally handed him the envelope at the dead woman's bedside, Dad, couldn't contain his curiosity and at the first opportunity steamed it open, found the will, found the note at the bottom of the will, found the smaller sealed envelope purporting to contain a revelation of the murderer's identity—who naturally steamed *that* envelope open, read the Old Woman's confession, realized that he couldn't destroy it, saw that he could only make it seem a forgery, and thereupon went through all the motions necessary to achieve that end; and when he had forged the stock memo, he resealed the small envelope with the confession in it, resealed the large envelope with the small envelope and will in *it*, and then produced the sealed large envelope at the formal reading, as if its contents had never been disturbed at all." Mr. Queen's voice became a whip. "You're a fool, Paxton, to think you could get away with any such involved stupidity!"

For a moment Inspector Queen thought the young lawyer would spring at Ellery's throat. But then Paxton's shoulders seemed to collapse, and he dropped into a chair to cover his face with his hands. "I'm tired. It's true. Everything he said is true. I'm glad it's over. I'm tired of being clever."

Mr. Queen thought this last remark might very well be added to the distinguished list of native American epitaphs.

30

There Was a Young Woman

"Say, Maestro," said Sergeant Velie the next day, stretching his legs halfway across the Queen living room, "I always seem to miss the third act. Why didn't you send me an Annie Oakley?"

"Because I didn't know myself," grinned Ellery. The lines of anxiety had disappeared from his lean face and he seemed passably pleased with himself.

"Seems to me," chuckled the Inspector, "you didn't know a whole lot of things, my son."

"True, how true," mourned Ellery.

"When you really take a look at it, your 'proof' was pretty much a matter of slats, cardboard, and spit."

"Mmm," said Mr. Queen. "Well, yes. But remember, I was working it out extempore. I'd no chance to prepare my attack; I couldn't let that wedding proceed; I had to do what I could on the spot, working my way from point to point."

"What a man," said Sergeant Velie. "He works his way from point to point. Sort of like a mountain goat, huh?"

"But I had certain advantages, too. Charley was caught off-guard in the middle of his wedding—at a time when he thought he'd pulled the whole thing off and had got away with it."

"And now he's chewing his fingernails off in the hoosegow," said the Sergeant. "Such a life."

"Circumstantial evidence," persisted the Inspector.

"But very strong circumstantial evidence, Dad. That last point—about the possession of the sealed envelope—powerful. It was my silver bullet. And it caught Charley Paxton dead center. Yes, he cracked and confessed. But I knew he would. No man can stand up under a confident attack at a time when he's unprepared, after a long period of strain. Charley's the intellectual type of killer, the type that will always crack under blows an ordinary desperado wouldn't even feel."

"Yes, sir," nodded Sergeant Velie, "here yesterday, in the hoosegow today. It makes you think."

"It makes *me* think I've never been so happy to see the end of a case," yawned the Inspector. "*What* a case!"

"You haven't quite seen the end of it," suggested his son respectfully.

"Huh?" The Inspector bounced to his feet. "Don't tell me you just realized you've made *another* mistake!"

"In a way, yes," mused Ellery. But his eyes were twinkling. "Sheila Brent phoned me. She's on her way over."

"What for?" Inspector Queen stuck his little jaw out. But then he shook his head. "Still got a hangover, I guess. Poor girl's taken a bad beating. What's she want, Ellery?"

"I don't know. But I know what *I* want."

"What?"

"To help her. I don't know just why—"

"Aha," said his father. "Velie, let's get out of here."

"And why not?" The Sergeant rose, stretching. "*I'll* tell you what you can do for Miss Brent, Maestro. You can help her spend some of those millions of bucks." And the Sergeant left, grumbling that the policeman's lot is not a lucrative one.

"I don't think, Velie," Mr. Queen called after him, "that that's quite what the doctor ordered for Miss Brent."

And he sat musing on various therapeutic matters until his doorbell rang.

"It's good to see you minus a hunted look," said Ellery. "I'd begun to be afraid it was permanent."

But Sheila was not looking too well. She was pale and her dimples spiritless this morning. "Thanks. Could you give a woman a drink of something wet and cold?"

"For a dry and thirsty day—certainly." And Ellery promptly set about mixing something wet and cold. He was nervous, and Sheila remarked it.

"I hope I'm not getting in your hair," she sighed. "I seem to have been hanging onto you—in a way—since…Oh. Thanks, Mr. Queen."

"Ellery."

He watched her sip the frosty drink and thought how pleasant it might be to repeat the service *ad infinitum*.

"I can't tell you how sorry I am about what I had to do yesterday, Sheila—"

"Sorry!" She set down the drink. "And here I've been so grateful—"

"You weren't too shocked?" he asked anxiously. "You see, I had no time to warn you—"

"I understand."

"Naturally I couldn't let you go through with it."

"Naturally." She even smiled. "If that isn't just like a man. Save a woman from—" she shuddered—"from the most horrible kind of mistake…and apologize for it!"

"Well, but I thought—"

"Well, but you're a love," said Sheila queerly. "And I can never thank you enough. That's why I asked if I might drop in. I had to tell you in person."

"Don't say another word about it," said Ellery in a nettled tone. "I don't know why you should thank me. I must be associated in your mind almost entirely with nastinesses, and clues, and policemen, and brutal revelations—"

"Oh, don't be an idiot!" cried Sheila. And then she said, blushing: "I'm sorry, Mr. Queen."

"Ellery." Ellery felt vastly pleased. "Sheila, why don't you start a new life?"

245

She stared. "If you aren't the suddenest man!"

"Well, I mean—you ought to leave that nest of blubbering imbeciles on Riverside Drive, put yourself into a new and cheerful environment, get a real interest in life—"

"Of course you're right." Sheila frowned. "And I'm certainly going to get out into the world and try to forget everything I ever...I've found that having money doesn't solve anything important. I've always wanted to do something useful, but Mother wouldn't let me. If I could only find work of some sort—work I'd enjoy doing ..."

"Ah," said Mr. Queen. "That brings up an important question, Miss Brent." He fingered his ear. "Would you—uh—consider that I come under the heading of enjoyable occupations?"

"You?" Sheila looked blank.

"How would you like to come to work for me?" Ellery added hastily: "On a salary, of course. That's understood. I'm not trying to take advantage of your millions."

"Work for *you*?" Sheila propped one elbow on her knee and put her fist under her chin and stared at him thoughtfully. "Tell me more, Mr. Queen."

"You're not offended? Wonderful woman!" Ellery beamed. "Sheila, forget the past. Break every tie you've ever had. Except with your father, of course. But even in that case I think you should live alone. Change everything. Surroundings, way of living, clothes, habits. Pretend you've been born all over again."

Sheila's eyes had begun to sparkle. But then they clouded over. "Listens good, Ellery, but it's impossible."

"Nothing's impossible."

But Sheila shook her head. "You forget I'm a marked woman. I'm Sheila Potts, or Sheila Brent—it doesn't matter; they know both names." *They* as she uttered the word sounded ugly. "I'd only mess your life up with a lot of notoriety, and I'd never be allowed to forget who I was...who my mother was...my half brother Thurlow...the man I almost married..."

"Nonsense."

She looked curious. "But it's true."

"It's true only if you let it be true. There's a perfectly simple way of making it not true."

"How?" she cried. "Anything—tell me how! You don't know how I've wanted to lose myself in crowds and crowds of ordinary, decent, sane people....*How*, Ellery?"

"Change your name," said Ellery calmly. "And with it your life. If Mr. Queen, the scrivener of detective stories, suddenly hires a secretary named Susie McGargle, a nice young woman from, say, Kansas City—"

"Secretary," whispered Sheila. "Oh, yes! But..." Her voice became lifeless again. "It's out of the question. You're a dear to make the offer, but I'm not equipped. I don't know how to type. I can't take shorthand—"

"You can learn. That's what secretarial schools are for."

"Yes...I suppose ..."

"And I think you'll find me an understanding employer."

"But I'd be a liability for such a long time!"

"Six weeks," said Ellery reflectively. "Two months at the outside—to become as efficient a stenographer as ever drew a pothook or made a typewriter sing for its supper. I give you two months, no more."

"Do you think I...really could?"

"Shucks."

Almost rapturously, Sheila said: "If I could...a new life...It would be fun with you! If you really meant it—"

"I really mean it," said Mr. Queen simply.

"Then I'll do it!" She jumped from the sofa. "By golly, I'll do it!" In her excitement she began to race up and down, flying from place to place. "Is this where you work? Is it hard? Doesn't anyone ever clean this desk? That's a terrible photo of you. Light's bad in here. Where's your typewriter? Maybe I could start today. I mean, the school...Oh, gosh, a new life, a new name, working with Ellery Queen...A new name," she said damply. "But I don't *like* Susie McGargle."

"That," said Ellery, watching her skim about with a delight that surprised him, "that was a low inspiration of the moment, chosen merely for illustration."

"How you talk!" Sheila laughed and for the first time in a long time Mr. Queen thought how delicious can be a woman's laughter. "Well, then, what's my name going to be? It's your idea—you baptize me."

Ellery closed his eyes. "Name...Pretty problem. Pretty problem for a pretty subject. Red hair, dimples..." He sat up, beaming. "D'ye know, here's a remarkable coincidence!"

"What, Ellery?"

"The heroine of my new book has red hair and dimples!"

"Really? What's her name? Whatever it is—even if it's Grimalkin—or Pollywog—I'll take it for my own!"

"You will?"

"Certainly."

"Well, you're in luck," said Ellery, grinning. "It's a darned sweet name, if I do say so as shouldn't."

"What is it?"

Mr. Queen told her.

"Nicky?" Sheila looked doubtful.

"Spelled N-i-k-k-i."

"Nikki! Oh, wonderful, wonderful. That's a *beautiful* name. Nikki...Mr. Queen, I buy it!"

"As for a last name," murmured that gentleman, "I can't give you my heroine's...it's Dempsey...perfectly good name, but inappropriate for you, somehow. Let me see. What would go well with 'Nikki' and you?"

"Nikki...Nikki Jones? Nikki Brown? Nikki Green—"

"Heavens no. No poetry. Nikki Keats? Nikki Lowell? Nikki Fowler?...Fowler. *E-r* ending. *Er*. Yes, that would be good. An *er* ending in a two-syllable name. Parker. Farmer. Porter...Porter! Nikki Porter!" Ellery sprang to his feet. "That's it," he cried. "*Nikki Porter.*"

"Yes," said Nikki Porter, all soft and tender and merry and grateful at once. "Yes, Mr. Queen."

"Ellery to you, Miss Porter," beamed Mr. Queen.

"Nikki to *you*...Ellery."